GUN THUNDER

Center Point
Large Print

GUN THUNDER

A Bartlett Brothers Western

CARSON McCLOUD

CENTER POINT LARGE PRINT
THORNDIKE, MAINE

This Center Point Large Print edition
is published in the year 2024 by arrangement with
Kensington Publishing Corp.

Copyright © 2024 by Collin McCurley.

All rights reserved.

This book is a work of fiction. Names, characters,
businesses, organizations, places, events, and incidents
either are the product of the author's imagination or are
used fictitiously. Any resemblance to actual persons,
living or dead, events, or locales is entirely coincidental.

The text of this Large Print edition is unabridged.
In other aspects, this book may vary
from the original edition.
Printed in the United States of America
on permanent paper sourced using
environmentally responsible foresting methods.
Set in 16-point Times New Roman type.

ISBN: 979-8-89164-275-1

The Library of Congress has cataloged this record
under Library of Congress Control Number: 2024938120

Chapter 1

The man called Noble dropped down out of the snowy Rockies and rode out onto the broad Colorado prairie. The posse would arrive back at Jamestown by now. They had given up the chase just shy of noon; the big black Noble rode proved more than a match for their mounts.

"A double ration of oats for you, next time we come across any," he said, and patted the stallion on the neck.

But there wouldn't be oats for miles yet. Boulder was to the south, but they knew him there, so he had turned north for the empty grasslands of Wyoming. At a frigid mountain stream he dismounted and allowed the big horse to drink his fill while he topped off his canteen. It was a silent place, almost holy in nature. The kind of quiet place where a man could sit back, rest, take it all in.

A man might settle here, run a few cows, watch them grow, and just listen to the trickling stream in peace.

Peace, Noble snorted. What right did he have to that? He didn't belong in such a place, no matter what he might want. Back in the saddle, Noble guided the stallion through a thicket of juniper before coming out into an open flat.

That was the first time he saw her.

She rode a little buckskin mare and, by the looks of both, they'd come a long way over rough country. Her hair hung long and loose, blonde locks filtering the setting sun's last rays. Noble could see little of her features, more hair covered her face like a veil. She was tall though; the stirrups were let all the way out and still came up inches short. She wore a flimsy dress, torn in several places around the knees and hem, dusty from travel.

Now, where would a woman come from out here?

Boulder, forty miles south, was the nearest town; Jamestown ten miles farther and more to the west. There were a few settlements scattered along the edge of Colorado's eastern slope, gold camps mostly, but these were all at least a dozen miles to the west.

Lost in her thoughts, she didn't see Noble until the tired buckskin stopped and she came right up on him.

"Sorry, mister," she said. She tugged the reins to one side, but the exhausted horse refused to go on.

"I'd say you got your money's worth out of that horse, ma'am."

"Bailey was my brother, Chet's, horse. Saddle too. I had to leave, though, and she was the only one saddled."

"If you aim to keep that horse alive, you'd best stop for a time."

"Can't stop. Not with them after me," she said. "I've got to . . ."

She swayed for a moment, then fell from the saddle. Noble let out a curse while scrambling down to see about her. On his knees, he cradled her head and looked her over. Nothing seemed broken, no sign of injury to her head; she'd fallen on soft sand and fresh spring growth. He lifted her up—shocked at how light she was—and carried her back through the thicket before setting her gently beside the stream.

Noble took off his coat, rolled it up for a pillow, and eased her head down. With his hand, he brushed the hair out of her face. She was young, not much more than twenty, and sweat caked a layer of rust-colored dirt to her features. Angry, red welts covered her bare arms and face.

She must have ridden through brush and branches.

"Ridden through at a run too, by the looks of those," Noble muttered to himself.

Walking through the juniper again, he retrieved both horses, watered the buckskin, and picketed each on some fresh grass. He stripped the saddle off his stallion and moved it near the girl. Then he did the same for the mare. There were sores along the smaller horse's back and flanks. That saddle hadn't been off for days.

He carried some salve in his bags and treated the buckskin as best he was able.

He opened the girl's saddlebags looking for a clue as to who she was or why she was out there; they proved empty.

She didn't have any weapons—didn't seem to have much of anything, really, only the tattered clothes she wore and the tired little mare.

Noble gathered an armload of juniper branches along with bits of tinder and started a fire. He took a battered coffeepot from his saddlebags, filled it at the stream, and soon had coffee going. Pouring himself a cup, Noble laid a pistol in his lap and leaned back against the trunk of a tall pine.

He had just finished the first cup when he heard them. They were beyond the thicket, but he didn't have to wait long. Three dirty men came through the junipers with enough noise to make a buffalo herd proud. They came out beside the stream, no more than thirty yards downstream. When the three saw the water, they scrambled down off their horses and put their faces in the stream. Over the rim of his coffee cup, Noble watched them.

The three were almost indistinguishable from each other. All of medium height, all thin, tawny men with patchy beards and covered in grime. Even from here he could see that their horses were in even worse shape than the girl's.

One of the newcomers noticed Noble's horse and elbowed the man to his left. Both studied the stallion for a moment, then the first man glanced around like some feral creature. Noble reached down and picked up his pistol. The man started for Noble's stallion.

"Touch that horse and I'll kill you," Noble said.

Instantly, all three froze in place.

Noble was back in the trees a ways, hidden in deep shadow. The three leaned forward to peer into the darkness; the three men's eyes were drawn to the orange glow of the fire, then to the girl sleeping beside it.

The one who'd moved toward Noble's horse spoke.

"Mister, we're just out here looking for our lost sister. That's her by the fire there. I don't know what she told you, but all we want is to take her home." Even as he spoke, his hand moved toward his belt gun.

"Touch that pistol and your 'sister' will be short one brother."

Noble stood, gun in hand, and walked close enough to the coals so they could see him.

"Look, we don't want no trouble. We're just out looking for our dear sister there. Got to take her back to Pa is all."

"And where would Pa be?" Noble said.

"Taylorville," the brother nearest the stream said. While he spoke, the third brother, the one who'd said nothing so far, slipped the thong off his pistol. All three had their guns free now.

Noble smiled. How many times had he seen men like this before? Men who thought themselves sly. Out here in the wild, with no one to see, they were dangerous, much like a pack of coyotes might be to a newborn calf.

Noble was no newborn calf.

"What's your sister's name?" Noble said.

"Her name? You don't know her name?" The one who seemed to be in charge tilted his head.

"Clarissa," the second said.

"And your pa's name?"

The third finally spoke. "Let's kill him and take her."

"Now, that's not very nice," Noble said. "Trying to kill people you don't know sounds like a good way to get yourself hung."

"Pa's name is Tom Clemsen. And what's your name, stranger?"

"They call me Noble."

The three suddenly went very still. The quiet, bloodthirsty one took a step back.

"Seems like you've heard of me."

"We have. We only want our sister back is all," the closest brother said. He licked his lips and glanced at the sleeping girl.

"There's three of us," the quiet brother said. "I don't believe the stories anyhow. No one is that fast." For all his talk, though, he'd taken another step back, placing himself directly behind the one that had done most of the talking.

The girl woke then. She rubbed sleep from her face, then saw the three men and jerked upright. "Get away from me!"

All three brothers went for their guns. Noble snapped two rounds off before they cleared leather, one bullet each for the nearest two. The third brother, the quiet one, got his gun halfway up before Noble's next two bullets struck him in the chest, and he fell dead. Noble's aim swung back to the closer two. They were down—one dead, one dying.

Noble walked to the still-living brother.

"Seems like she doesn't want to go with you."

"Damn you. She was our—"

Noble put a bullet through his eye.

He turned back to the girl while reloading each cylinder.

"I take it those weren't your brothers."

"Brothers? N-n-no," she said. "You killed them."

"I gave them a chance; they could have run away. I would have let them go."

The girl's face hardened. "I'm glad you did."

"Who were they?"

"Saul, Jack, and Silas Clemsen. Their pa claimed I owed him a horse. He said he'd trade it for me cleaning their house. Only he didn't really want me to clean their house. He wanted me to . . ."

11

A tear rolled down her cheek.

"And your real brother? The one whose horse you have?"

"He's gone. Chet caught sick last spring. Silas took Bailey, and I stole her back," Clarissa said. She moved over to the brother with the missing eye, kicked him and then spit into his face. "Silas was the worst, always leering at me."

"How far to this Taylorville?"

"A few hours," she said and gave him a leery look.

"North?"

She nodded slowly. "Right up against the mountains."

Noble went toward his horse and the girl's mare. "Coffee on the fire if you want it. I'm riding out."

"You going to Taylorville then?"

"I am."

"I need to go to Boulder," the girl said. She filled a cup of coffee and then eyed the dead men again. "You won't take me?"

"Take one of their guns," Noble said, and threw the blanket on his horse. He did the same for Clarissa's mare and then led both horses over to the fire. He handed the reins to the girl.

Noble saddled his stallion, reloaded the rest of his gear, and swung up. "It's forty miles to Boulder. Your horse won't make it without rest. You might go a little further if you ride one of theirs."

The dead men's horses grazed near the stream.

"Forty miles?"

"Forty or more," Noble grunted. "Good luck to you, ma'am."

Noble spurred the stallion into a trot then, passing through the screen of juniper and out onto the open plains. The night was bright, and the plains took on a ghostly glow. Most people wouldn't ride at night—too much risk of breaking a horse's leg—but Noble was used to it, and the stallion had excellent eyes. He heard the girl swear. She used—in his opinion—a particularly colorful word, one he was surprised she knew. Women rarely surprised him; men didn't either, for that matter. Over the years, he'd met all manner of people through dozens of towns all over the West. Gold-boom towns, cattle towns, rail sidings. He'd seen them all.

Then she and the little mare came crashing through the thicket behind him.

"So we're off to Taylorville," she said when she'd caught up to him.

"Looks like it."

"You know my name already. The least you can do is tell me yours."

"Noble."

For the third time in her life, Grace Bartlett rode along the old, secret trail west of her home. The first time she'd ridden this way, Gabe had been with her, the second time had been eight years ago. Gabriel had been along that time too.

This time, she traveled alone.

The first time she had done it on a dare of sorts. Gabe teased her for weeks before getting her to agree to follow him. He had been fifteen then, she thirteen, and his younger brother, Daniel, fourteen. Daniel had been working. Even as a boy, Daniel had always been working. He was—much like his father—born serious. But the three of them had been fast friends. Daniel stern and proud, she both cautious and adventurous, and then Gabe . . .

Gabe swept through life like a summer storm, raw and primal, wild, and utterly fearless.

The three of them had once ridden to the edge of their valley to gaze out upon the far western Bitterroots.

Daniel glanced at those high places, then turned his eyes back inward toward his father's lands, lands he would one day call his own. Grace stared at the snowy mountains, awestruck by their majesty but unwilling to go further. One look and Gabriel yearned to climb those icy peaks and see what lay far beyond.

They had been so young then. With so much ahead of them.

The second time they'd come thinking of running away and getting married. Gabriel's parents had been furious. They were too young.

They didn't know what it took to make a marriage and a family. They needed to wait and be patient.

Grace sighed. She couldn't remember why she and Gabriel decided against it in the end. Fear of his parents?

Gabriel's parents, as they usually were, had been proven right.

Grace's horse stopped at the crest of a long rise. How far west was she? Fifteen miles, at least. She'd started early, and it would still take all day to return.

The trail dipped down along a stream ahead of her, and from there it wound north until reaching the cabin and corrals she and Gabe had discovered those long years ago.

She patted Rose on the neck, then spurred the bay onward.

Grace knew the horse sensed her nervousness, and there was every reason to be nervous, if not outright frightened.

My family's future depends on this. Depends on me succeeding.

Rose wound her way down the trail, and with every step, Grace's fear grew. Who might be at the cabin? And worse, what if no one was?

Going back without finding out was not an option. If no one was at the cabin, she would have to return again later to find what she needed.

And if someone is there, I will have to convince them to help me.

It had been easier those years ago. Womanhood . . . motherhood had made her more cautious. And she knew now what manner of men lived in the world and what manner of men used the lost cabin.

The trail dropped down and turned north, following the stream. Movement drew her eye; a man had been watching from atop the hill ahead. Grace took in a long breath, fighting to calm herself. It seemed she would not have to make a second trip.

When the cabin came into view, it lay in worse shape than she remembered. The window overlooking the trail had fallen out, or had been shot out, and the roof sagged deep in the middle. The walls bulged outward at the top, and the whole thing looked like it might collapse under the next snowfall.

There were horses in the corral though. Three of them, all tall, handsome animals that looked like they could run all day. Finer horses than any honest man could afford.

Four disheveled men came out to meet her, each holding rifles. She knew none of them. A young man in a red shirt wore a bandage over one eye, he couldn't have been more than twenty. Another had a buckskin shirt, leggings, and two guns tied down on his narrow hips. He gave her a wolfish smile. The third man was black. He wore a wide-brimmed planter's hat and a bandolier of shells for a rifle. The fourth man took off a battered old cavalry hat and held it over his chest. He was the oldest of the group, with bits of gray in his lank hair and beard.

"Ma'am," the older man said. "We weren't expecting any visitors up here. You mind telling me what you're doing up this way?"

"I understand," Grace said. She took a breath, then started. "I am looking for someone. A man."

The buckskin-clad man's grin widened. "Looks like you found one. Four men, in fact." He looked her up and down, and she fought back a shudder.

"The specific man I'm looking for is a big man, good with a gun."

"I'm big enough when it matters, and as it happens, I'm plenty good with a gun," the buckskin man said. He sauntered a step closer. "If you'll tell me what you need, I'm sure we can reach some sort of arrangement."

Grace ignored him. She kept her eyes on the older man; he seemed in charge. "The man I'm looking for has a scar on the back of his hand shaped like a crescent moon."

"Ma'am," the older man said, "I don't recall anyone like that. Did this man of yours have a name?"

"He isn't mine. I don't know what name he uses anymore."

The older man's face turned ashen. "Ma'am, I surely wish you hadn't ridden in here today. We can't afford to have anyone knowing where we are."

"Joss, you sure about this?" the wounded man said. "She's a woman and all."

"Mose, take Jake back inside," the older man said.

The black man, Mose, leaned down and pulled the young, wounded man back toward the cabin.

Jake tried to resist, but Mose held him fast. "Dammit, Joss, this ain't right. I didn't sign on for this. Pit, don't you dare."

"Pit," the older man said, "we can use that horse. I am truly sorry, ma'am."

The buckskin man, Pit, was close now, and before she could pull away, he snatched the bridle of her horse. Rose shied back, but he held the bridle fast. "Why don't you come on down off that horse and let us get a better look at you."

Grace turned to him. "Let me go. I have no interest in you."

His face turned red and ugly. "Think you're better than me, do you? I'll teach you something."

He grabbed at her leg then; he moved very fast. She tried to hold on to the saddle horn, but he pulled her down. She hit the ground hard. The air rushed out of her lungs, and she gasped for breath. She remembered the derringer. Her hand went into her pocket. She fumbled for the small gun, found it, and drew it out.

He was ready for her. Snake-quick, he clamped an iron grip over her wrist.

"What's this now? A pretty little lady's gun." He shook her and the derringer fell useless to the ground.

Not liking the commotion, Rose jerked back and tore free from the gunman's hand. He swore, snarled, and then grabbed Grace's shoulder. His grip was tight enough to hurt. Grace fought to get free, but he was so strong. What had she been thinking coming here? She would fail her family.

She fought with all she had. She raked at his eyes. She stomped at his legs and groin. Nothing worked. He was too strong. Too fast. He trapped both her hands in his left and raised his right hand, palm open, ready to strike her.

"Pit," the older man said. He had caught her horse and was looking at its hip. "Pit!"

"What?" Pit snarled. "Dammit, Joss, I was about to teach her some manners."

"Let her go."

"What?" Pit cocked his head to the side.

Grace tried to take advantage of the distraction, but he put a hard knee on her stomach and pinned her to the ground.

"Pit, let her go."

"No. Joss, we can't let her go, and since we can't, I'm about to have some fun with her." Pit leered down at Grace.

"Let her go and help the lady up," Joss said.

He had a gun in his fist, leveled at Pit's head. He cocked it, and Pit went still as a stone. "Pit, we've been friends a long time, don't make me kill you."

Mose had come back out of the cabin now. He looked from Pit to Joss in confusion. "What's this about now?" he said.

Pit licked his lips. "Joss here has lost his nerve. Or he's wanting the woman all for himself I—"

"Look at that bay's brand, Pit," Joss said.

Mose came up beside Rose, patting the frightened horse on the neck and talking soft and slow. He turned the horse to study the brand. "Lord almighty."

"What?" Pit asked. "What's so damned important about a damned brand?"

Mose turned Rose where the gunman could see the brand for himself.

Grace did not see it. She didn't need to. The Rafter N, the Bartlett family brand, Daniel's brand, her husband's brand.

"I'll be damned," Pit said, and released her. "Joss, I didn't know. How could I know?"

"You and us all," Joss said. "Go back in the cabin with Jake. Mose and I will see to the lady."

The gunman left without a word, and Joss offered Grace a hand to help her up. When she stood, her head felt groggy, and the ground spun.

"Ma'am, I apologize," the outlaw said. "We didn't know. We just came down from Helena after seeing to a bank there. Pit just got riled up and all. We've had a rough go of it. The posse killed Mose's horse and all."

Grace fumbled for Rose, and the two men carefully helped her up into the saddle. She mumbled her thanks, head still swimming. How could she ride home like this?

"Mose, get my horse," Joss said, answering her unspoken question. "I'll see you get home, ma'am."

When the black man returned, he led a gelding that was all black but for two white hind feet.

Joss mounted up. "I'll make sure she gets home. While I'm gone, Mose, keep an eye on Jake."

Grace tried to clear her head. She'd come here for a reason, one that seemed lost to her now, but she knew it was important. She had to do something; she had to save the Rafter.

"The man, the man I'm looking for?" Grace said. She fought back her dizziness. "You know him. Will you find him?"

"We will," Mose nodded. "I'll send word with anyone who comes here between now and then."

"Tell him . . ." Grace said. Her thoughts were clearer now. She knew what was needed. A hundred times she'd thought about what to say, about what might bring him back, "Tell him Grace needs him to come home."

"We'll be riding out tomorrow," Joss said.

21

"When we do, I'll pass word along the trail as well. We'll make sure he knows."

"Where's your ranch, ma'am?" Joss asked.

"Rafter N. East of here. Just north of Bigsby."

"I'll get you there," Joss said.

Chapter 2

Despite the late hour, Noble knew at a glance that Taylorville wasn't much of a town. The settlement lay in a narrow valley, high, gray mountains pressing in on either side like the jaws of a granite vise. There were two saloons, a restaurant, a hotel sporting a coat of fresh red paint, and a general store barely larger than a wagon bed. There were homes and shacks of various sizes clinging to the mountain's skirts; the whole town couldn't have held more than forty people.

Back in Jamestown, Noble remembered hearing about this town. Last year, a passing miner claimed he'd panned out a few flakes in the nearby creek and then started a rumor of gold. Taylorville popped up overnight. Never mind that no one had actually seen either the gold or that first lucky miner.

Noble stopped at the hitching rail in front of the restaurant and tied off the black.

Clarissa brought her buckskin up beside the stallion but stayed in the saddle. She kept glaring toward the shacks nearer the mountains, saying nothing and twisting her reins tight around the pommel.

She'd said nothing on the long ride in, and that

had suited Noble just fine. He wasn't much on talking.

"I can buy you a meal," Noble volunteered.

"No. No, I cut out so fast I left some things back home," Clarissa said. One hand rubbed at the pistol hanging on her hip. She'd taken it from one of the three Clemsen boys, and Noble hadn't commented on it.

He wasn't sure she actually knew how to use it.

"I wouldn't be too hasty to pull that," Noble said. "You're liable to kill the wrong person. The law won't look kindly on that."

Clarissa turned to give him a faint smile. "There's no lawman in Taylorville. If there was, they'd have hung the Clemsens by now."

Noble gestured toward the restaurant. "This place any good?"

"Not really. Stay away from the ham. It's half rancid at the best of times. They scrape the mold off every morning so you can't tell."

"Good to know."

"Thank you again," Clarissa said suddenly.

"All right." Noble tapped his boot against the top step. A few clumps of dirt fell from the heel, and he used the toe to push them clear.

She gave him an odd expression, tilting her head to one side, and Noble was reminded of a puppy he owned a long time ago.

"You aren't used to being thanked," she said.

"I'm not."

toughness to her that they'd lacked. She had at least a measure of sense, too. Enough to snatch up that pistol and follow him instead of trying for Boulder alone.

On their ride, she'd proved good company too. She had said little and didn't bother him with needless questions. Most folks were always asking needless questions, or complaining, or thinking out loud.

That girl didn't complain once.

Noble finished a refill of his coffee and paid the waiter. He had a few coins, not much to show after keeping his head down all winter. He needed a job, and a good one.

Last summer, he'd brought a herd up from Texas, then fought in a range war over in Kansas before winding up in Colorado just before winter. In Denver, a local tough looking for a reputation had recognized him. The fight had been a fair one; Noble gave him every chance to back down. The local refused. He'd been younger than that girl, twice as foolish. They'd met in the street and the kid proved too slow. Afterward, before the local's friends could gather up for a hanging, Noble rode west into the mountains around Leadville.

There was a log cabin in a hidden valley west of town, one well known to men who rode his kind of trails, and all winter he'd sat by and watched the snow pile up.

Come springtime he'd ridden on to Jamestown and been desperate enough to play a few hands of poker. A local man, fancying himself a gambler, had cheated, and poorly. Noble called him on it; they'd both gone for their guns. The gambler was overmatched, but once again he'd been a local man with local friends, including the local sheriff. Noble left town a half hour ahead of a noose and posse.

The restaurant was quiet and empty. The cook, a broad man in a greasy shirt, came out and glanced around once while the waiter wrung out a towel and wiped down the tables. Without a word, he yawned and disappeared back into the kitchen. When the tables were cleaned, the waiter pushed in each chair.

Noble took the hint. He stood and went outside. Deep under the shadowed eave of the restaurant he waited, and let his eyes adjust to the dark.

He didn't consider himself an evil man.

Most folks wouldn't agree. He'd certainly killed too many men to call himself a good one. But he hadn't gone up against anyone who didn't deserve it. The men he killed were mostly outlaws or cardsharps or just general varmints, like the Clemsen boys.

No one, not even the saintliest sky pilot, would miss those boys. Not after they set out to molest a woman.

Some of the men he'd fought and killed,

though, had just been riding for the brand, same as him. Only they'd been on the other side. That didn't mean they were on the wrong side, no more than it meant Noble had been on the right side. Range wars didn't seem to follow right and wrong. Usually it was just two sides, both with money, fighting like old bulls over who controlled the local range.

Noble never shot anyone in the back though. He always squared up to them and let them make their play. But he had never backed down either.

Still, he didn't have much to show for his life: a fast horse, a well-used gun, a cold saddle, and no future. That needed to change. Better than most, he knew where he was headed—a shallow plot on some Boot Hill.

If I can get just one big windfall, it'll all change. I can find myself a little place against the mountains, maybe like that creek back there, and settle down.

Maybe raise a few beef cows. From his younger days—those seemed like a lifetime ago—Noble knew a lot about beef cattle. He could have some peace and quiet without worrying about some reputation-hungry gunhand wanting to make a name for himself.

He was thinking where he might go to bed down for the night—a copse of alder they'd ridden by east of town seemed promising—when the first shot echoed through the town.

Noble checked to make sure the riding strap was off his Colt. He was careful not to draw it. Anybody running to a window and looking down would see a man holding a gun, lounging in the dark along the street. That seemed like a good way to get shot at.

For the same reason he didn't rush to his horse and head out of town. He had done nothing here. No reason to act guilty.

The drumbeat of hooves sounded up the street toward the houses. It was one horse, running hard, coming his way. Noble moved deeper into shadow.

The rider slowed just behind Noble's horse, then stopped and glanced around. Noble recognized the horse at once.

What had she done now?

Clarissa called out, "Noble, are you here?"

More noise came from near the houses. More and more lanterns lit that end of town.

"Noble?" she repeated.

"What happened?" Noble said. Someone was yelling up the street now, a man. He sounded drunk.

"I've got to go. I've got to leave. Will you help me?"

Noble thought about it for half a heartbeat. What had the girl done now? Whatever it was, he couldn't avoid being drawn into it. When they caught her, they'd learn he killed the Clemsens, and then they'd learn who he was, and then they might try arresting him, and then hanging him. That sheriff up in Jamestown would see to it.

He jerked the horse's reins loose and jumped up into the saddle.

"Sorry, boy, no rest for us tonight and no sweet oats again."

Noble had learned a great deal about tracking over the years. He'd used those skills often enough, sometimes hunting after bounties and sometimes evading the law.

Being hunted was something he knew all too much about.

He moved out ahead of Clarissa, and when they dipped in the bottom of a graveled streambed, he swung north, toward the Wyoming border. Two miles up the stream, he brought them out up a steep rockslide onto the western bank. Without comment or complaint, the girl followed. Noble gave her credit for that. Scrawny and young she might be, but she was tough as old boot leather. Her head bobbed as she fought off sleep.

How long since she last slept? She'd rested a little in the trees before the Clemsen boys showed up, but that hadn't been more than an hour. Noble fought back a yawn. It had been far longer since he'd slept last, but he was used to it. Used to it or not, though, he couldn't ride much farther.

These horses need to rest.

He slowed down beside the girl, reaching over to shake her.

"Hey," he said.

"I'm awake," she said with a wide yawn. "I'm awake."

"Good. Now tell me what happened back in town."

Instead of speaking, her head eased back down until her chin touched her chest.

Noble shook her again. "What happened back there?"

Clarissa's head jerked up a little more this time. She looked around at Noble, as if surprised to find him there. Her eyes flared open, and she drew back from his outstretched hand. "What?"

"Taylorville. What happened?"

"I shot him," she said.

"Shot who?"

"Pa Clemsen. I went back for my things, expecting he was gone down to the livery. He mucks it out at night. But he wasn't there. He asked where his boys were, and I told him they were dead. He was angry. He cussed me and said I was a tramp. Then he tried to grab me. And so I shot him."

"Killed him?"

She shook her head. "Missed. But it slowed him down, and my second shot got him in the side." Clarissa pointed down to her waist. "It spun him around like a top, and then I grabbed my things and lit out. People were coming out into the street, and then he came out before I could get my things on Bailey. He had an old pistol in his coat. He shot at me."

"Are you hit?" Noble hadn't seen any signs of injury on her, but his thoughts had been on getting clear of town. If the girl was shot, and if it was serious, she would need to see a doctor. He could do a few things. He once pulled a bullet out of his arm up near Powder River, but he was no sawbones.

"He missed," Clarissa said. "I don't know what happened after that. I was scared, and Bailey and I ran."

"Good thing you did. Can you stay awake another hour or so? There might be men after us from town, and we've got to put more distance between us and them."

Clarissa nodded. "I'll make it."

Noble looked at the faint wisps of cloud high overhead. The horses' breath fogged in the night air. *It's going to get cold tonight. Awful cold.*

They skirted the edge of a sandstone bluff, again making their way north. The horses wove their way through boulders that time had whittled from the tall bluff. To the west, the snowy Rockies rose up, huge and black against a star-filled sky. East, the land lay flat and empty, bare but for rippling grass.

Another half hour passed, and Noble stopped

to let the horses drink from yet another stream.

Upstream, toward the mountains, a stand of thick aspens grew. He brought them into the white-trunked trees, climbing higher until he saw the very edge of the high bluff. In the midst of the aspens' ghostly trunks he saw a wide space where wind had downed one of the older trees.

He climbed off his horse and set to work on a simple lean-to. He used the edge of the bluff for one side, cutting a few thick boughs for the other, then weaving a mat of thinner branches for the roof. Clarissa tried to help but only got in the way until he finally got her to sit back against an aspen and wait. Moments after sitting, the drowsy girl dropped off into a deep sleep.

Noble finished the shelter, swept the ground inside clear, and covered it with piles of leaves and cut juniper boughs; several grew along the bluff's base. As shelter went, it wasn't much—just enough to block the worst of the wind and keep the snow off. To get through the night, they would need heat. Smoke and fire meant risk of being seen, but going without meant a cold, miserable night. Odds were against anyone coming after them. If this Clemsen was as bad as Clarissa made out, no one was likely to help him.

Not in this cold, anyway.

He tucked the girl into the lean-to and then started a small fire. Then he cared for their horses. Fresh spring growth showed at the very base of the bluff. It wasn't much, just enough to give each horse a few bites, but they would be warm and out of the wind.

Like stretched cotton, wisps of clouds hung in fat, low rolls overhead.

"Yessir, going to be a real cold one tonight," Noble said to himself.

He piled up more brush and debris around the lean-to and banked the fire so it would burn for a few hours. This deep in the trees, no one would see it unless they were right on top of them and— if he'd guessed right about the coming weather— no one would be out tonight. Tomorrow morning, they could easily wake up to a foot or more of snow.

Then he would have real problems. He had winter clothing. He knew how to survive. The girl did not. A tattered dress and the paper-thin coat she must have retrieved from her home would not keep her warm.

Where could he find what they needed?

The closest settlements were all to the west. There were mining camps all along the Rockies, like fleas on a dog's hairy back. But snow would still block the high passes, and it would be colder still in those windswept heights. East lay open prairie, the absolute coldest place to be.

South was out. *Nothing but trouble down there.*

There was a place north and a little west, a camp of sorts, where men on the dodge might ride out the long winter. A woman named Kettle ran it. Few people knew the place; fewer yet actually went there. Only the kind of people that rode the outlaw trail. How long since he'd been there last? Two years. There had been talk of a rail line coming through.

Kettle would have what they needed. She took in orphans sometimes. They worked in the kitchen or garden for her. She might also have a decent place for the girl to work.

Noble slid down to rest beside Clarissa. Somewhere along the way, she'd taken time to clean up. Her clothes were the same, torn and stained from travel, but she'd washed her face and brushed back her hair. She had an honest face. Young, but not so young as he'd first believed. She couldn't be more than five years younger than him.

She hasn't seen the things I have though. Few have.

Kettle's place it was then. Kettle would either give her a job or get her to whatever friends or family she had in Boulder. Either sounded better than living with Clemsen. He could drop her off with Kettle, see that she was settled in, and then be on about his business. It wouldn't be anything to brag about, but she'd be fed and kept warm.

Certainly, life on the road isn't any fit place for a girl.

Chapter 3

Grace Bartlett followed the man called Joss to the edge of her family ranch. They paused on an overlook at the entrance of a long, broad valley. There were cattle below, scattered dark shapes, stark against the pale grass.

"That it, ma'am?" Joss said.

He'd said little during their ride. Asking every few miles about directions, making thin bits of small talk about the range, the grass, the cattle business in general. Grace knew little of such things; Daniel handled the cattle and she their home. Grace suspected Joss spoke more from concern for her than genuine confusion about the trail. On the trail, the man seemed to know his business well.

"That's home," she said, and meant it.

Several buildings stood at the valley's farthest end. In her kitchen, a lantern shone bright and inviting. *Daniel must be up late.* He would be worried about her. She should have left him a note or something . . . anything to set his mind at ease. He had too many worries these days.

She told him she was going to see her friend Mary Hempstead. She had not told him the truth. If he'd known that, he would never have let her go.

Her mind had cleared over the long ride. Enough that she wanted to ask her escort a question.

"The brand, Rafter N. What made you stop your friend when you saw it?"

Joss took the makings out of a shirt pocket and built himself a cigarette. He struck a match, lit the end, and took a deep breath.

Grace was close enough to see his eyes. He studied the grass bucking in the night wind; he took in the stream that ran through the ranch yard before splitting the valley down the middle.

"Nice place. A man could run a good number of head on a place like this. Your husband's?"

"Yes, his family settled it," Grace said. "You didn't answer my question."

Joss used a thumb to push up his hat. "Ma'am, that man you described . . . that could be any one of a hundred men I know, maybe one of a thousand out along the owl hoot trail."

He dismounted and took a long drag on the cigarette. The tip flared orange and bright. Then he dropped it into the grass and rubbed it out with his boot toe.

Grace had seen cowhands do that before. Cowhands cared about the range. They would never risk a grassfire. She'd never considered an outlaw caring about a grassfire. This man knew cattle. He'd either worked for or owned a place like the Rafter. What had caused him to lose it? What drove him to the outlaw life? Her family might very well find itself in the same situation unless matters improved. That's why she had gone to the hidden cabin.

"That brand though . . . the one on your bay. There's a man rides a horse with that same brand. He's known to me. He's known to a lot of men."

"Men in your line of work?" Grace interrupted.

Joss smiled for the first time. "My line of work. Pretty words for what I do, but no. Me and the boys, we do small jobs. We have humble needs. We aren't really bad men, not even Pit. We don't hunt trouble. The man with that brand though . . ."

He climbed back into the saddle and adjusted the reins. "The man with that brand is another type entirely."

Grace paled. She'd been worried about this. How much had he changed over the last seven years? Would he care about their troubles?

"He's a bad man then? A really bad one? A killer?"

Joss's eyes narrowed. "He's killed men, sure enough. I've met him, but I won't say I know him well. He's a loner. Some of those men needed killing, I reckon. Some others, well . . . I guess he had his reasons."

Grace wasn't sure what to say.

"That might not answer your question," he finally said.

The outlaw turned to go then, and Grace

watched after him. After a few steps, he paused and looked back.

"He's a hard man, a dangerous man, but reliable in his own way. I wouldn't say he's an outlaw though."

Joss spurred his horse then, and his voice lifted in song.

"I got a girl in Chey-enne, she can dance, she sure can. I got a girl in Chey-enne, love her the best I can-can."

He had a good, strong voice and—like the way he'd cared about the range and known about the cattle—it surprised her.

Then he was gone, one more shadow melting into the black night.

Grace started her horse down toward the house and the lone lantern. At her mother-in-law's request, she'd gone to the cabin to call him home.

Did Emilia know? Did she know what he'd become?

She did. Grace was sure of it.

Emilia Bartlett always seemed to know things others didn't. She would have been keeping tabs on him the whole time. How did she do it though? And how had she kept it secret from all of them?

"Tomorrow I will ask her," Grace said aloud. "She owes me an explanation after what I've done."

A dangerous man. A killer.

That's what Joss had called him. Grace couldn't

reconcile that with the boy she'd grown up with. He'd been angry often enough. More than once he'd been angry and fighting mad and on the verge of outright violence. She and Daniel had always pulled him back from the brink. All but that one, last time. She hadn't been there for that, only Daniel, and he hadn't been able to stop him.

If Joss was right, he was a hardened killer now. How could he have gone so far?

We weren't there for him. We weren't there to pull him back to himself.

With no one to calm him, he had acted on the rage he carried, and men had died.

She was close to the ranch house. She could see her son, Jack, through the kitchen window. He was braiding a rope with the leather strips she'd bought in town last week. Someday he might rope one of his own calves on the Rafter, but not if things continued as they were. Their troubles were not just growing but multiplying. Daniel had tried his way. He'd gone to the law. He and his father had gone to the banks for more money to see them through. The Rafter N wouldn't be theirs much longer. Her son might never call this ranch home, nor would Ester.

Daniel had done what he could. This wasn't the empty valley his grandfather had settled, nor the peaceful one his father inherited. Men were coming to the valley, men of violence, men who wanted to rule and would kill to take what her family had.

"A dangerous man. A killer," the outlaw Joss had called him. It broke her heart to hear it of the boy she'd known.

These days, though, that's what we need. That's what we must have to survive what's coming.

It took two days for Noble and Clarissa to reach their destination.

Kettle's place sat where the edge of the mountains met the Laramie River before it swept out eastward into the plains. Old cottonwoods lined the river's rocky banks, their thin limbs showing faint signs of spring in every green bud. The Medicine Bow Mountains were to the west, more open plains to the east. The place was an intersection of sorts. Within a few miles several trails all came together, some known only to those who rode the dark trail, others used by all manner of travelers.

"What kind of place is this?" Clarissa asked.

There were four buildings: a stable, two storage sheds, and the large main building where Kettle fed customers and sold a few select goods.

"The kind where people don't ask questions. Kettle runs it. She's tough but fair. She can give you a job and get you up on your feet. Can you cook?"

"I can," Clarissa said, nodding. "I did all the

cooking for myself and my brother and later the Clemsens."

"Good. That'll get you a job in the kitchens and keep you out of sight. The girls up front catch a hard time from the men passing through here though Kettle puts a stop to it before it goes too far."

And in those rare instances where the formidable Kettle wasn't enough, one of the visiting gunhands would intervene. If, that is, he wasn't the one causing the problem.

That didn't happen often. Most men were well-behaved at Kettle's place. She wouldn't do business with anyone after they bothered her girls. Nor did she tolerate fighting at her place. Noble had seen bitter enemies ride in, share a meal, and then ride a few miles out before settling their affairs.

"Why can't I just ride along with you?"

"I'm no fit companion, and the trail I ride isn't right for a young girl."

"I'll be eighteen this summer. You're not that much older than me," she said with a pout.

Noble thought back through the years to when he was eighteen. He'd been gone from home by then, and he'd already killed more than one man. At that age, he thought he knew everything. Five years later, he realized he hadn't known a damned thing.

Age wise, she was right; there wasn't much

between them. But in life experience, they were worlds apart. Kettle's place would be better for her. Safer.

When they were in front of the main building, Noble knew something was wrong. Five horses, all saddled, stood hitched out front, but there were no other signs of activity. Kettle had always kept her people busy. Every other time he'd been there, her people had been chopping wood, hauling water up from the river, stringing laundry on the line, smoking meat out back, and tending the livestock.

Now he saw no one, and other than the five horses, there was no stock at all.

"Careful here," Noble said. "Something's not right." Normally he would have waited on the trail until he knew exactly what he was riding into, but having the girl with him had distracted him.

One more reason she can't be with me.

Noble swung down out front of the main building and as he did, he slipped the riding thong off his pistol. They were well into Wyoming now, and in Wyoming he wasn't a wanted man, but it might not be the law laying up inside.

Kettle's had been a popular place for men on the dodge. For that type, few places offered a home-cooked meal and an easy escape.

Clarissa climbed off her horse and came up close beside him.

"This is it?" she said.

"No, something's wrong here. I've never seen it like this. There should be people everywhere." Then louder he said. "Coming in."

"Come ahead," a voice called from inside.

Noble went into the trading post slowly, keeping Clarissa well behind him.

Five men were inside. Two sat near the center playing cards, another stood beside the south-facing window. He was the oldest of them; steel grey hair curled out from under a wide-brimmed brown hat. The last two were directly in front of him. A bottle and cork sat on the table between them.

They were gunmen. Noble knew it at once. Their horses were too good, their pistols used, and well cared for.

One of the two at the table spat while the other poured himself a drink into a thick glass.

"Saw you riding up," he said, and set the bottle down.

"Where's Kettle?" Noble said.

"Moved on towards Utah," the man said. He had a southern accent and a broad cavalry hat hung on the empty chairback beside him.

"This girl needs some things," Noble said. He didn't like the way this was shaping up but couldn't see a way clear—not without putting his back to these men, and that he would not do.

"There's some clothes in the back storeroom,"

the older man by the window said without turning. "Might be some that'll fit her."

"Go on," Noble said, and Clarissa circled around the pair in front and went to the storeroom.

"She your girl?" the man with the bottle said.

"She is," Noble said. Anything less than that would only encourage them.

The man drained his shot and poured another. "You come up from the south?"

"We did."

"Those horses look tired," he said. "You running toward or from something?"

Noble didn't see badges on any of them. Their horses and gear seemed far too fine for a group of marshals, so he decided on the truth, or at least part of it.

"The girl had trouble with a man down south. She wanted to leave, and I was headed this way. I thought Kettle might take her in."

"Only Kettle ain't here," the southerner said. His companion gave Noble a grin broad enough to show a missing front tooth.

"We could take her in," toothless said.

Noble ignored the comment. He wondered how long it would take Clarissa to find some clothing and then how he could see them both clear of this without getting shot. It occurred to him then to consider why these men were there. Had they finished a job or were they about to do one?

They haven't done it yet. None of them have the heady excitement that comes after a job.

Noble considered what might be worth stealing in the area. There were a few mines to the north; none shipped much more than a few thousand in gold or silver at a single time. Of course, one might have gotten snowed in during the winter—it had been a bad one—and would then have a big haul ready to come out. That would make a tempting target.

But there were other options.

The railroad wasn't too much farther north. At times, they hauled payrolls on those trains, not to mention wealthy passengers. Noble knew several men who'd made a great deal of money holding up trains. Trains were dangerous though. Besides the wealthy passengers, there might be anyone aboard: soldiers, gunmen, Pinkertons, even other outlaws.

Where else was there a lot of loose money lying around?

Laramie. That had to be it. The bank in Laramie was a rich one. With cattle prices up the previous fall, the ranches had done well for themselves. And now, with spring on, they'd want to add young stock to their herds. Between all the buyers and sellers—the mines too—the banks would be flush with cash, and the Laramie bank most of all. It was the biggest bank in the biggest town for a hundred miles.

That's a risky job. They'll need more men than this. At least this many more.

"I said we could take her off your hands," the southerner repeated.

"No," Noble answered, and glared at the man.

"He don't think we're good enough company for her," toothless said, and he spit another wad of tobacco on the floor.

"Is that right, mister? You don't think we're good enough to take care of that girl?"

"If I kill these two," Noble said, "I want their share."

"What'd you just say?" the southerner said.

"Shut up. I'm talking to your boss, and I said if I kill you and toothless here, I want both your shares."

The two men playing cards were suddenly silent; the old man at the window turned to him then. He had cold, blue eyes. "What makes you say something like that?"

"I don't think you're planning on hitting one of the mines, and the railroad's been sending Pinkertons after train robbers. That leaves the bank in Laramie. You've chosen some trouble-hunters here though. They'll either get you caught or killed."

The old man smiled a little. "The one you call toothless is our safecracker. I need him—unless you could handle that?"

"I can if need be. The other two out of it?"

"I do need enough men to keep the townsfolk at bay. They've got a smart sheriff in Laramie—tough too—and if you know the bank, you know what the townsfolk are like. Fighters all. Of course, if you think you can take all four of my men, I suppose you could handle all that as well."

"Nah," Noble answered. "They can go back to their cards. These two are enough, and I'm not greedy."

The front two were sweating now. He'd sized them up right. When it had been five against one, they were confident; now it was down to just the two of them, and they were right up front and close together.

Noble regarded them again. "What do you say, Johnny Reb? Still want to go now that your boss won't back your play?"

The man didn't answer for a time. The shot went untouched on the tabletop.

"Forget it," he finally said. "Me and Bill. We were just funnin' you."

"Good," Noble said. He reached over and slugged down the poured drink before either of them could move. "Clarissa," he called. "We need to be leaving these men to their work."

"Now, I don't know about that," the older man said. "Seems like you might know a little too much to go riding off so fast. Especially if you're headed north."

The two nearest men, Toothless Bill and his southern friend, grinned at the sudden turn back to five against one.

Noble let out a sigh. It didn't look like he'd be getting out of this without getting bloody. He certainly couldn't beat all five at once. The two nearest wouldn't be a problem, but he had a feeling the others might know their business. The old man almost certainly would.

Noble thought through his next move. It would be better to start the ball rolling without Clarissa in the room. The storeroom door was thick, as were its walls. She'd be safer in there.

The old man and the two hard cases were all watching him closely. The nearest two had their confidence restored, but they had to know that they were in the line of fire. If Noble didn't get them, their "friends' " return fire might.

The old man suddenly glanced out the window again, then his gaze swung back to Noble. "Riders coming. Friends of yours?"

"Maybe." Noble shrugged. "I've got a few here and there."

"Might be friends of mine," the old man said. He watched Noble with an expression of amused eagerness.

Noble decided to wait. His odds were already poor, and the newcomers could tip things in his favor. The old man wouldn't want anyone else knowing his plans. He only had five men; not enough to hold both Noble and the newcomers here.

Then again, it might be the rest of this group, but Noble didn't think so. By his earlier words, the old man seemed to want to keep his men as few as possible. Fewer men meant a larger split for each of them. Fewer men also meant fewer men he had to trust. Those cold, blue eyes weren't those of a trusting man. Outlaws who trusted rarely lasted long.

Noble could testify to that.

The horses drew closer. Noble could hear their hooves beating on the packed ground.

The old man gave another of his small smiles and moved away from the window. "No luck for you, I'm afraid. Friends of mine."

Noble's chest tightened. If the old man decided to kill him, he had little chance now. If he let it play out, his only chance of making it through was by the old man's good graces.

He did not seem like the kind of man with much in the way of good graces.

Gravel crunched outside, there was the creak of leather. Boots sounded on the planks out front.

Noble took a slow step away from the door to allow the newcomers in while also keeping them all in front of him. If the shooting started, he would need room to draw, and then he'd dive in among the newcomers. The old man and his men might hesitate to shoot into their friends.

Not enough to see him clear. He had little chance of surviving this, but he would take more of them with him. Not the worst outcome.

A shadow darkened the floor, and the first man entered. He was a little older than Noble by maybe five years, dressed in brown buckskins, and he had a smirk on his unshaven face. Noble did not recognize him.

"Took you long enough, Pit," the old man said with a little smile.

"Jake caught one up in Montana," Pit said.

"Jake?" the old man said. He surprised Noble with a sudden look of outright fear.

Then a big black man came in, followed by an even younger man with a dirty bandage over one eye. Noble had seen the black man before but couldn't remember where. Tucson maybe?

"Pa," the young man said, and went to the old man.

"Jake, what happened?" the old man said. He put a hand on either side of the young man's face and stared at the bandage.

"I was too close to the lock when it blew, fragment caught my eye. I can still see. It's just an ugly, bleeding mess."

Noble took it all in without a word. If Clarissa hadn't been in the back, he might have ducked outside and slipped away unnoticed. Then the black man spotted him. He leaned down to whisper something in the one called Pit's ear.

Pit's head whipped around to Noble. His face whitened, and his mouth fell open.

Then a fourth man entered. He took in the crowd, spotted Noble, and smiled. "Noble, I am lucky to find you here. I thought I'd have to comb through half of Colorado to hunt you up."

"Joss," Noble dipped his head. He knew the old outlaw well. He'd staked him a couple times in the Powder River country, and they'd ridden as shotgun guards for a payroll down in Arizona. They'd always been friendly, if not exactly friends.

"You know this man, Joss?" The old man came over from the window.

"I do," Joss said, his smile slipping a notch.

"We were just about to see if he's any good with a gun when you arrived."

Joss took a long step out of the line of fire and said, "Oh, I wouldn't do that, Colonel."

"He can't take all of us," the old man said.

"No, but he'll be the fastest, and he'll get you for sure," Joss said. "Jake, you and Pit get clear beside Mose." The black man was already moving back behind Joss, closer to the door.

It was Noble's turn to smile then. The odds were bad, but Joss would keep his group out of it. Moreover, the old man was at least a little worried now.

The old man's eyes narrowed. His two hard cases were on their feet, staring at their boss and Noble in turn.

Clarissa chose that exact moment to come into the room. The hammer of her old Colt came back with a heavy click. The long black barrel was aimed directly at the back of the nearest hard case. "I'll see to these two," she said. Less than a dozen feet separated them. At that range, she couldn't miss.

"Shall we keep it between us, Colonel?" Noble asked. "No need for your boys to catch a bullet in the back."

"I don't think she'd do it," the old man said.

"She shot her stepfather a couple days back. I guess he thought the same."

The old man's smile faltered.

Noble could see he didn't like it, being backed down in front of so many men. But Joss had warned him, and everyone knew and was known by Joss.

"Father," the younger man who'd arrived with Joss said. "Don't do it."

The old man's eyes flared. Noble knew that he was going to draw. He wouldn't be shown up for yellow in front of his son.

"Father, that's Noble."

Chapter 4

"What exactly did she say?" Noble asked.

He and Joss stood beside the river. Noble watched the reflections, sparkling white in the dappled water's surface. Clarissa sat on a smooth boulder some distance away, staring out over the clear water, throwing in an occasional stone, listening while acting like she wasn't.

Joss drew deep on a hand-rolled cigarette and went on. "She said to tell you 'Grace needs you to come home.'"

"That's it? Grace needs me to come home? Nothing more?"

"Just that," Joss said. His cigarette flared orange against the dying light. "I made sure she got back home to that ranch of hers safe and sound."

"Grace needs me to come home," Noble muttered to himself. Grace.

She'd gone to the lost cabin to find him. The place always terrified her; it took him weeks to convince her to go. How desperate must she be to go there, and then ask for him?

"You saw the ranch then? The Rafter N? How did it look?"

"Prosperous. Lots of young, strong cattle, all growing fat on a carpet of high, green grass. I'd say they were doing well."

Noble scowled. Daniel had done well for himself then. But if things were going so well, why would they want him back?

"You know much about that country?"

"Some," Joss said. "We scouted it a little before deciding to hit Helena. Nice little bank in Bigsby. Not nearly so rich as the one in Helena though. There are rumors about that country though."

"Rumors?"

"A few stories, I know nothing for sure. Rustlers, according to what I heard though, and a lot of them. I heard they cleared out one of the smaller outfits completely. Webster's, I think it was."

"Eli Webster. Circle Bar. I know them. That wasn't a small outfit," Noble said. Old Eli was a tough man, and he had three tough sons, all scattered around Noble's own age. He'd been close with two of them. The Websters were a feuding, fighting bunch who came out of the Ozarks after the war. If rustlers had cleared them out, they knew their business.

"Seems like several of those Webster boys got killed under mysterious circumstances. Lots of bullets in the back, I'd heard." Joss dropped the finished cigarette and ground it to gray char beneath his boot toe. He looked toward the trading post. "I helped her set that foundation. Kettle, I mean. Me and Tim Redmond spent a week cutting and planing on those hardwood floors. A plain dirt floor wasn't good enough for her, no sir. She was sure proud of those floors."

"Yes, she was," Noble said, and meant it.

"She did a lot of good here. Helped a lot of people. Wasn't particular of who she helped either. Didn't care if you were rich, poor, a settler, a lawman, or even an old outlaw. To her it never mattered."

Noble said nothing. Joss wanted to get something off his chest; Noble was patient enough to wait for it.

"Noble, the work we do—the work I do at least—it's coming to an end. The day of the outlaw is just about done. We had our fun. We had our easy jobs and easy money. I spent more than my share of it on cheap women, cheap booze. But that time has run its course now."

"I'd say so," Noble said.

He wasn't like Joss. He hadn't been so much an outlaw as a man caught on the losing side in a few fights between big ranches or between big ranchers and small homesteaders. He'd always tried his best to choose which side he thought was right, but he'd also always drawn fighting wages. Sometimes his side won. Sometimes they lost. In either case, when the shooting was over, the smoke cleared, and the bodies buried, he'd always ridden on. No one wanted a killer around. Not once the need for killing was done.

"What will you do?"

"Oh, a few last jobs I guess." Joss grinned toothlessly. "Might as well play my cards out to the end."

"Try not to make it a bitter one," Noble said.

"And you? Now that I've delivered that lady's message, what will you do next?"

"Go home and help Grace."

"Seemed like a nice woman—one with sand, too. Took courage to ride down into that hollow like that. Any manner of men might have been down at that old cabin."

Noble shifted his feet. "She's always had sand. Sometimes more sand than sense."

Joss laughed. "I know a few people like that."

"Your friend won't mind us leaving?" Noble nodded toward the other men.

"Nah. Colonel Henry's a likable enough sort. Stern though. Very stern. I laid it all out for him." Joss shifted a bit to peer over Noble's shoulder toward where Clarissa sat on her rock. "That one seems to have sand too."

Noble turned enough to see Clarissa. "Seems like. She's just a kid though. Scared."

"Holding that pistol like she was, didn't seem that scared to me," Joss said. "She don't look like much of a kid to me either. She can't be too much younger than you. No more'n five years anyways."

"It's the miles that count, not the years."

"And who told you that?"

Noble smiled. "Some old catamount outlaw

down in the Animas country. Seems like he owed me a favor or two."

"He still owes you as I recall." Joss gave the girl another appraising eye then offered a hand to Noble. "If you'll take another piece of advice from an old catamount then take this: Settle down before it's too late. Find yourself a woman like that and settle down and stay clear of the outlaw life."

"Joss, take care of yourself," Noble said, and clapped his friend on the back.

Noble and Clarissa rode for several hours after leaving Kettle's place. They bedded down among a stand of high pine trees. In the abandoned trading post, Clarissa had found several pairs of pants that almost fit her, a couple of dresses, and a winter coat that was about two inches short in the arms but still warm enough.

When they lay down, Noble found his mind wouldn't let him sleep. He listened to the horses cropping spring grass. Heard them stamp their feet and whisk their tails.

Grace.

Seven years since he'd seen her last. Seven long, empty years.

He'd never written her. How could he? The girl he'd grown up with and then left without so much as a word.

She'd married Daniel, of course. That was to be

expected and always had been. There had been moments, a few at least, when Noble thought he might have stood a chance. He'd always been restless though. Daniel had been the respectable one. Steady.

Noble, not so much. Grace might have loved him, could accept him for what he was, but she could never go with him. Noble understood now what he hadn't then. They never would have lasted. He would have resented her for tying him down, and she could never be content with the life he'd chosen: always on the move, always looking over his shoulder.

Nor should she have to.

A woman needed a place of her own, a home. Grace deserved nothing but the best and, at the Rafter N, Daniel could provide just that. Noble could not.

Damn him for that.

"Why did they fear you?" Clarissa suddenly asked.

"What?"

"Those men were frightened of you. So were the Clemsen boys. Why?"

"Reputation."

"Are you an outlaw then?"

Noble paused and considered. Others might disagree, but he didn't think of himself as an outlaw. Was he though?

"I fought in a few of the big cattle wars.

Sometimes, if a local marshal or sheriff was on the other side, they called us all outlaws."

"You've killed a lot of men then?" She raised up on one elbow to look at him.

"More than a few."

"Most gunfighters like to talk about how many they killed."

"You've met a lot of gunfighters?"

"Well, no. But Chet always said they like to notch their guns and brag about how tough they are."

"Your brother wasn't wrong. Some do. That type doesn't tend to last long. They try to fight everyone and end up crossing someone who shoots faster or a hair straighter, or someone who's just plain lucky."

"Lucky?"

"I once saw a boy named Nebraska Lane square off against Big Bill Coulee down in Dodge City. Coulee was vicious, a great big bear of a man. Shoulders like railroad ties and fists like sledgehammers. Coulee was good, too. Fast, and could hit what he aimed at. Nebraska was just a little guy, maybe five two, and skinny as a rundown milk cow. Nebraska, I don't think he'd ever killed anybody. He was just a dumb kid fresh up the trail from Texas. But he thought he was grown up enough to carry a gun. Coulee, drunk at the time, started a fight, thinking Nebraska would back down."

"And this Nebraska out drew him?"

"Nope. In fact, Coulee still drew faster, but he missed with his first two shots, striking dirt on either side of Nebraska. A normal-sized man they would have hit, but like I said, Nebraska was rail skinny. Nebraska got his gun up before Coulee fired a third time and the kid didn't miss."

"Did he become a famous gunfighter? Nebraska, I mean?"

"Coulee's friends weren't happy with the outcome. Seems he owed them a considerable sum. Tough to collect anything from a dead man. So for their trouble, they hanged Nebraska from a cottonwood down along the creek."

"That's a terrible story."

"Most true ones are. Point is, Nebraska got lucky when he fought Coulee and unlucky when it came to Coulee's friends. That's the way it goes sometimes."

For a long time neither spoke. Noble watched the stars through the treetops and thought of times long ago. Would he recognize her?

"Who's Grace?" Clarissa said. The question had a strangeness to it that Noble wondered about.

"An old friend. My oldest friend, in fact," Noble said.

"And we're going to see her?"

"We?"

"Unless you plan on dumping me somewhere else," Clarissa said.

"Not too many stops the way we're going. Empty country."

"So you're taking me with you?"

"For now."

"Good."

For the tenth time since leaving Kettle's, Noble considered where he could leave the girl. He hadn't exaggerated: there was next to nothing the way they were riding. Certainly nowhere he could leave a young girl alone, and he'd forgotten to ask Joss when he'd seen Grace. How much time had passed since she'd sent for him? A week? A month?

He couldn't afford a long detour. Even now, Grace would be needing him.

Joss's partners said Kettle had moved west. He could still find her and leave the girl, but only after he dealt with the Rafter N trouble.

The wind picked up, and the treetops swayed.

What exactly was the Rafter N trouble? Joss said there were rustlers in the area, and no ordinary rustlers could have beaten the Circle Bar. Was that the problem? Surely Daniel could hire fighting men to take care of his stock. But would he? Would Daniel have the stomach to fight a cattle war?

Likely not. Takes too much after his father. Always ready to turn the other cheek and let someone else do the fighting and killing.

Another thought occurred to Noble.

Does Daniel know Grace sent for me?

The answer seemed obvious: He was her husband, surely he knew. But did obvious make it true?

Daniel never would have allowed Grace to ride to the lost cabin—not by herself, and not with an army. She'd done it all on her own.

"She didn't tell him," Noble said to himself. "Whatever the trouble is, she's scared and sent for me, but she didn't tell him."

The thought didn't comfort him.

Chapter 5

Clarissa and Noble rode north, across the wide swath of empty green plains and beneath an endless canopy of white-blue sky. They'd risen early and set out after a light breakfast of hardtack and salty bacon. The trip would be a long one.

Noble kept them to a quick pace, and the wind howled around them like a rushing river.

After midday, the wind finally abated.

"Where are we going?" Clarissa asked.

"Montana." Noble took off his hat and slapped it against his thigh. Pale dust flew from both.

"Grace is in Montana?" The girl studied the ground ahead of the little mare. She wore a distant look on her face, but she seemed to listen closely. Her manner was much the same as it had been when he'd been talking to Joss, and she'd eavesdropped on them.

"The Rafter N is in Montana and so is Grace."

"What will you do when we get there?"

"Joss said there was trouble, and I guess I'll see about it. After that, we'll ride west."

"Both of us? Together?"

"For a time."

The girl nodded to herself then, apparently satisfied with the answer.

"The Rafter N is a good ranch. I'll help them out and be well paid for it," Noble said.

He'd been thinking about that over the long miles. To his mind, Joss's earlier words rang true. The frontier was changing. The day of the outlaw was at an end. Outlaw or not, soon no one would want a gunslinger like him around. He needed a big stake, enough to set himself up on a quiet little ranch somewhere, and then he could fade into the background unnoticed. What would it be like to sleep without worrying about the next young trouble-hunter trying to kill him?

They passed east of the Hole-in-the-Wall into southern Wyoming. In the late afternoon they crossed a recent grassfire, and their horse's hooves raised puffs of ash and gray soot. Already the prairie was replenishing itself. Tiny shoots of grass, hair fine, poked up through the black wound like so much fur.

"What caused that?" the girl asked when they were on the other side.

"Lightning, most likely," Noble said. "Could be a careless cigarette though."

"People come through here? Through this?" She swung her arm to encompass the broad prairie, the low hills in the far distance. Other than themselves and a few scattered antelope, there seemed to be nothing in all the emptiness.

"We're going through it. Indians been coming

out here to hunt for a long time. Used to be buffalo thick as fleas all through here."

"There's nothing out here. Is Montana like this?"

"Parts of it. But not around Bigsby."

"Bigsby. That's your home?"

"My home is this saddle." Noble's voice was sharp, and Clarissa retreated at his words. Her head hung a little, like she was studying the ground for tracks.

"Sorry," she mumbled.

Noble dismounted to walk. He was stiff from so much riding, and it felt good to be on his own two feet again.

Without another word, Clarissa did the same. She walked behind him, like a shadow, still studying the ground.

"It's all right," Noble finally stopped and said.

"I just wanted to know more about where you're from." She would not meet his eyes.

"I should be the one to say sorry. I'm . . . touchy about where we're going is all. Going back isn't always a good thing."

She looked up at him then. Her eyes were red-rimmed and damp. He could see she wanted to ask more questions, but she held herself quiet.

Noble didn't volunteer anything further. Sooner or later she might find out more, but today the past was too close, too painful for words. He turned and marched on toward the north and a home that he'd left long ago.

Before this was over, she'd have all the answers she wanted. Grace would tell her everything, of course. All that she knew, at least. Unless Daniel had confessed their secret—not much chance of that—there would be one thing, the event that set him on this path, that Clarissa would never learn.

It didn't matter, of course. Clarissa was nothing to him. Just some girl he'd rescued from an unpleasant situation. Somehow, though, the thought of her learning his history bothered him. He'd never been ashamed of anything before. Living as he had, he'd never had close friends. A gunfighter could not afford friends, not if he wanted to stay ahead of his enemies, and every gunfighter had enemies. Most of their names would never be known, but they were there all the same, lurking, waiting for a moment of weakness. All desperate to prove themselves quicker, deadlier. All wanting to know who was the very best.

Noble walked on, and the girl followed silently behind.

Grace was in trouble. She needed his help, and that was enough to draw him back home, but the money had better be worth it.

Grace Bartlett admired a long table full of eggs, hot buttered biscuits, and slabs of salt pork. She'd had years to perfect her breakfast routine and was known throughout the valley for her cooking. Cowboys sometimes rode a dozen miles out of their way to put their feet under her table.

Her husband, Daniel, had recruited more than one hired hand using his wife's cooking, and closed several business deals besides.

He entered then, their kids in tow. In look and bearing, Ester, the youngest, took to her mother's side, but she had Daniel's eyes and nose. Little Jack, older by two years, looked much as his father did at that age. He looked even more like his Uncle Gabriel, though Grace would never speak those words aloud.

"Eggs," Ester said.

"And bacon," Jack added, and both kids helped themselves.

"Big meal today," Daniel said with a grin. "Many more like this and I'll have to buy bigger pants."

"Or you'll just have to work that much harder," Grace said, and piled eggs onto his plate. "The cattle don't tend to themselves."

It was a running joke between the two of them, and they shared an easy laugh.

Grace sat down to her own meal. Over the rim of her coffee cup, she studied her husband. Few others might notice it, not over the smiles and laughter, but she was not fooled. Daniel wasn't a talkative man, lately even less so than normal. He was worried—more worried than she'd ever seen him.

Their early years had been tough. Daniel's grandfather Jack Noble founded the Rafter, driving a herd of branded mavericks up from the Texas brush country, and he had done very well for himself. But Sam, Daniel's father, had not been cut out to be a rancher. He was a circuit-riding preacher, a fine one, and a good man in his way, but no rancher, as he himself admitted.

The proud Rafter N had fallen into disrepair under Sam until he'd turned everything over to Daniel. Night and day, Daniel had worked tirelessly to restore the place to its former glory. Grace did her part, of course. She would have it no other way. Sam and Emilia, Daniel's mother, too did their own respective parts. But Daniel had done the bulk of the work. Until they'd saved up enough to hire more cowboys, he'd done all the branding and culling. How many times had he come home bruised and battered after a hot, dusty day?

In the first year alone, Grace lost count.

Three long years later, they'd finally achieved some sense of stability. Two more after that, they'd begun to prosper. And now? Now, the Rafter stood on the precipice again.

Daniel refused to acknowledge the danger, of course; he refused to admit it. He didn't want her to worry. It showed though. At least it did to her. Grace saw it in every line on his face, every gray hair, even the way he walked, proud at times, but not so straight as he might have just a year ago.

"I thought I might ride into town today," Daniel said after he'd emptied his plate. "Is there anything you need?"

"We're low on all the usual. Flour, salt, sugar, and coffee."

"The stuff just keeps getting more expensive. Everything does." Daniel gestured out the window toward the bunkhouse. "Even the hands cost more every year. If a man can even find one."

The Rafter had two hired hands these days, Cactus Huff, old enough to be Grace's father, and half-blind to boot, and Vern Ollie, a boy of sixteen, who knew next to nothing about ranching. In times past, they might have had a half dozen—the range was certainly big enough—but now they had only two. Cactus had been on the Rafter longer than anyone, even Emilia. As a boy, he'd come up the trail with Jack Noble as a cook's helper, staying on as a cowboy, and he'd been instrumental in restoring the ranch to its former glory.

"Can we come?" Little Jack said.

Both children looked at their father expectantly.

"Not unless your mother does."

"Not this time. We've got too much to do here today," Grace said. "Jack, you need to study your numbers."

Jack scowled at that. He had no use for math.

Grace thought that was probably true of most young boys who preferred fishing in the creeks or hunting deer out on the plains.

In truth, Grace did not want to go to Bigsby.

Once Bigsby had been a friendly town, a quiet town. The kind of town where everyone knew each other and acted like neighbors. The kind of town where no one bothered locking their home. A year ago, that changed. Grace couldn't have her finger on why, but these days Bigsby had a strange feel to it. There were five other ranches nearby—four now that the Websters were gone—and though they each described the feeling differently, the other ranch wives felt the same. It was almost like the town didn't want them there anymore. Almost like resentment.

Riggins, a newer town west along the base of the mountains, was even worse. Grace knew all about Riggins. When she was a child, there had been a few old shanties up there, including the one she and her father lived in. Now there were at least fifty, each the same, with their paper-thin walls and patched-over roofs. Riggins began when someone claimed they'd found gold along the creek and the miners had come in like heel flies. When the truth came out—there was no gold—the miners had left and only a few, those too poor or too worn out or just flat busted, decided to stay. Since then, more drifters moved in and settled. Now the rumors of treasure in the mountain had returned, and Riggins had grown to almost as many people as Bigsby, a rough crowd of gamblers, miners, and tramps.

Grace was grateful that the Webster place was between the Rafter and Riggins, though now that buffer was gone.

Jack and Ester finished their meals and were off to other parts of the house, leaving Grace alone with Daniel. Her husband took up his coffee and walked outside. He paused and leaned against an awning post to stare out over their range. Grace took up her own cup and joined him. The view was impressive. Eight thousand acres of prime Montana grass stretched away from them down a long, rolling valley. Clusters of cattle could be seen among the grass, growing fat and ready for market. To the west, the Bitterroot Mountains rose high in the distance, their icy peaks a stark contrast to the warm valley below.

"How bad is it?" Grace finally asked.

"Nothing to worry about," Daniel said.

"You've never been a good liar, Daniel."

Daniel studied her for a moment, then went back to staring at their cattle. "We've lost a hundred head in the last month. All from the west range."

The west range couldn't be seen from their home. It lay on the far side of a line of hills running down north to south from a high bench. It was a wild country, rough and free, bigger than the home range at ten thousand acres, but not so lush. The Rafter had always kept most of their cattle at the home place, where they could be easily watched, but Daniel usually ran four or five hundred head back in the rough west range.

"Stolen?" Grace already knew the answer. Rustlers had taken all the Websters' cattle. That was how it had begun. That was what had sent her on the trail to the lost cabin.

Daniel nodded. "I'm going to speak to the sheriff today. He's got to put a stop to this, or we'll be in the same shape Eli was."

"Why didn't he help Eli?"

"I don't know." Daniel sighed. "I think the old man was too proud to ask for help."

"What if he asked for help and the sheriff didn't do anything?"

"I don't know, but he has to help us."

"And if he doesn't?"

"Then I'll write to the marshal service or the governor. The law has to put a stop to this." Daniel scowled and went off to the barn. Moments later, he emerged on his favorite horse.

"I'll be back this afternoon," he said, and rode south toward town.

Grace watched him go. Her husband wasn't a weak man. It took strength to build up a ranch, to save it, to keep it growing and prosperous. But he wasn't a fighter. Not like his grandfather had been.

When she returned to her kitchen, Daniel's mother, Emilia, sat at the table drinking coffee. Grace hadn't heard her come in, but that wasn't a surprise. The older woman could move quiet as an Indian when it suited her, and it usually did.

"I guess you heard all of that?" Grace asked.

"Enough," Emilia said with a shrug. "Did you go to the cabin? Did you send word to him?"

"I did. Several days ago."

Neither spoke for a long time. Grace wondered why Emilia hadn't just gone to the cabin herself. The old woman knew where it was. She knew Montana like few others. In her wild youth, she'd drunk from every stream, crossed every mountain. All of that was before Sam Bartlett though. Before she'd settled down to raise a family.

"Do you think he'll come?" Grace said.

"He'll come."

"Will it be in time?"

"Yes." Emilia sounded certain as the sun would rise tomorrow.

"What can he really do? What can he do that the law can't?"

Emilia turned cold, blue eyes to Grace. "He'll do everything the law can't. That's why we need him. Daniel is my son; he's a good man, like his father, but good men aren't enough to win this kind of fight. I love him and you and my grandchildren all dearly, but we need someone like my father now—a violent man to confront violent men."

Grace shuddered. "I wish it weren't so."

"So do I," Emilia said, and reached over to squeeze Grace's hand. The old woman's grip was warm and strong and reassuring. "Have faith. He will come, and he'll be here in time."

Chapter 6

Noble paused in the wild foothills of the Bitterroot Mountains. He and Clarissa sat their horses on an overlook, with wide-open prairie rolling away toward the east like rippled sand on the bottom of a clear stream.

Seven years had passed since he'd gone from here. Seven long, hard years. He'd never been back, not once. And when he'd ridden out that last time, he hadn't paused to look back. Over the following years, he regretted that. On the dark nights huddled over a lean fire and surrounded by bitter cold, he would have liked one last memory of seeing the home place.

Two towns lay in the distant south; Noble could just make them out. Tucked into the mountains, Riggins was closer by several miles, while Bigsby lay out alone on the flatlands. From a distance, little seemed to have changed. The same craggy mountains, the same shallow hills and winding creeks. Even the sky held the same Montana blue. There were a few changes though. Riggins had grown. Judging by the amount of smoke rising from chimneys and stoves, there might have been as many people living there as in Bigsby at that point.

"This is it?" Clarissa said. "Your home?"

Noble started to speak and then coughed to clear his throat. "The Rafter is up north a bit, but you can see what's called the home range from here. The west range is over that long ridge you see."

"How long till we get there? I could use a meal and an actual bed," Clarissa said, stretching.

"This afternoon. We've still a long way to go, down through the canyon country." Noble pointed at the broken landscape beneath them. "Easy to get lost in there, and there are only a few ways to get across."

They dropped down off the overlook, and Noble led the way into the canyons. These too, had changed in seven years. Water and wind had done their part scouring the rocks, but the biggest landmarks remained. Balanced rock marked the entrance to the main canyon, and a toadstool column stood on the east wall. Noble used these and other points to navigate and soon recognized which part of the canyon they'd entered.

At noon, they stopped to let the horses drink from the stream that ran through the deepest part of the canyon. There were signs of cattle in the bottom, a great number of them walking through, and Noble thought that odd. No one ran cattle near the canyon. No one allowed their cattle anywhere near it. Prone to flash flood as it was, a hard summer storm could wipe out an entire herd.

Noble found tracks from shod horses and a swatch of cloth hanging on a sharp branch, red-and-black plaid, torn from a passing rider's shirt. Cattle hadn't just wandered into the canyon, they'd been driven.

When the horses were satisfied, they started on toward the southeast.

An hour later, Noble brought them up the winding breaks and out onto the flat country west of Bigsby. The sun shone down directly overhead, warm and inviting, but the bitter north wind tugged at their coats. Occasionally Noble heard the sound of cattle and, on a hunch, he swung due south and skirted along the canyon country.

Three miles south of where they'd emerged, he hopped down off his horse and handed the reins to Clarissa.

"Wait here," he said and drew out his rifle. "I need to check something."

Despite the risks of flooding, Noble had always liked the canyon country. He enjoyed the wild feel of it. Some of those old canyons hadn't seen a white man before, some had never seen a red one either, for that matter.

Noble had been born with the heart of an explorer, his mother said. She would have known—her father had been much the same.

On one of his overnight forays into the canyons, he'd discovered a big hollowed-out place in the rock, an amphitheater of sorts. It was several acres in size, with a spring in the back and a rock basin where the water pooled. The grass there was lush and thick. There was a cave too, decorated with paintings of bighorn sheep, elk, and other unknown symbols, a place hunters had used even before the Sioux migrated west out of the Great Lakes region. On a ledge inside the cave, he'd found one of their spear points.

Noble crept toward the amphitheater's rim until he could peer over the edge.

There were cattle held below—a lot of cattle. Someone had strung up a rough wooden fence at the amphitheater's narrow entrance, and there were at least a hundred head inside. A hint of smoke rose from the old cave's entrance, and there were several horses picketed on the grass outside. A group of cowboys was near the entrance, two taking turns roping cattle while three more worked over their brands from a circle bar to what looked like a double eight. Double Eight was a common rustler brand. A good man with a branding iron could use those eights to cover almost anything.

Noble watched the process for a few minutes; the rustlers seemed well practiced. Then he worked his way back to Clarissa.

"What did you see?" the girl asked.

"Trouble, but none of mine. Not yet, leastways," Noble said. "Though I may now have a better idea of just what I'm walking into."

If the Rafter needed him to clear out the rustlers, it would be a tall task. There had been five men working those brands and, unless he missed his guess, another group resting down in the cave. That many would be a tall order. Though if he killed the right one or two, the rest would likely scatter.

So many would also mean more risk and more pay. And that, Noble didn't mind at all.

Golden evening had come, and Grace stood alone at the sink, finishing up the dishes from supper. The children were in their rooms, asleep or reading by candlelight after a long day. With the onset of spring, the days were growing long and warm. The heat of summer would be there far too soon.

After supper Daniel had gone out to check on the herd in the west range.

"Got some cows were due to drop their calves any day now," he'd explained, but Grace knew the real reason. He wanted to see if the rustlers had taken any more.

What he would do with them if he found them she couldn't guess. He'd taken his rifle and a scattergun, but Daniel had never shot at anyone in his life. Their two cowhands, Cactus and Vern Ollie, went with him, and she felt better about that. Vern might be young, but he showed good judgment most of the time, and Cactus had a lifetime's worth of knowledge about rustlers.

She had little fear for herself, at the home place. Emilia and Sam weren't far away; their house was just a few hundred yards farther north. And surely their peaceful valley had not gotten so out of hand that a woman had to worry in her own home.

The sun was a red-orange torch shining back behind the Bitterroots when Grace toweled off the last of the dishes, and movement outside the window drew her eye.

A girl, young and lean, dressed in rough travel clothes, walked into the open and stood waiting.

Grace went out to speak to her, taking down the rifle from above the door as she did so.

"Can I help you?" Grace said.

"You sent for a man." The girl's voice was smooth but nervous. She seemed to be studying Grace closely.

Momentarily confused, Grace said, "I didn't send for anyone."

The girl tilted her head to the side, and her look turned scornful. "You sent word for help from him didn't you?"

Grace then thought about her trip to the cabin, her talk with the outlaws.

"Is he here?"

"He's waiting for you. He said you'd know the spot." The girl turned then and started to leave.

"Wait, I'll go with you—" Grace started, but

the strange girl had already gone into the growing dark.

Grace ran back inside and grabbed her shawl. She thought to leave the rifle but decided to keep it. She didn't know this girl and wasn't sure she could trust her. She checked in on Ester—fast asleep—then peeked in at Jack. He was awake, reading a book about King Arthur.

Where had he found that?

"I've got to go check on a few things," Grace told him. "I'll be back soon though."

"I can go with you," Jack said.

Grace patted his hair and said, "Not this time. Watch over your sister."

He went back to reading without further comment, and Grace draped the shawl over her shoulders and slipped out into the night.

The ranch lay dark and still now. The stars were faint, the moon not yet risen, but she knew the way. How many times had she taken this path? She moved quickly east, up a rolling hill, then down into a copse of pine and alder to a shallow creek. She followed the creek, skipping across on boulders scattered in the water, then coming out into an open area that overlooked the southward valley. Two silhouettes stood there. The girl from earlier she knew right away. The other was a man, big, with broad shoulders and a narrow rider's waist. He might have been her husband by his build, but the failing light twinkled off a pair of pistols he wore draped around his waist.

"You should have waited for her," the man said. His voice was deep and solid like a stone. Grace felt her heart quicken hearing it.

"You said she could find the way," the girl answered. There was heat in her voice, but the big man didn't seem to hear it. He stood near an old pine, running his hand over the bark.

Grace knew what was there. She'd been here when he'd carved it for her.

"You should have waited. There's no telling how long it will take her—" His voice trailed off and he turned to face Grace then. Somehow he had always known whenever she was around.

"I am here," Grace said.

"Grace," he breathed, and for a moment Grace had the wild idea to run and embrace him. But she was a woman grown now, married to a decent man, and with his children. She did not embrace other men.

"Gabriel," she answered.

"Gabriel?" the girl interrupted.

He turned his head to the girl for a moment. "That is my right name." Then he looked back toward Grace. He was close now, close enough for her to smell the scent of him.

"Grace," he said. "It's good to see you again."

Grace felt her cheeks redden.

"You too, Gabriel," she stammered. "I wasn't sure how long it would take for word to reach you. I wasn't sure what name you went by either."

"I heard less than a week ago, down in Wyoming. Lucky I was that close. I came as soon as I could."

An awkward silence passed. The girl crossed her arms and moved off a bit to lean against the trunk of a huge pine, though she was not so far that she couldn't hear what they said.

"How have you been, Gabriel? We never heard much after . . . afterwards."

He let out a long sigh. "Tired mostly. It's a tiring business roaming place to place. Never sure when your next meal might come. Never sure if the man beside you might shoot you in the back. Takes a toll on a man."

Grace sat down on a downed log; the same one she rested on so many times during their childhood. How many times had the pair of them come out here to watch the sunset or talk the night away?

"And you?" he said. He did not sit down beside her. He always had, back then.

"We are fine. All of us."

"And Daniel? He takes care of you?"

Grace's chin lifted. "He does. He is a good man. A good husband and a good father." The words stung him, even in the dark she could see it, and she didn't regret them. There had been venom in his question, and she'd answered it in kind.

"But not now?" Light glinted off Gabriel's smile. "Otherwise why would you send for me? I know it wasn't Daniel's idea."

"It wasn't my idea either, it was—"

Gabriel cut her off with a raised palm. He stared off into the deepest trees, saying nothing. Grace followed his gaze. She saw nothing but shadows. Gabriel eased back out of the pale light where she could barely see him.

"Might as well come out," he said. "I should have known you'd be joining us. How long have you been here?"

Emilia Bartlett laughed and stepped from the shadows into the light. "Just got here. It takes an old woman a while longer to skip across that stream. Not so light-footed as I was in my younger years."

For a moment no one spoke.

"Gabriel, would you do an old woman a favor and move where I can see you?" Emilia finally said.

Gabriel stepped forward into the light. He took off his hat so his face was visible and waited, tall and unashamed.

The faint light caught and shone in Emilia's damp eyes. "Oh, my lost boy. You've gone off and become a man, and the very picture of my own father."

"My road hasn't been an easy one," he muttered.

Emilia walked closer. Her expression was

of purest wonder. A look Grace had never seen on her mother-in-law's face. She reached up and gently ran her fingers over his sun-dark face. Like grains of rattling sand, the rough whiskers scratched against the older woman's fingertips.

"My boy," Emilia whispered. "I have missed you so very much."

Gabriel cleared his throat. "I've missed you too, Mother. It's been too long. I . . ."

He coughed then and replaced his hat. The dark brim shrouded his face, but Grace recognized the set of his jaw. For a moment he'd been the old Gabriel again, the boy who loved life so much. Now the mask was back on. The one he wore to protect himself from the world.

"Who's your friend?" Grace said.

"Clarissa, come meet my family," he said.

The girl came forward, timid now. She offered her hand to Grace, and they shook stiffly. She did the same to Emilia, but the older woman ignored the hand and wrapped her up in a hug.

Clarissa giggled, a sound that made her seem even younger.

"Good to meet you. Has my boy been taking care of you? Like his grandfather, he's a bit rough and coarse at times."

"Yes." Clarissa nodded. "Noble—I mean Gabriel helped me out of a bad situation, and we've been on the road since."

"Noble?" Grace said. She had heard that name before. In town perhaps?

Emilia took Clarissa by the arm. "We'll get you settled down proper, my dear. I've got some clothes that might fit you. Maybe have to take them in some. You're a skinny thing. Tall though."

The girl looked at the ground and rubbed her toe against the dirt.

Grace thought back to what she'd heard. Noble. Yes, in town they'd told stories about a man named Noble. A gunfighter. A man who'd killed. . . .

"You're Noble." Grace pointed at Gabriel, at Noble.

"Yes," he said. A note of resignation filled his voice.

"Noble the gunfighter. Noble the hired killer. Noble the outlaw."

Clarissa drew protectively to Noble's side, and Gabriel seemed to draw up taller and harder with every accusation. He denied none of them. Emilia put herself directly between Grace and Noble.

"Noble the cold-blooded murderer," Grace finished. She couldn't have her children around a murderer. She had to protect Little Jack and Ester. Who had she invited back to her family ranch?

"Now, Grace," Emilia said. She gestured for calm.

"No." Grace shook her head. What had she done? "No. He can't be here. Not a man like him."

The girl, Clarissa, clung to Gabriel tighter. "We didn't ask to come here. You sent for us," she said.

"Grace, please—" Emilia started. She reached for Grace's arm, but Grace snatched it away like she'd been bitten. A horrified look crossed Grace's face, then quickly one of white-hot anger. Emilia. She had sent Grace to find him. This was her doing.

"You knew," Grace said. "You knew all along. You knew who he was. You knew who you were inviting to the Rafter. To my home."

"I knew," Emilia admitted.

"He's a killer. You know the stories they tell about him."

"He is. And he is what we need," Emilia said.

"No. No, we don't need his kind," Grace said. The sweet, wandering boy she'd grown up with was one of the most famous outlaws in the west. Gabriel had moved away; he stood tall and unashamed. He still hadn't denied any of it.

"I've killed plenty," he said. "Never anybody who didn't need it or anybody who wasn't trying to kill me first. I never robbed any banks or stages or stolen cattle or anyone's ranch either."

He was angry now; Grace heard his pain and hurt.

"I hired on to the big ranches, sometimes the little ones. I helped them as a puncher, and then I helped them when some two-bit sharp tried to take what they'd sweated and bled for. People learned I was good to have on your side in a range war. That I was good with a gun. Men came then, looking for trouble, men looking to build themselves a name, men who gave me no choice. I won. I won't apologize for it. I'm not ashamed of it. But I'm no outlaw. I fought for the Double B in Texas and my side lost. The other side bought himself a county sheriff and charged us all with murder. But I didn't murder anyone. I fought for money or to stay alive or to help others and that was it."

"This is who you've brought to help us?" Grace gestured to Noble. "This is who'll save the Rafter?"

"Who better?" Emilia said.

"I don't fight for free," Noble said. "Family loyalty got me here, but my gun and my life don't come cheap."

"He wants to be paid?" Grace asked. "On top of everything else, how can we pay him? We don't have any money." It was true. In land or cattle, the Rafter was rich. But they had practically no cash.

Emilia turned to Noble. "How much?"

"Six thousand."

"Six thousand!" Grace coughed. She'd never

seen that much money all at once. The ranch couldn't afford half—a quarter—of that.

From a pouch at her waist, Emilia drew out a small bag and tossed it to Noble. It clinked when he caught it. "Two thousand in there. The rest when it's done."

"What does 'done' mean?" he said.

"When the ranch is safe," Emilia said. "No threat of rustlers. We've lost too many head of cattle already."

Grace couldn't believe what she was hearing. How could this be happening?

"Done." Noble nodded. He looked at Grace, and his voice grew cold. "Clarissa and I will stay at the west cabin. We'll keep to ourselves, much as we can anyway. It will be better that way."

They left then, and only Emilia and Grace remained beside the stream.

"What have you done?" Grace finally said.

Emilia gave her a hard look. Her voice was every bit as cold as Noble's when she said, "I just saved the Rafter."

Chapter 7

Noble led Clarissa away from the stream and into the deepening evening, back where their horses waited. They rode north then, circling around west toward the Rafter's west range.

An hour short of midnight they crested a rocky hill and looked down over a little valley and a small wood-and-rock cabin. Though the moon was high now, casting blue light down on the still snowy Bitterroots farther west, the valley lay dark and forbidding.

Noble had never thought of it that way though. Daniel and their parents might have the better grazing, but to him this was the wild heart of the Rafter. This was his grandfather's home, and this was where Noble had spent most of his days, learning from the old man.

The trail wound down the rocky valley, passing between boulders, clumps of rough brush, and the occasional juniper grown twisted and gnarled by the wind. Their roots fought hard against the rocky soil, clinging deep on the one hand, and reaching for the high sun on the other.

There was a corral out back of the house. Noble rode a quick circuit, inspecting the railings for anyplace a horse might escape, then dismounted near the gate.

"Looks solid enough. They'll be fine in here for tonight," he said.

"If you say so," Clarissa said. Her eyes were enormous and shining in the moonlight.

After settling the horses in, Noble carried most of their belongings into the cabin. The place had been swept recently.

Mother's work, Noble was sure of it. *She would have expected me to stay here.*

Beside the small iron stove, tinder was laid out for a fire; Noble quickly had a warm blaze going.

"Now let's see about some more light," he said.

An oil lantern hung above the stove. Noble took a long stick from the fire and lifted the glass. The thick smell of lamp oil filled his nostrils. The wick lit easily, and finally he got his first good look at the place he'd left so many years before.

Little had changed.

The table was just where his grandfather had left it. The doors to the two bedrooms were open. The shelves in the kitchen held a variety of cans and sacks.

More of mother's work to fix the place up for me.

Several skillets and pans hung on iron hooks over the stove. From above the door of one bedroom the head of an old bison looked down on the scene; an elk head hung above the other.

"Hello Buff," Noble said. When he was a child, he'd named the old bull. More than once he or

Grandfather Jack held evening conversations with the bison.

A creak sounded behind him, and Noble spun. His pistol was halfway out before he realized it was the girl, Clarissa. She'd sat down in his grandfather's old hidebound chair.

"Only me," she said with her hands raised and palms open.

"Sorry," he told the frightened girl, then shoved the pistol back down. He'd gotten lost in the memories. "This place brings a lot of things back to me, is all."

He went into the kitchen to see about their supper.

"That older woman at the creek, she's your mother?"

"She is."

"And the younger one, that's . . ."

"Grace. My brother's wife."

Noble found a can of beans and a slab of bacon. There were fresh onions and potatoes. He took down the skillet.

"I can cook. Let me do that," Clarissa said. "Just sit by the fire here."

Noble looked at her and then at the skillet. He was tired. Bone weary from the trail. She would be just as tired, but she was younger than he, and she'd dozed in the saddle some.

Clarissa moved into the kitchen and shooed him off with her hands. "I'm tired of that trail food you cook, anyway. I can fix us something nice and proper."

Noble retreated to the second chair by the fire; he did not sit in his grandfather's place.

When he was fifteen, he'd found an oak tree toppled over a few miles south of there. Proper oaks were scarce in this country. What trees grew were types of pine on the slopes, soft old cottonwoods along the creeks, and stately aspens scattered in among both.

The oak had been a real find and rather than letting it go to rot away or sending it up through the chimney, he'd cut it up into planks and boards. Most went into the corral, but some of the wood he'd saved to turn into his own chair beside the hearth.

The chair was comfortable, if a little smaller than he remembered.

Noble drew his pistols, examining both. Then he cleaned and oiled each in turn. Finally, he did the same for his rifle. When he was done, the smell of cooking onions and potatoes and hot bacon grease filled the cabin, reminding him of old times.

"This Grace, you knew her for a long time?"

"We all grew up together. Me, Daniel, and Grace. She came up from Riggins. She walked onto the ranch one day, half starved and asking for work. I guess she couldn't have been more than twelve or eleven. I was fourteen at the time.

Daniel a year younger. Out of pity, my mother took her on to help with the kitchen work."

"And Daniel grew up and married her?"

"He did." Noble's voice was flat and cold.

"You didn't want to?"

"Daniel is steady, dependable, and I was . . . wild and free," Noble said. "I wanted to see over the mountains and ride where the wind blew me. I wanted to see what lay beyond. Beyond the mountains, the valleys, the deserts. My grandfather, Jack Noble, he started the Rafter; he was the same way. He traveled all over the country, up and down the Rockies and across the Great Plains."

"But he settled here."

"Finally. He rode into Texas, rounded up a herd and some hands to drive them, then brought the whole outfit here to settle."

"Your mother with him?"

"Yes, she grew up on the ranch. Her own mother passed just before they reached Montana. Cholera, I think. She doesn't remember much of the great drive, just the long days in the saddle and the endless dust."

"And your father?"

"A circuit-riding preacher. I don't think my grandfather liked him much, but back then there wasn't a whole lot to choose from. Preachers and cowboys."

"No outlaws?" Clarissa asked with a raised eyebrow.

"Not enough time for them to get acquainted. Grandpa Jack liked to hang those."

Noble sat back in his chair, relaxed, watching her in the kitchen. How long since a woman had cooked for him? How long since he'd spent any time with one?

"Six thousand dollars is a lot of money," Clarissa ventured.

"Enough for what I want."

"And what is that?"

"A place of my own. Maybe up in the mountains in California or Idaho. Lots of wild places there. I can start my own little outfit. Do it just like the old man did."

"Alone?"

Noble didn't answer. Instead, he asked a question of his own. "What do you plan on doing?"

"You mean after you drop me off with this Kettle person?"

"Unless you know some other place."

"I suppose I'd like to open a cafe. Nothing fancy, just simple food."

"You can cook that good?"

"I guess you'll soon see." She smiled, and her whole face lit up.

"There's gold camps all over. If you set up in one of them or along one of the new rail routes, you could do well."

"Maybe I'll do that," Clarissa said. She took

the skillet off the stove to cool and scrounged around until she found a pair of plates and forks.

Noble shifted over to the table, and she served up their dinner.

The girl hadn't lied. She was a wonderful cook. Noble ate with abandon until, completely stuffed, he eased back from the table.

"That was good," he said.

"Told you. I know my cooking." Clarissa cleared away their dishes.

"I'll say," Noble answered. He watched her pour water and soap into a basin, then start in on cleaning the plates and pans.

"What will you do tomorrow?"

"Ride back to where we saw those rustlers. I can start there."

"You think they're the same bunch? I thought they didn't have any of your family's cattle."

"Yesterday, they didn't. But that doesn't mean they don't have them held someplace else." Noble took off his hat to be polite. "The valley seems big, but it really isn't. There are just a few large outfits in here. Little chance there's more than a single band of rustlers causing all the problems."

Neither spoke for a long time. Noble watched Clarissa work her way through the dishes. He smelled the sharp soap mixed with the scents of their meal.

Finally, while she dried everything off with a

small towel, he stood and went to the door. He slid the heavy wood beam down, then made for the bedroom on the left, the one with the elk head above it. The one he'd stayed in as a boy.

"Good night," he said, halfway through the door.

"Noble, what happened here? What made you leave?" she asked.

"Good night, Clarissa," Noble answered, and closed the door behind him.

At first glance, the canyon amphitheater seemed empty. Noble wasn't surprised.

He crawled forward, as close to the edge as he dared, and craned his neck to peer over the rim and look farther down. But the cattle—the rustlers too—were all gone. Gray ash from their fire and the short section of crude fencing near the canyon's mouth were the only signs they'd ever been there.

How had they gotten that herd brand switched so quickly? And where had they moved the cattle afterward?

Noble considered the possibilities.

Anyone who saw those fresh double-eight brands would be suspicious. Especially if they knew the local ranches.

So they moved them out of the valley then.

But where?

The canyonlands followed the base of the

Bitterroots south before turning, widening, and branching off in different directions, but going generally westward. The Sioux reservation lay in that direction. Surely the army would be suspicious of those fresh brands.

Noble crawled back from the edge and replaced his hat. No point speculating further. The best way to find the herd was to drop down into the canyon and follow them along. That many cattle would leave tracks a newborn could follow.

He retrieved his horse, and as he climbed into the saddle, a bit of sunlight reflected off something metallic in the Bitterroot foothills. Nothing lay in that direction, no farms or ranches or even much by way of game—not this time of year, anyway. There was no reason at all for anyone to be out there.

Whatever the source of the reflection, Noble did not like being out in the open. He spurred his horse into a quick trot toward the notch he and Clarissa had recently ridden out of.

Soon enough he was in the canyon bottom, crisscrossing the shallow stream and searching for signs of cattle.

Noble sighed. The problem wasn't the lack of sign, but an abundance of it. There were tracks and cow chips strewn all across the canyon floor. Some fresh, some days or even weeks old. The rustlers must have used the trail often for there to be so many. The only thing he could determine was a general direction. Downstream. South. With nothing else to go on, he could only follow.

Three hours passed before he found the second fence.

As fences go, it wasn't much. A few lashed-together pine poles, but it crossed a narrow section of the canyon and diverted the cattle up into one of the feeder canyons. This particular feeder cut off to the east, toward the old Circle Bar.

What was it Joss had said about the Circle Bar? Something about the Websters being run off.

Eli Webster was a feuding man from the Missouri hill country. He'd been an artillery gunner during the war, one of a handful to survive his unit being ambushed at a river crossing in Kentucky. A hard, tough man, Eli had loved his ranch. It would take an awful lot to run him and his boys off their land.

Noble followed the cattle tracks east. Nothing about this particular canyon seemed different from any other. The walls were soft sandstone in alternating layers of yellow, white, and red; a deep purple band, less than a handspan wide, separated the yellow and white. Scattered trees grew on the bottom and where they could find purchase on either side. There was no standing water or pools here, but he could see clumps of debris in the lowest tree branches from where floodwaters had rushed through the canyon during a hard storm. The grass was cropped down to its exposed roots, more sign of the cattle's passing.

The stallion stumbled on a loose stone, and it saved Noble's life. He heard the bullet whizz by his head and strike a nearby tree. The crack of the shot came next.

Noble spurred the big black into action, leaping the horse forward behind a screen of cottonwood and leafy willows.

The shot had come from behind and, by the delayed sound of it, the shooter had to be some distance off. In the canyon ahead, the trees curved around a sharp bend. Whatever happened, he had to keep moving. The attacker, on higher ground, had too many advantages there. Noble pushed the stallion deeper into the trees; he needed to stay out of sight until they were safely around that bend. He rode at a fast trot, and juniper branches stung against his face and arms.

To Noble's surprise, no more shots came. The bushwhacker knew his business. Moving as he was, more shots would have little chance at success, but they would have given him a better idea of just where the shooter was.

Once he cleared the bend, Noble kept the horse moving. He couldn't hide and turn the tables on his attacker, much as he would've liked to. Against the sandstone and green growth, the black horse would be easy to spot. Distance. He needed distance now. Enough to put himself out of rifle range.

The stallion was a good mountain horse—surefooted, despite the earlier stumble. They ran up the canyon, and Noble saw where the cattle had been driven up on the flat country. It wasn't a natural entrance to the canyon. The rustlers had used shovels to cut a section of ramp into the canyon wall and give access below. Noble weighed his options. To continue down the canyon was to die. Soon it would taper out into a trap. Going up on the flatland had its own risks. When he topped that ramp, he would be skylined, and if the shooter was close, he'd have a clean shot.

There really wasn't a choice though. Not if he wanted a chance at escape.

Noble leaned down against the stallion's back and spurred the big black upward. They shot up the ramp at speed, and Noble heard the whine of another shot. Dirt exploded to his right with the miss.

Then he and the black were out on open prairie and still running. Noble recognized the hills all around. They were on the south end of the Circle Bar. Before leaving Montana, he had been close with Josiah, Eli's middle boy, and they'd prowled all over the Circle Bar hunting elk or deer. He remembered a stream a few miles farther east and rode for it.

He paused at the edge of the water, long enough to allow the stallion to rest and drink while Noble drew his rifle and watched over his back trail. He suspected the shooter would not follow. The country was open enough that a man on horseback could be seen a long ways out, and he would know Noble carried his own rifle.

Noble traveled against the stream in a northerly direction, toward the Websters' ranch house. The rustlers hadn't taken the cattle to the reservation, and he had an idea of where they might be.

Eli Webster's house stood alone in a shallow basin beside a deep pond and a set of large cattle pens. South of the basin, Noble belly-crawled up to the crest and looked down over the house and pens.

Given what he'd heard about Eli letting the ranch go, the place should have been deserted. But it was not. Smoke rose from several fires, and cattle bawled beneath the hot branding irons. Hundreds of milling cattle filled the pens. Noble caught sight of a couple of rustlers. They looked like the same ones he'd seen back in the amphitheater.

Once Noble had seen the fence and the notch the rustlers had cut in the canyon, he'd half expected this. Everyone knew about old Eli's pens. Now that he was gone, it was the perfect place to work over the rest of those brands.

From a distance, Noble couldn't tell exactly

whose cattle they'd stolen, but it seemed likely he'd find Rafter's missing animals there.

How to get down closer though?

He couldn't just ride down. If it was the same group of rustlers from earlier, he would be outgunned eight or ten to one. Not to mention the hidden rifleman. If he was protecting this operation, he would have ridden here after losing Noble.

Noble crawled back from the edge, retrieved the black from a thicket, and rode out.

He'd watched the rustlers long enough that he was confident he could recognize several when he saw them. Sooner or later, they would head into town. It took a lot to feed so many men, and men like that liked to spend their money on whiskey and women. They would go to Riggins. It was closer than Bigsby and served more of the rough crowd. The kind of crowd a rustler would enjoy. And when they came into town, he would be waiting.

Chapter 8

In Noble's youth, Riggins had been a dirty, run-down kind of place. The people that lived there were all dirty and run-down as well. The town had been born in a mining boom, a short one even by boomtown standards, and then it died slow and hard, as such towns usually did.

Only now it didn't look like it was dead. It was still dirty and still run-down, but with a lively feel to it. There were far more people here than Noble remembered, and some of the shops looked like they were actually making money. Looking up slope he saw several fresh muck piles.

Someone must think they can make the mines pay again.

Noble knew little of such things. He was a man of mountains and prairies and open sky. He'd been in a mine once or twice, guarding ore shipments, but he didn't like the cooped-up feeling or the thought of walking beneath a mountain with countless tons of deadly rock poised overhead. There were too many stories of crushed men or fires or pockets of boiling water down in those sunless places.

A water trough lay out front of a saloon, the Rusty Nail, and Noble pumped fresh water for the stallion. Then he loosened his pistols and went inside.

The bartender, a portly man with a walrus mustache, took his order and poured three fingers into a glass. Noble slugged it down. The whiskey was better than he expected, and he took a refill.

"Town's quiet," he said.

"It doesn't last," the bartender answered as he wiped his bare forearms with a towel. "The miners fill it up quick after shift change."

"I don't know how they do it," Noble said.

"Same. You won't catch me underground. I'm happy to stay up here and serve them though." The bartender draped the towel over his shoulder. "You here looking for work? Not much here, except for the mining."

"More of a cattle man myself. Thought I might find a riding job."

"Some big ranches around but they aren't doing so well."

"Oh?" Noble said.

"Too much missing beef lately."

"Missing?"

The bartender chuckled. "I suspect it winds up in the miner's bellies, but I hear things time to time."

"About missing cattle?"

"Circle Bar got cleaned out completely. Big outfit back in the day. Man named Webster, southerner, came here after the war. He lost his sons and then his best hands. Soon he didn't have any cattle either."

"What happened to him?"

"Died. I've seen it before. Even tough men lose the will when they're beaten bad enough."

"Must be some outfit hiring," Noble said. "I thought there were other ranches in the valley."

The bartender leaned over and lowered his voice. "There are. But they've all got cattle missing too."

"What about the law? Why don't they go out and find the missing cattle."

"Not much law here. A sheriff over in Bigsby. Never leaves town though. Just sits in the shade all day, counting his pay."

"He can't be paid much for sitting all day."

"Might be he's paid twice, once by the town and again to keep to the shade. None of my affair either way." The bartender shrugged.

"Got to be some way for a man to make a living here," Noble answered.

"Take my advice, friend, and ride on. They're suspicious of strangers here—especially cowhands."

"To good advice then," Noble said, and raised his glass.

"I'll drink to that," a fresh voice said. The newcomer stood in the doorway, silhouetted black against the sandy street.

Noble held his drink in one hand; the other

hung near his pistol. He'd heard that voice before, long in the past.

"Gage Banier," he said.

The newcomer stepped forward into the light. Three years had done little to Gage. His hair was still the same sandy blond, the creases on his face might have been carved a little deeper. The eyes were the same cruel brown, cold and lifeless, even when he was smiling. He smiled at Noble now.

"It's been some time since I saw you last," Gage said.

"Texas. I've been traveling since. Have a drink with me?" Noble tilted the raised glass toward him.

"Why not?"

The bartender gave Noble a wary look and poured a second glass. Gage sidled up to it, careful not to get too close to Noble though. Banier was a small man, whipcord thin, not in any way imposing. Not physically at least. But one look at those eyes and men knew he was a killer. They sensed the danger.

Gage Banier was a gunman of the first order. Around the campfires they said he'd killed eight men. Noble thought it was at least ten. He'd known one of them, Tennessee Smith, a fast man with a reputation of his own.

"To Montana," Gage said and drank.

"To Montana," Noble repeated.

"What brings you to Riggins?" Gage said.

"Business. Looking for some work."

"Not much call for our kind of work."

"Only enough for one?" Noble cocked an eyebrow at him. "I know you don't come cheap."

Gage only smiled. He lifted the shot glass, examining it. "See you round Noble."

Then he stepped back out to the street and was gone. Noble stared after him. Never would he have put his back to Gage Banier. Other men had, and they'd died for their mistake, but evidently Gage knew Noble wasn't that sort.

The bartender glared after Banier. "He never pays for his drinks," he said.

"On me then." Noble gave him a handful of coins.

When he was halfway to the door, the bartender called after him. "Watch yourself with that one. He'll shoot you quick as look at you."

Noble smiled and tipped his hat, "I know."

Gage Banier's presence changed things.

Staying in Riggins to wait for the rustlers wouldn't be possible. Noble wasn't afraid of Gage—he wasn't afraid of any man—but he knew enough about Gage to keep clear of him. The gunman was too quick to pull the trigger, and he had no problem shooting a man in the back. He wasn't the hidden rifleman though. Noble had never heard of Gage using a rifle. He liked to kill up close, where he could see his enemy and claim credit for it. He wanted everyone to know how many men he'd killed. He wanted to be feared.

If Noble stayed in Riggins, he'd have to guard his back every minute, and that was no way to watch for a gang of rustlers.

Gage being here raised a question though.

Who's paying him?

Gage never did anything for free. He might have ridden there thinking the return of mining would mean work, but more likely someone paid him to come. Few men could afford gunfighters of Banier's caliber—almost none in this valley. Noble wanted to know who.

If he couldn't wait for the rustlers in Riggins, he would ride to Bigsby and see what he could learn.

Time had changed Bigsby very little.

The general store was still Matthew's, with the same sign hanging over the door, the same wooden bench out front, even the same goods displayed through the same dusty window. The town's three churches, Baptist, Methodist, and Mormon, each looked the same, with fresh white paint and stained-glass windows.

Noble had spent a lot of time in that Methodist church. How many years had his father been pastor there after his run as a circuit rider ended?

It took riding to the middle of town to see

anything truly different. About to enter the saloon, Noble noticed the bank had changed names from Bigsby Independent to First National of Bigsby. Another sign, smaller, hung below the new name.

LOCALLY MANAGED
BY GRANT M. HICKMAN

Noble smiled. He knew the name. He and Grant had been of the same age. Grant had been wild—almost as wild as Noble himself. His old man had been one of the hard-luck miners in Riggins before giving up on his claim and opening a blacksmith shop there in Bigsby. Everything Grant's father made from smithing he spent on mining claims. Maybe one had finally panned out. The Hickmans had come up in the world if Grant ran the bank, and Grant himself must have tamed down considerably.

Batting the trail dust from his jeans, Noble crossed the street and entered the bank.

He hadn't been in the bank since he was a kid, but it all looked much the same. Light poured through the windows on either side of the building. The mirror in the back shone bright with the afternoon sun. So did its brass frame. The bank was warm, despite the cool of the day and the hot sunlight streaming in through the windows. The walls were thick-cut limestone, Noble remembered.

A pair of bank robbers had learned that the hard way when they tried to break in through the back. The sheriff had found a couple of discarded picks from where they'd spent all night trying to bust in.

A squat safe, black and dull like fresh-dug coal, sat against the back wall, the door hanging open. Noble couldn't help but notice the high stacks of bills sitting inside.

Thirty or forty thousand at least. The bank is doing well.

A young man in a suit approached him, arm outstretched for a shake.

"Welcome to First National. Is there anything I can help you with?"

Noble ignored the hand. "Grant Hickman. He runs this place?"

"He does. I'm afraid he's not seeing anyone today though."

"Where's his office?" Noble craned his neck to see better. The bank had three offices along the back wall. The largest was also nearest to the safe.

A man stepped out from the big office then; Noble knew him in an instant.

The years had been kind to Grant. He'd always been a big man. When he was old enough to swing a hammer, his father had put him to work in the smithy, and Grant bore those same thick shoulders and deep-barreled chest.

"Grant," Noble said, and stepped around the greeter.

Grant's mouth fell open, but he recovered himself quickly. "Gabriel Bartlett. Is that you?"

Noble threw out a hand. "Good to see you, Grant."

The banker hesitated, eyeing Noble's guns before clasping the hand. "It's been a long time."

"Seven years."

"Have you ate yet?" Grant said. "The Benton's got the best food in town."

"Lead the way then."

Noble followed his friend down the street toward what had been the Drover's Hotel and was now called The Benton. Drover's had been one of two Bigsby Hotels. The Continental Divide, on the other side of town, catered to travelers with more expensive needs, and Drover's picked up the rest.

"Drover finally gave it up?"

"Three years ago." Grant waved a hand. "New ownership fixed the place up. It's not the hole it used to be. In fact, most people agree it outclasses the Continental these days."

"Really?" The outside of the building looked little changed. A fresh coat of paint, clean windows, and of course a new sign, The Benton, in bold red lettering.

Grant held the door open and gave Noble a half bow. "You'll see soon enough."

Noble stepped in and for a moment he could have sworn he was in Cheyenne or Dodge or even on the Comstock. A huge crystal chandelier hung from the ceiling, throwing off light like a second sun. Whoever owned the place had torn out the cedar-plank bar and replaced it with some dark, exotic wood Noble didn't recognize. There were tables for poker and Faro, and more for eating. It was full to bursting, men crowded in shoulder-to-shoulder while saloon girls took their orders and carried trays of food.

The air stirred, and Noble caught the scent of hot steaks, garlic, and beer. His stomach groaned in applause.

One of the saloon girls, a leggy and dark-haired beauty, spotted them and started over.

"Where are we going to sit in all of this?" Noble said. There wasn't an empty seat in the house.

"I'm sure we can squeeze in," Grant laughed.

With eyes only for Grant, the brunette blushed when she got close. "Mr. Hickman, your usual table?" she asked.

"For me and my friend, Clair," Grant said, and tapped Noble with his hat.

"Follow me then." The girl gave them both a beaming smile and led the way to a second room, off to the left side, this one empty and quiet.

She brought them to a table near the window and laid out two menus. Grant sat first, taking the chair where he could see out toward the bank, while Noble sat opposite.

"Your usual table?" Noble said.

"They know me pretty well here," Grant said with a wink.

A waitress approached, this one dressed not like a saloon girl but in a long gown of blue and purple silks.

"Mr. Hickman, what will you be having today?" Her voice rolled out like poured honey, and there was a faint accent Noble thought he recognized.

"The usual for me, Audra."

"And your guest?" Audra turned to Noble, favoring him with a smooth smile and soft brown eyes.

"Whatever he's having," Noble said.

"Of course." She turned, and Noble watched her sway back toward the kitchen.

"She's not from around here," Noble said.

"No," Grant chuckled. "Baton Rouge. She owns part of this place alongside a mostly silent partner."

"Mostly silent?"

Grant smiled. "The bank keeps me much too busy to involve myself beyond my special table."

Noble eased back in his chair. "Banker, restaurant and hotel owner. You've done well, Grant. What else have you been up to?"

Grant laughed into his fist. "Rancher, most recently, and I could actually use a man like you."

"A man like me?" Noble's eyes narrowed.

"A man who knows how to use a gun." Grant smiled and waved a hand. "Oh, don't worry, your secret is safe with me."

He gestured to the street outside, where a good number of people were moving about. Townsfolk mainly, but plenty of cowboys mixed among them. "Most of these people didn't keep up with you after you left. They forgot. But I didn't. I heard of a gunman matching your description, a man named Noble. Unusual name. It didn't take much imagination after that."

"And what would a respectable banker need from a man like that?"

"I see you don't deny it." Grant laughed again.

"Not much point." Noble shrugged. "And I'm not ashamed of it. But you didn't answer my question."

"I've recently acquired ownership of the Webster place, Circle Bar. You remember?"

"I do."

"Anyhow, I've come into ownership, and unfortunately, the place is overrun with rustlers. They even went so far as to chase me off my own land."

"How'd you come to own the place, anyways?"

Grant leaned back before answering. "Old Eli was broke. For years, he struggled. But I don't have to tell you that. Even when we were kids, the place was barely making ends meet. Solid a man as he was, he didn't know much about raising cattle. And he knew even less about selling them. He came to the bank needing money, and I loaned him enough to get through."

"He put up the ranch against the money?" Noble knew a little of such things. His grandfather had always cautioned against debt and the bankers that held it.

"I didn't want it that way. The cattle market was terrible at the time; I told him he should sell off parts of the ranch to keep as much as he could. But he insisted. All or nothing." Grant shook his head in resignation. "You know how proud he was."

Noble grunted. Eli had been all of that.

"And now you own it, and rustlers have cleared the cattle out."

"Completely." Grant nodded, then he leaned in and lowered his voice. "I think they're even using those corrals Eli built to bring in more cattle stolen from the other ranches."

"Really?" Noble said casually. "Who else has been losing stock?"

Grant shifted his eyes left to right then back again. "Everyone. Even the Rafter."

"Any idea who's behind it?"

"Some ideas. There's a man here calls himself John Trevor, cattle buyer up from Colorado, or so he claims." Grant leaned in. "Only he never seems to have any cattle or cowhands. Dresses well, plenty of money, but no one's seen him do any kind of work. Then there's Miles Falk."

"Miles Falk?"

"Rich young fellow, from back East. Lives in the hotel here. Rode in about a month before everyone started losing cattle."

"Not much to go on," Noble said.

"Agreed. But he hasn't moved on. You know the valley. Why would anyone stop here, of all places?"

"Mining maybe. Riggins seemed busy enough."

"Maybe." Grant shrugged. "Like I said earlier, I might have some work for you. If you're interested."

Noble leaned back in his chair. "And just what do you want to hire me to do?"

"Run the rustlers off. Clean them all out of the valley."

"You have the law for that."

Grant's face twisted in disgust. "Local law isn't up for it. Won't leave town, in fact. He says he's the town marshal, not county."

"Seems like a town banker and hotel owner could do something about that," Noble said.

"Who is there to replace him? You interested?" Grant studied him for a moment.

Noble leaned back and laughed. "No chance of them pinning a star on me. Not with my past."

"No, I didn't think so." Grant eyed the door where Audra had gone. Then he turned back to

Noble. "What about my offer though? How's five thousand sound?"

Noble thought about it. Five thousand was a lot of money, especially alongside another six thousand from the Rafter for doing the same job.

"Six sounds a little better," Noble said with a smile.

Chapter 9

Noble rode north, back toward the Rafter, after his meal with Grant.

He had a lot to think about: Grant's offer, the rustlers, the unseen rifleman, Gage Banier . . . But instead he let his mind go back to his younger days. He and the stallion snaked their way through the sand hills where he'd killed his first antelope. Then he cut west a few miles to the stream and the deep pools where his mother had taught him and his brother to swim. Later, Daniel had been baptized in that same stream by their father.

Noble never had.

He was soon on Rafter's home range, and he noted the improvements his father and brother had made. The ponds were cleared out, and the creeks dammed with rock in places to hold extra water for the hot summer months. The cattle were fat, and each had a fat, healthy calf pressed tight against her hip.

Jack Noble had been many things, but after starting the ranch and defending it from outlaws and the Sioux, he hadn't done much to improve it. There hadn't been time in those early years, and after the territory was finally settled, he'd been an old man. Still fierce enough but not much interested in the ranching life. He'd spent most of his time hunting or just riding the country.

The seed Jack Noble had planted, Daniel and Sam Bartlett watered—Daniel mostly—and pruned until it had grown into a mighty oak—an oak that a gang of rustlers now hoped to cut down.

When Noble was a boy, the Rafter might have run a thousand head. Now, after all the improvements Daniel had made, he could easily count double that number and room for more yet, judging by the grass. And this only on the home place. The west range could run several thousand more, and it hadn't been improved at all.

Once that's done, the Rafter will be one of the best and biggest ranches in Montana.

The thought was a bitter one. His brother would be a rich man someday, and he'd have Grace alongside him. She'd chosen well. Noble couldn't fault her for that. He'd taken his freedom and gone riding to the high places while Daniel had made the most of what he'd been given.

So did Grant, from the look of things. Hotel owner, banker, now rancher. Who knew what else?

Noble crested a long rise and turned west; the Rafter's main ranch houses lay over the next ridge, and he had no desire to be seen.

He swung around a hill and almost collided with a young man on horseback.

"Watch yourself," the young man said, and swung his horse sharply about. He might have been seventeen but was likely a year or two younger. Freckles covered his face and locks of flame red hair stuck out from beneath a gray sweat-stained hat. His horse wore the Rafter brand, a mirror of Noble's own.

"I will," Noble said as he studied the young rider up and down. "You ride for the Rafter?"

"What of it?" The kid's hand twitched toward his gun.

"Just being polite."

"And who do you ride for?"

"Myself, mostly," Noble said.

"And just who might that be?"

"Look kid, I don't want no trouble with you, and you don't want any from me."

"I ain't no kid. And I ain't scared of trouble, no way. Try me, and I'll give you all you can handle."

"Fine, you go your way, and I'll go mine."

"You're on Rafter range."

"Yes, I believe I am," Noble agreed.

The kid's eyes grew when he finally noticed the brand on Noble's horse. "That's a Rafter horse. You're a damned thief—"

The kid reached for his pistol, but Noble acted faster. He jumped the stallion forward into the kid's smaller horse and his fist sent the youngster flying from the saddle. The kid hit the ground hard, rolled once, came up spitting grass, swearing, still grabbing for his pistol.

Then he saw Noble's gun was out and covering him. He squinted up at Noble.

"Look kid, next time you jump a man, make sure the riding strap is off your gun."

The kid looked down at his holstered pistol. He hadn't been able to draw with the strap over the hammer. He swore again.

"Kid, you got a foul mouth," Noble said. "Now, have you ever seen this horse before?"

"No."

"And I'll bet you've seen every horse on the Rafter, haven't you?"

"I have." The kid rubbed the spit from a busted lip.

"Then I can't have stolen it from the Rafter, can I?"

"No."

"Better be sure next time you accuse a man of being a horse thief." Noble wagged the pistol at him.

The kid squinted up at him and spit a leaf from his mouth.

"So we're settled, then?"

"No, I owe you a sucker punch in the mouth."

"Well, at least I didn't shoot you. I could have, and you'd owe me one from that forever. Now, take off your gun belt and drape it over the saddle."

"Damned if I will."

"Damned if you don't." Noble held the pistol on him.

"I won't," the kid said.

Noble eased back the hammer on his pistol with a loud click. The kid was tough, that much was certain, but he was also smart enough or could see something in Noble's face to know he'd best do what he was told. He unbuckled his gun belt and hung it over his horse's saddle.

"Good," Noble said. "Now I'm going to ride off that way, and I'll be taking your horse with me. I'll turn him loose when I'm a ways off, and you can have your gear back."

The kid licked his lips.

"What's your name anyway?" Noble said.

"Vern Ollie. You best remember it because next time I see you, I'll have my gun ready. No leather strap is going to save you."

"Uh-huh. I'm sure you will, Vern. But I don't plan on seeing you again."

Noble took the young man's horse by the reins and rode off. When he'd ridden a half mile west, he looked back toward Vern Ollie. The young man was jogging along after them. Noble tied the Rafter horse to a stunted pine and then set the stallion to a quick trot to the west.

He couldn't remember a time when the Rafter sent out a cowboy alone. His grandfather liked to keep them working in pairs, one older rider along with one younger, less experienced. There was more to it than just breaking in the new man; there were dangers working cattle alone. Indians—at least in Grandfather's early days—rustlers or thieves later, and grizzlies or lions always. One man, even armed, against a big brown bear stood little chance.

So why was Vern Ollie out here riding alone?

The day was almost gone when Noble rode back down into the shadowed valley and up to his grandfather's cabin. After leaving Bigsby and then having his run-in with Vern Ollie, he'd ridden west along the Rafter's range to see where the rustlers might strike from next.

So far they'd confined their thieving to the west range's wild backcountry, but sooner or later, the fat cows milling on the home place would draw them. Noble was certain of that.

Even from a distance, he could see Clarissa had been busy. The porch had been swept and cleared, and she had transplanted wildflowers from the field into the boxes hanging beneath the windows. The windows themselves were clean and bright with inviting lantern light shining through.

The kitchen window was open a crack, and the cool evening breeze carried scents of baking, and cooked meat.

Noble put away his horse, giving the stallion a thorough rubdown and a double ration of oats. He saw to Clarissa's horse even though she'd already cared for the animal herself. An extra portion of oats would do the skinny buckskin some good.

"Washbasin by the door. Soap too," Clarissa said when he entered.

"All right," Noble agreed. He set his rifle up on the pegs above the door and hung his hat on a lower peg before lathering up.

"Smells good," he said.

"Grace brought some supplies over. She seems nice."

"Yes." Noble wasn't sure how safe the subject of Grace was. Clarissa seemed to get offended anytime he brought his sister-in-law up, or any other woman for that matter, but now she had done so herself.

Should he say more or let it go?

The latter seemed the safer course, so he tried changing the subject. "I followed the rustlers today. Found where they're keeping the cattle. Old Webster place. He's got a set of big corrals over there where they can alter the brands."

"That's good. How do they do that, anyway? Change the brands, I mean?"

"Use tongs and a cinch ring, usually. They heat it up and draw the new brand over the old one."

"I imagine you'll have them cleared out soon enough," Clarissa said.

"Hope so." Noble eased into his chair by the fire.

Clarissa was frowning at him now. What had caused that?

"There's a lot of them. I can't just ride in and start shooting. I've got to catch them alone or in small batches. Go slow and sure."

"It's dangerous then?" The frown was gone now, replaced by a look of concern.

"Only if I'm careless. Someone took a shot at me today."

"They didn't hit you."

"No. I was lucky the first time, and the second, I didn't give him much of an opportunity."

"They shot at you twice?" Now the concern had deepened.

"I get shot at a lot. Comes with the territory."

"Have you been shot before?"

"Three times," he grunted. "Shoulder, leg, and side. Once each."

"You need to be more careful."

Noble grinned. "Can't avoid trouble forever. Not doing what I do."

"You still need to be more careful." Her look was stern.

"What's dinner looking like?"

"Beefsteak. Roasted with carrots, potatoes, and onions. I've got a pie cooling on the sill. Apple."

"Sounds real good. My grandfather always had trouble with the stove. Said he didn't get the draft right."

"I fixed that," Clarissa said.

"How?" Noble raised an eyebrow.

"Cleared out the bird nests in the pipe and opened the damper up."

"Huh. Guess he never considered that before. He wasn't much hand at cooking. Mostly I did it when I lived with him, or my mother when she was around. I got pretty good at it."

Clarissa gave him a flat look. "I've tasted your cooking enough to know better."

Noble laughed. "That was traveling food. I do better with a real kitchen."

"I'm sure you do," she said like she didn't believe it.

"The cabin looks good," Noble said, changing the subject again. He could tell he wasn't going to convince her.

One night I'll cook for her, and then I won't do it again until she asks.

"Grace helped me get it looking nice. I wanted it to be right when you got home. I tried to take that awful buffalo head off the wall, but she said you wouldn't like that."

"You tried to move Buff? He's an old friend. And he's lucky."

"Lucky how? His head is mounted on the wall."

"Buff was the first critter on the ranch. The first head of Rafter stock. My grandfather, Jack Noble, came up the trail from Texas with his herd, and when they crossed into Montana, he rode on ahead to find the right place. He got crossways with a band of Sioux, and they chased him for two days."

"He escaped them though," Clarissa said.

"He did," Noble nodded. "Killed three of them, and after that, they decided he wasn't worth the trouble. But they'd killed his horse. He wandered around afoot for a time and stumbled on this young buffalo bull, Buff, there. Grandfather Jack was hungry—and thirsty—but he'd shot all his rifle shells holding off those Sioux, so all he had was a pistol. He crept up close to Buff, but the bull wasn't a fool. He'd let Grandfather get close and then shuffle off a ways." Noble laughed aloud. "I can imagine how the old man cussed him up and down.

"Around nightfall Buff finally crossed over a little ridge and Grandfather followed. On the other side, a stream ran through a wooded cut and the deer were so thick and tame you could hit them with a rock. That's the same stream we waited beside the other night. So—with a belly full of venison—Jack swore to share his newfound ranch with old Buff."

"A buffalo?"

"Yep. Buff got the run of the place and all the grass he could eat. The cowboys even forked hay for him in the snowy winter. Grandpa said he could never kill an animal that saved his life."

"How did he end up on the wall, then?"

"Hunter," Noble said, and his expression

darkened. "Grandpa Jack came up on the man right after he'd shot Buff. He almost hanged him."

"He hung a man over a buffalo?"

"Almost. The man had three kids and a wife in a wagon some distance away. They'd gotten lost off the trail and been starving. Grandfather couldn't hang a man for feeding his family."

"So he let him go?"

"He did. Said Buff was getting old, and it was a better end than the wolves and buzzards, anyway. Saved Grandfather from putting the old bull out of his misery."

Noble had heard that story only once in his life. It had been the only time he'd seen that tough old man cry.

"So Buff's good luck. Good luck for the Rafter and good luck for some traveling family that needed him. Can't move him now."

But for the crackling of the fire, the cabin was silent then. Noble's mind went back to similar nights when he was a boy. Sometimes Grandfather would go to bed early and he'd stay up, listening to the night sounds, watching stray embers fly up through the chimney.

A creaking noise came from the porch outside, and suddenly Noble was up, gun in his fist. He waited, eyes shifting from the door to the windows then to the door again.

Someone is out there.

"What's—" Clarissa started, and he silenced her with a raised hand.

"Come away from the window," he whispered.

The noise from the porch continued.

Noble crept toward it, moving his feet slow and silent. He eased the door open a crack and peeked out. He didn't see whoever was out there, but their shadow lay stretched out before him, a big man, without weapons showing in either hand.

Pushing the door farther, Noble took a quick step outside and spun to face the intruder.

The porch was dark now, and the man's height hid most of his face; only a strong, wide jaw was visible.

"I might have guessed," the man said.

Noble knew that voice, that tone of pitiless disapproval. He'd heard it often enough from his father, but this wasn't him. This was a younger man, and it could only be one.

"Daniel."

"Why are you here?" Daniel asked.

Noble glared at his brother. Daniel was taller than he, and thicker across the chest, but there was a layer of fat around his gut, the type that comes from too much riding and too much good food. Daniel had been living an easy life.

"Good to see you too, brother," Noble said. He holstered his pistol.

"I said, why are you here?" Daniel's deep voice rumbled.

Noble looked him up and down again. Daniel hated to be kept waiting. He'd never had much patience. "I was sent for."

"Sent for by who?"

"If you don't know, then why should I tell you?" Noble grinned.

Daniel's hands clenched into fists. The muscles along his jaw flexed.

"Tell me."

"No." Noble opened the door farther and let the light spill out where he could see better. "I was sent for to clean up a mess that you either can't or won't."

"What mess?"

"You tell me. How many problems does the Rafter have that you're scared to face?"

Daniel stepped off the porch toward his waiting horse. "The rustlers then. This is a family affair. A family you gave up being a part of. I will handle it. Legally, without killing. Go back to wherever you came from, big brother."

"You do remember why I left, don't you? Someone had to, and I was willing to do what you wouldn't. Now I'm back again to fix another of your problems."

"I don't need your help!" Daniel shouted. "I'll be back at noon. Be gone by then."

"Or what? You'll run me off? Burn down our grandfather's cabin?" Noble roared back. "I'll be

133

gone when the job's done and the Rafter is safe again."

Daniel left then, without another word.

"Good to see you too, little brother," Noble said to himself.

Chapter 10

Grace heard her husband's heavy bootsteps on the porch. They matched the steady beat of her heart. The door banged open, and she knew, the way any wife would immediately know, that something was deeply wrong. Her husband had painstakingly fitted that door, spending hours on it; he would not be so callous with it. Not unless he was angry.

"Grace," he said. Loud and hard, his voice rang through the house.

"Daniel, the children are sleeping," she said.

He knows. Somehow he knows what I have done.

One glimpse was all she needed. She wrapped the shawl tight around her shoulders like a suit of heavy armor.

"Did you send for him?" Daniel thundered. "Did you send for my brother?"

"I did."

She thought he might rage then. Her Daniel was not quick-tempered like Gabriel or Jack Noble, that hard old man; he was an even-keeled man like his father. Few times had she ever seen him truly upset. But on those rare occasions he was a fright to behold, raw and primal and raging against the whole of the world.

Never had he directed that rage against her. She drew a breath, long and deep. She wasn't sure if she could survive it.

He looked at her, eyes full of raw disappointment and hurt. Her heart almost broke at the sight of it. He stunned her then when he simply turned and retreated back outside, stumbling at the threshold as if he'd been shot, the door still hanging open in his wake.

What have I done?

Grace ran after him.

He was pacing in the open space between the house and barn, cursing under his breath, staring at the ground, and raising a cloud of thick dust with every step.

"You saw him then?" Grace ventured.

Daniel tore off his hat and threw it. It sailed high and then arced down into the corral.

Grace took a long breath. She had to handle this with care. "We need his help."

"Help?" Daniel turned to her. His eyes reflected the light from the house. "He can't help us. He's never helped anyone but himself. He'll cost us everything."

"We need him to drive off the rustlers."

"At what price?" Daniel's look held such intensity it caught her up short. "You don't know what he is now. I do. After he left, I kept track of him. I know what he's become. A killer. A callous killer. He'll destroy us."

A callous killer, maybe that's what we need.

That's what she wanted to say, but the words wouldn't come. She couldn't do it. There was too much hurt in him.

"He won't hurt us," Grace said. It was all she could muster.

"He already has. Here a day, maybe two, and he's already got you keeping secrets. Turning against me."

"I am not turned against you." Grace felt her confidence return. She'd known this moment would come. She'd known it the moment she set out for the outlaws' lost cabin. "I am your wife, Daniel, and I will never be against you."

"Then why? Why would you send for him?" Daniel went to the porch and slammed a fist against one of the wood posts. It boomed out a heavy thud.

"I thought it was the right thing to do. We need help to save this place. To save our family."

He looked at her then, his head tilted to one side. "You don't think I can do that?"

"You can do many things, Daniel. You've worked hard to turn this place into a home for us. I don't want to see you lose it now." Grace took a tentative step toward him. "You can't ask me to watch them take it from us."

"You regret it. You regret choosing me over him. You think he could've done better. He wouldn't let the rustlers take a single calf?" The anger was back now and rising quickly.

"Daniel Bartlett, you will stop this now." Emilia stood at the corner of the house. "I sent for your brother, not Grace. If you're angry at someone, be angry at me."

Daniel's head whipped around. He studied his mother up and down. She was a small thing, weighing less than half of what her son did, but she was all iron and rawhide and that unbreakable Bartlett will. "I might have known, Mother. You always loved him best."

"I love both my sons. I still do. But it's time you grew up."

"Grew up?" Daniel gestured at the house, the barn, the ranch itself. "Look around you. I built this. All of it. Me and Pa. We built it while he went off gallivanting over the hills, fighting and killing all the while."

Emilia took three quick steps to her son and slapped him across the face.

That slap had not been playful. The sound of it stunned Grace. She had never seen Emilia strike anything or anyone.

"And what did we do, Daniel? What did Grace and I do while you and your father 'built' this place? Did we not put as much blood and sweat and tears into it? Do we not deserve a say in it? Do we not own even a piece of it?"

Emilia turned her back to him and walked out

to look down on the home valley. Grace stepped through the corral bars, picked up Daniel's hat, dusted it off.

"Are you alright?" Grace asked, and held out the hat.

"I'm fine." He rubbed his face.

"Good," Emilia snapped, and then spun back around. "I sent for your brother. There's trouble coming, and we need him. The Rafter needs him. Unless you plan on fighting and killing the rustlers yourself?"

Daniel growled. "The law will take care of them."

Emilia laughed. "My sweet son—the law doesn't care about us. We're not town folk, and the law only cares about town folk now. Your brother knows what to do, and he's willing to do it."

"And what is that?" Daniel asked. "Is he going to kill them?"

"Yes. He's going to kill every one of them. He's going to hunt them down and kill them like the thieving dogs they are."

"Those days are gone. Grandfather Jack's ways won't work anymore. The law—"

Emilia spat on the ground. "I spit on the law. That's for the law. You tried. You went to the sheriff already and what did he say?"

"He said it's a county matter."

"A county matter," Emilia said. "By the time

the county sorts it out, your brother will have it resolved."

"What about after?"

"What about after?" Emilia said.

"When it's over, will he leave?" Daniel said. "There's no place for him here."

"That will be up to him," Emilia said. "There will always be a place on the Rafter for my boys. Both of them."

The stallion woke him. Noble had taken to sleeping with the window open. The cabin was too quiet, and comfortable enough that he couldn't hear the night sounds. For a man living like he did, the normal nighttime sounds and his attention to them kept him alive. The stallion wouldn't have that problem. So Noble came awake when the stallion whinnied to let him know someone was around.

Drawing a pistol, he eased out into the main room. Clarissa's door remained closed. He'd never met anyone who slept so soundly.

Is she just blissfully unaware or blessed with a clear conscience?

Either way, the girl could sleep through a hailstorm.

Drawn gun leading the way, Noble peered out into the gray dawn through the windows, seeing nothing and no one, and then he opened the door.

His mother sat on a chair, stretched out, with her feet crossed at the ankles and resting on the front railing.

"A normal person would have knocked," Noble said.

"Normal," she huffed. "Few people ever accused me of that. Besides, you sleep hard enough it would take a marching band to wake you. Figured I'd just wait out here. Didn't plan on it taking you so long to notice me."

"No need to bluff me. You've been here less than five minutes," Noble said, and eased the hammer down on his pistol. "That stallion let me know as soon as you arrived."

"A good horse is worth a lot," she replied with a grin. "You're the only one I couldn't bluff, Son. You and your grandfather."

"Don't know about that. Seems like you held your own with him. You're the only one who could."

"Your brother came by for a visit?" Emilia asked. She was dressed in a brown shirt, matching pants, and knee-high boots with buckskin fringe.

"I wouldn't call it a visit," Noble said. "He didn't seem to want my help."

"It isn't up to him. Our deal—yours and mine—is a private one. You clear out the rustlers, I pay you. Simple."

Noble gave a low chuckle. "Nothing simple about any of this."

Emilia sighed. "Simple as I can make it, then. Did you find out anything so far?"

"They're smart. Using the canyons to move cattle along the west side and then hiding them on the Webster place."

"Eli's pens. I should have seen that," Emilia said, and got to her feet.

Noble ignored the comment and went on, "From Webster's I don't know. They've got to get them to market somehow. South or west, I can't tell yet."

"It doesn't matter. What matters is stopping them from emptying us out."

"There's a group of them. Too many to tackle all at once. I've got to single them out and cut them down to size."

"How many?"

"Ten, at least. And one of them likes to shoot people in the back."

Noble explained about the hidden rifleman and his escape. He leaned out over the porch railing. "There's another complication, too. Gage Banier, a gunfighter. He's over in Riggins. Doing what I'm not sure, but he could be part of it."

"He's fast? This gunman?"

"He's fast," Noble said, nodding.

"Enough to worry you?" Emilia looked up at him.

"I worry about everybody. And when I stop worrying, I'll hang up the guns."

"I hope you hang them up long before that." Emilia gave him a pained look.

Noble regarded her for a moment, then said, "So do I."

Neither spoke for a time. The gray lightened enough that they could see the surrounding mountains, and the first birds came out to hunt their morning meal.

"Way you ride over this country," Noble finally said, "I thought you'd have this all figured out by now. How'd you miss where they're taking the cattle?"

"Your father isn't well. I can't stray so far from home these days."

"I'm sorry to hear that. How bad is the old—"

Emilia slapped him.

"Be respectful of your father," she said. "I know you two had your differences, but that was a long time ago, and he is your father."

"Yeah." Noble rubbed his jaw. The slap had been genuine.

His mother acted tough, but he saw her rubbing her hand while she thought he wasn't looking. He couldn't remember the last time he'd been slapped, but he was pretty sure he'd killed the man who did it.

"You two were also too much alike," Emilia said.

"How so?"

"Prideful, stubborn, set to prove everyone else

wrong. All three of you got that in common, and your grandfather, too."

"Fair enough. But I'll wager I'm the only one of us who would admit to that."

Emilia smiled warmly. "You'd win on that wager. How's your girl getting along? Awful lonely out here. No other folks around and all."

"She's fine, and she's not my girl. I'm just helpin' her out some."

"Uh-huh," Emilia said. "Well, today's Sunday, and you know what that means."

"I haven't been to church in a while, Ma. I doubt they'd have me."

"I wasn't referring to that. I meant the family supper."

"Up at your place?" Noble's brows lifted. "I'm not sure Daniel would like that. I doubt Pa would either."

Emilia sighed again. "I will take care of your brother and your father. But the secret's out now. Daniel knows you're here, and he'll be sure to tell Sam, so you might as well come to supper tonight. Do your girl some good to get out."

"I'm not sure—"

"Don't make me ask again, boy." Emilia gave him a look of warning. "Seems all I do is slap you boys these days. I am an old woman. You should both be taking care of me, not me still taking care of you two."

Neither spoke for a time, and the sun sent streaks of red-gold fire over the horizon.

"Sunrises in this country make it all worth it," Emilia mused. "All the cold and the pain and the struggle. Words are helpless to match the beauty and wonder of this place."

"The desert is like that. Mountains too," Noble said. "Midnight in the Sonora smelling of blooming cactus after a cleansing rain, or sunset over the Sangre de Cristos. The light bathes those high, jagged peaks in red and purple."

"Did you become a poet in your travels?"

Noble's face darkened. He lifted his gun. "Only with this. But I did see beauty, Ma. All of it wild and wonderful."

The door opened then, and Clarissa came out. "Oh, I didn't expect company," she said, and flushed.

"My son tells me you are quite the cook. I thought I'd ride over for a free breakfast and some coffee," Emilia said with a warm smile.

"You're always welcome. This is your house and all."

"Not mine," Emilia said. "If it's anyone's, it belongs to Noble. He and his grandfather were always close, and he'd be proud for him to have it."

Emilia followed Clarissa into the cabin. Noble remained on the porch, admiring the magnificent morning a minute longer. It was beautiful, no doubt about it. He also couldn't deny how much he'd missed the place.

Sounds came to him. His mother talking to Clarissa, their giggling laughter, the rattle of pans, plates, and dishes. Then came the smell of bacon frying and hot bread rising in the oven.

This was a good life. That too he couldn't deny.

He glanced inside. Clarissa was kneading more dough, and his mother was using a fork to turn over the bacon. Both were smiling in that secret way women had with each other.

Supper tonight with the family.

He wasn't looking forward to it, but his mother wanted him there, and that was enough. Getting out would do Clarissa good. She was right in that.

Noble took another look at the sunrise.

He would miss all of this when his work was done, and he rode away. There was pain for him here: the cold judgment of his brother and their father. But so too was there good: his mother, Grace, the memories of his grandfather. More than the proper Rafter houses, this cabin was home as he'd always remembered it.

I don't think I'll ever come back again though. Not when this is done.

Chapter 11

Noble spent the day surveying the Rafter's west range. It was rough country, shot through with broken canyons, flat plateaus, and dense thickets of pine, alder, juniper, and fir. Water was plentiful. Most of the canyons carried spring-fed streams and beaver ponds. Where the trees grew thin and the soil deep enough, grass grew, high and thick and lush.

All told, the Rafter had just over five hundred cattle on the west range. The land would support more, five or six times that number, but between the bears, the wolves, and a few mountain lions, along with Daniel holding most of his growing herd on the home range, the herd hadn't grown beyond those five hundred.

A few good men to keep an eye on the cattle here and a little time and this herd would soon swell. The ranch could get quite wealthy with just a little more care in the west. But Daniel and the two hands seemed to have all they could handle with the home place.

Checking the cattle wasn't the main purpose of Noble's ride though. He studied where a group of rustlers might strike next, and where they might get any stolen cattle started south into the canyon country and those branding pens.

There were several places Noble remembered from his youth. He found more during his ride, places where rainwater had reshaped the land from what he remembered. He marked each in his mind. The farthest west of these showed signs of recent travel by shod horses. He found where the branches of a fir might have been broken by a man riding through on horseback.

This was where the rustlers had last struck.

A few dozen cattle lingered in a meadow nearby, and Noble started them east, away from danger. The harder the rustlers had to work, the more time they took, the easier it would be to catch them.

In the early afternoon, he headed back to the cabin. Clarissa waited for him there, her horse saddled and ready.

"What do you think?" she asked, and held out the hem of a long, blue dress. He hadn't seen her wearing this one before. She must have gotten it from Kettle's place.

"Very pretty," he said.

She smiled and blushed. "I had to take it in a little around the waist, but it fits nice."

"I'd say so," Noble said. The time here, short though it was, had been good for her. She looked less like a young girl and more like . . . well . . . like a young woman.

"Is it time?"

"It is," Noble said. He dismounted and then helped her onto her little horse.

"Do you think they'll like me? Your family, I mean?"

"Probably more than they like me," Noble said truthfully.

"How long has it been since you've seen them?"

"Seven years since I rode out." Noble swung into the saddle. He tugged his hat down, took up the reins, and spurred his horse. They rode up out of the canyon and onto the flat plains. As soon as they crested the top, the wind picked up, warm and fresh from the south.

Noble led the way south and then due east. They crossed several hills, circling a few, each with broad flats of grassland stretching out between them. Cotton-colored clouds rolled overhead. Finally, in a notch in the hills, they saw the Rafter's ranch buildings.

Clarissa let out a wild whoop when she saw them, and she spurred her horse into a run. Noble followed, and instead of chastising the girl for her recklessness, he found himself grinning. Though the stallion was bigger and faster, he couldn't overcome the buckskin's head start. When they passed the barn, Clarissa looked over her shoulder and smiled in triumph.

"I won," she said, and reined up in the ranch yard.

"You did," Noble admitted. "I didn't think the little horse could do it."

"He's small but mighty. Aren't you, Bailey?"

Clarissa said, and patted the buckskin's neck.

Noble hopped down and eased Clarissa down from the saddle. She stood close to him for a moment; he could feel her breath over his bare neck, hot and quick.

"You made it," Emilia said, coming out of the house to meet them. She too wore a dress, a plaid one that he recognized. The rest of the week she donned her buckskins, but on Sundays she always wore a proper dress.

She wrapped Clarissa in a hug. "And you, young lady, can really ride. I thought I recognized myself out there. Gabriel, you didn't tell me she could ride."

"She can ride," Noble said, and grinned.

Grace came out next, followed by two small children, a young boy and an even younger girl, and then two somber-looking men. Vern Ollie came over from the bunkhouse looking angry. Noble did not see a gun on him. Cactus Huff trailed him a few steps.

Cactus held out a ready hand.

"Gabriel Bartlett, is it really you?"

"Cactus, you're still above ground?"

"So far." Cactus looked around suspiciously. "Don't say it so loud though. The Good Lord might hear you and decide it's my time." Cactus came close then, looking Noble up and down. "You've seen some country, boy. You'll have to tell me about it."

"When there's time," Noble gestured toward the old man. "Clarissa, this is Cactus Huff. He's original Rafter. Came up with Grandpa Jack from Texas. Been here ever since."

"They keep feeding me, and I'm too lazy to get a job anywhere else," Cactus said, smiling. "Nice to meet you, ma'am."

Noble made an effort to keep the grin on his face and his tone light when he spoke to the two men on the porch. Were it not for the gray in his father's hair, the two could have been brothers rather than father and son.

"Daniel, Father, you both look well," Noble offered.

"Well enough," Sam Bartlett said in a somber baritone.

Noble fought back a surge of anger at his father's hard voice.

How many times have I heard that somber disapproval?

Clarissa moved to Noble's side, close enough that their shoulders touched.

"This is Ester and Little Jack," Grace said.

"Ester, that's a pretty name," Clarissa said, and knelt down to the girl's eye level. Ester retreated back behind her mother's dress and blushed.

Noble shook Little Jack's hand. The boy looked very much like his father at that age. "I doubt you'll be Little Jack for long. They'll be calling you Big Jack in a year or two."

"They call me just Jack now," the boy said.

"Just Jack," Noble repeated. "Good a name as any."

An awkward moment followed. Noble looked toward his father and brother, and they studied him from the porch in stony silence.

"Well, let's all go inside and eat," Emilia said. She smoothed the front of her dress, then took Clarissa by the arm to lead her in. "Now you'll have to tell me where you learned to ride like that."

Grace and her children followed behind the pair, Noble trailing in their wake. Cactus and Vern came next, with Daniel and Sam the last to enter.

The table stood as Noble remembered it, long and piled high with rolls, potatoes, steaks, carrots, and other vegetables.

Emilia took a seat at the end, with Clarissa and Noble filing in next to her. Grace sat opposite them, along with Jack and Ester, and Cactus took up the spot on Noble's right. Sam sat at the head of the table, Daniel on his right, and Vern Ollie on the left. Vern gave Noble a venomous glare.

"This is the fellow who jumped me yesterday," he told Daniel. "Stole my horse and left me afoot."

Noble ignored him. He would not be baited into a confrontation at his mother's table.

"Where all have you been Gabriel?" Cactus asked.

"All over. California, Arizona, Nevada, Oregon, Texas."

"Texas," Cactus echoed, and held one hand over his heart. His eyes took on a far-off look. "The home country. I'd love to see it one last time."

"You never went back?" Noble said.

"Never. Someday I might. Maybe. Or more likely they'll just plant me with Old Jack and my pards up on the mesa. Whole lotta Texas blood and bones buried down deep in that black Montana soil. Makes it Texas enough for me."

"Why do you travel so much?" It was Little Jack that asked, but Noble knew every ear in the room was straining to hear the answer.

"I like to see new country," Noble started, "and I suppose I've got a bit of a knack for things."

"What's a knack?" Ester said.

"It's a talent, like being good at whistling or roping."

"And what's your knack?" Jack said.

Noble suddenly liked his nephew, straight to the point of things. The boy might grow up to look like Daniel, but he sounded an awful lot like Grandfather Jack. Noble smiled and said, "Since I was your age, I always had a knack for finding trouble."

"It went back much further than that," Sam said from the end of the table.

Noble couldn't deny it, so instead he gave his nephew a wink and said, "See? It's a knack."

Emilia cleared her throat. "Pass one of those steaks will you, young lady?" she asked Clarissa.

For a few moments afterward, no one spoke as the food was shared all around. Clarissa started cutting hers with knife and fork, and Noble bumped her with his elbow and coughed. She looked around at the others, face a little red, and put her fork back down.

Both hands raised before him, Sam closed his eyes, knelt his head and began to pray.

"We thank thee Lord for gathering us all together this blessed evening, and we beseech thee Lord to forgive our trespasses against others and against you. We know, Lord, that any injuries we've done to others we've so inflicted on you as well. Your son spoke such to Peter in the garden when he committed violence in your own name."

Sam took a breath and went on.

"Violence will ever beget more violence, as it has since wicked Lucifer fell, cast down from your heavens for his rebelliousness. Now he walks the land, inciting coarse men to the wicked ways of alcohol, adultery, and the sinful ways of violence, the way of the gun. We ask forgiveness in your Son's holy name and that you keep the ways of violence far from our home."

"A-men," Daniel said at the end.

Emilia shot both of them an angry look while Cactus studied his plate and Grace followed his example.

Noble didn't bother feeling offended. He'd always known what his father saw when he looked at him. Too much Jack Noble, hard-case rancher, and not enough Sam Bartlett, peaceful pastor. Not for the first time, Noble wondered how his mother could have married a man like his father. She'd carried her own rebellious streak. She and her father hadn't always gotten along; they were far too much alike for that. Was her choice of husband her way of striking back at the hard old man?

They ate in near silence, Clarissa speaking to Grace or Emilia at times, the children occasionally asking a question about Texas or California or what lay over the Bitterroots to the west.

Noble answered each question thoughtfully. Out of politeness, he asked a few of his own. Were they good at riding horses? Could they rope?

Jack seemed interested in everything, and he offered to show Noble his new Appaloosa after dinner.

"Not too many of those around anymore. The Nez Perce took most of them to their reservation. I had one a few years ago. Won him in a card game."

"A card game?" Little Jack asked.

"Sure. Five-card stud."

The boy cast a look down the table toward his father. "We aren't allowed to play cards."

"Really? Your mother was the best bottom dealer I ever saw."

"Ma was?"

"Slick as a greased pig. I lost count of how many times she cheated me at cards. She never lost."

"We don't have cards in this house," Daniel said.

Noble ignored him. If he could overlook an insult during prayer, then Daniel could overlook an honest answer about a card game.

"Your mother knows every card game ever invented. She taught them to me and your pa."

"Gabriel," Daniel said.

"Pa played too?" Little Jack looked like his whole world had just shifted.

"He did, but your ma always won against him too," Noble turned to look at Daniel. "You remember, don't you, Daniel? We finally caught her slipping aces up her dress sleeves one day."

Daniel coughed, and Sam looked like he'd eaten a bug. Grace only smiled.

"I had to," she said. "Daniel would never place a big enough wager for me to win. He was always folding. And you always lucked into the best cards."

"Grace!" Daniel finally said.

"I'm still lucky when it counts." Noble grinned.

"I don't like this talk of gambling," Sam said.

"Who taught you to play, Ma?" Jack said.

"My father," Grace said. To Noble's eye, she looked a little grey at talk of her father.

That hasn't changed.

"I recall someone else who used to enjoy playing with us, and she always wound up taking the pot." Noble looked at his mother, who was feigning innocence.

"I never cheated," Emilia said. "You got your luck from me. I just had a little more of it."

"Old Jack made all of us teach your grandmother everything we knew. I showed her how to rope."

"Enough." Sam slammed a hand on the table. "I'll have no more of this coarse talk at my table." Slowly he rose and went to his bedroom. The door slammed behind him.

No one spoke.

Daniel let out a sigh. "See what you've done, Gabriel? One day back and now look."

"You know, little brother, I remember when you weren't so high and mighty. I remember our mother taking you over her knee and spanking you aplenty."

Jack and Ester both giggled.

"And what does that mean?" Daniel said.

"It means you weren't always so damned sanctimonious. There was a time when you were fun to be around."

"You mean a time when I was young and let you lead me into foolishness?"

"I seem to remember several of those fun times were started by you. Who thought it was a good idea to make a fire in the hayloft? Who decided we should build a raft to float down the river? You were going to be a gambler like Grady. Now you won't even let your kids learn how to play poker. What happened to you?"

Daniel stood, fists clenched, so quickly Vern Ollie had to jump clear. "I grew up, Gabriel. I had to be responsible. Something you wouldn't understand. You never had to."

He too stormed off, out the front door and toward his own house across the way.

Grace gave Noble a disapproving glance. "You shouldn't provoke him." She turned to Emilia. "Thank you for the lovely meal, and Clarissa, it was very nice to see you again. I don't get the chance to talk to other women much these days." Then she and the children went scuttling along after Daniel.

"Let's go, Vern," Cactus said with a sigh. "We'll catch up some other time," he told Noble. "I want to hear all about California. Emilia, dinner was perfect, as always."

Vern said nothing but gave Noble one last hard look before departing.

"We should be going," Noble said.

"Not until I help clean up," Clarissa protested. "I won't leave your poor mother with all this work alone."

"Thank you, dear, but that isn't necessary," Emilia said.

"Nonsense, I won't hear of it." Clarissa donned an apron and set about in the kitchen. "Noble, bring me the plates."

Noble gathered up the plates and shuffled them to her, two at a time.

Emilia watched him with interest. When he was done, she smiled at him over the rim of her coffee cup.

"What?" he said.

"Nothing," she laughed. "I didn't expect my big, bad gunfighter son to be clearing tables."

"Clearing table for my magnificent mother." Noble swung down and kissed her on the forehead. "I'm sorry about tonight."

"No you're not. I know you better than that."

"All right, I'm not sorry. They shouldn't have started it with that dam—with that prayer. An old man taught me to always finish a fight, even if I didn't start it."

"A wise man."

"And a wiser woman made it stick."

Emilia rose to help Clarissa with the plates and bowls, and Noble slipped outside. To his surprise, Cactus and Vern were both waiting for him there.

"Your mother said you knew where the rustlers were," Cactus said.

"He don't know nothing," Vern interrupted.

"We haven't been able to find them. How could he? We know the place better than anyone."

"No one knows it like him 'cept Emilia," Cactus answered. "Even Daniel and I don't know it like he does."

"Webster place," Noble said. "They're using the pens behind the old house to work the brands over, though they're also doing some down in the canyons. Place where it opens up into a wide bowl, like an amphitheater."

"I know it. Smart of them," Cactus said. "Your mother sent for you to clear them out?"

"Yes."

"Good," Cactus said, nodding. "How many do you figure?"

"I've seen ten at least, and I'm thinking there's more behind this," Noble said. Then he went on to explain about the hidden sharpshooter.

"I don't believe a word of it," Vern said when he was done. "He's lyin'. He comes riding in here acting tough, claiming he's done figured it all out."

Noble's face grew hard. "Next time you call me a liar, better have that riding strap off your gun, kid."

Cactus moved between them. "He didn't mean it, Gabriel." Then he rounded on Vern and jabbed a finger into his chest. "Not another word."

"Fine. Fine," Vern said, and went off toward the bunkhouse.

Cactus watched him go. "Thank you."

"For what?"

"Not killing him." Cactus looked Noble in the eye. "You know, even when you were a kid, younger than Jack even, I always knew what you were."

"And what's that?"

"A fighter. A man who'd do anything to win. Just like him, the old man." Cactus nodded toward the cemetery on the hill. "Vern's just a kid, but he's got the makings of a decent man. He'll grow out of it someday."

"If he lives long enough. There's cemeteries full of those that never made it."

They studied the sunset as it faded over the gray mountains.

"I heard stories," Cactus said. "Stories that started after you left. Stories about a man calling himself Noble."

"Word travels," Noble said simply.

"Ten is too many, even for a gunman with your reputation. When you're ready, me and Vern will be around to help."

"I'm not looking for an outright battle. I plan on one at a time, safe and smart."

Cactus snorted. "Daniel's wrong then. You have grown up some. I won't tell you how to do your business, but when you want help, you'll have it. I ain't so old and infirm as to be completely useless yet. I'll hold my own in a fight."

"I'd never doubt it."

Noble shook Cactus's hand again, and the old cowboy went to the bunkhouse. Noble breathed deep, taking in the scent of the mountain pines, the cool grass. The air had moisture to it, enough that it might storm soon.

Clarissa came out and stood beside him.

"The view isn't as nice as the one from our cabin," she said.

"No, but it isn't bad. I'm not sure there's a bad view on the place, actually."

"Why don't you teach me to play cards?" Clarissa said.

"Never. You might win too much, and my pride couldn't stand it."

Clarissa laughed then, a sweet, throaty sound that Noble liked.

"I'll let you win plenty," she said.

Noble wasn't sure he believed her.

Emilia came out to see them off. "You two travel safe."

"We will," Noble answered, and looked around the ranch. He'd grown up wanting to be anywhere else, but now he was glad to be back.

It is good to be back, even if I won't be here long.

Noble set out well before dawn. He rode slowly, working his way through canyons and brush toward the west and the spot the rustlers had used most recently.

The canopy of stars lay masked beyond a veil of thin black clouds. The air was crisp and cold. Whatever the calendar might say, this was still Montana. This far north, the high peaks might see snow on the Fourth of July. Noble knew well the seasons of things here, but he couldn't swear to what month it might be. May, to his best reckoning.

He swung wide around a ridge of rough granite and then down into a tree-lined gully. Beyond the gully was the meadow where cattle had been grazing yesterday and, on the opposite side of that, the place where he'd seen signs of the rustlers.

Picketing his horse, he drew his rifle from its scabbard and stalked toward the meadow's edge.

From the tree line, he looked out into the open. Yesterday he'd started these cattle drifting east, away from danger, but the meadow lay in a favorable spot, catching the day's best light and protected from the cold north wind. Just the kind of place cattle preferred. Clipped down to a uniform height, the grass showed just how much they liked it.

Noble waited for more light, watching the meadow, glancing occasionally to either side, but generally staying dark and silent beneath the tree's canopy. He held the rifle close and butt down. The barrel felt deathly cold in his hands.

Dawn began like an invading army with a

bright artillery blast of white-yellow and quickly swelling into charging brigades of reds, purples, and oranges. As always, night kept an orderly retreat, the last star fading only at the bitter end, leaving the pale, ghostly moon behind.

Light fell on the meadow last, and Noble rose up to see better. Not one head of cattle lay in the open.

Noble put the rifle away and swung back up on his stallion. Movement to the east drew his eye, something big and black sifting slowly through the trees.

It was too tall to be a cow, and it moved much too quickly to be a grizzly walking on its hind feet. Bears liked to stand up for a better look at things, but they usually traveled on all fours.

Noble waited. Whatever it was, it would soon be out of the trees and into the sunshine where he could see it. A twig snapped beneath the thing's foot, and for a moment it paused and seemed to peer around. It was a man then. Unless it was escaping danger, a wild creature would not step on a twig. Noble's position was excellent, thick shadows behind him and ahead. The tree trunks would break up his silhouette. The stallion knew something was out there but didn't make a sound.

The shape finally moved again, and a horse and rider came out into the bright morning sun. It wasn't a rustler. It was Daniel.

Noble watched his brother for a time.

Daniel leaned over—to check a track Noble guessed—then started for the western edge of the meadow. The very place the rustlers had used last time. Once Daniel rode ahead, Noble let him pass, curious as to what his brother might do.

Once Daniel was on by and ahead, Noble rode out into the meadow and followed.

The surefooted stallion made little sound when he walked, and Daniel seemed to be focused on the meadow's edge and what he might find there. He reached the end and swung down to look at the trail before he noticed Noble. He gave a start and reached for his pistol.

No matter Daniel's thoughts on violence, even a man of peace carried a rifle and pistol when he went out riding. Montana grizzlies were notoriously quick to anger, the sows the more dangerous by far, and more than a few cowboys rode up on a mama bear and came to regret it. There were other dangers of course: rattlesnakes, wolves, wild steers with wicked horns, the rare mountain lion. Most of nature didn't go along with Daniel's or their father's views on violence.

Claw and horn and fang, most animals were willing and able to fight to the death.

"Gabriel," Daniel said when he recovered.

"Little brother," Noble answered. "I laid a few logs across that yesterday. Guess they cleared them out when they came back for more."

"Yes." Daniel looked at the tracks. "A couple

dozen this time. No more than that. You think they took them to the Circle Bar?"

"Through the canyon first. You remember that amphitheater place we found that time?"

"I do."

"I think they hold them there for a while, branding a few while they rest, then move them out to Webster's."

"Why delay? Why not go straight for Webster's?"

"If they've got a few rebranded, they could claim they were only returning their own cattle to their range. Someone else's just got mixed in, and they were doing them a favor by getting them out of the canyon."

"Smart," Daniel grunted.

"Who owns the Double Eight?" Noble asked. "That's who's behind the rustling."

Daniel frowned. "I don't know anyone with that brand."

"It covers up the Circle Bar pretty well. Rafter too, with a little work. Slick idea, whoever had it."

"What are they doing with the cattle after they work the brands over?" Daniel asked.

"I wasn't able to find out. There were an awful lot of them around, and a sharpshooter who likes to shoot people in the back."

"What are you going to do now?"

"Ride for the amphitheater. If I can't catch

them there, I'll follow," Noble said. He'd given the idea a lot of thought. Out there in the open, there wasn't anything for a hidden marksman to hide behind. And a man on that high rim with a rifle could cause a lot of problems for men down below.

"I'm going with you."

Noble rested the reins on his pommel. "You sure about that? This is bound to end in gunfire."

"It need not come to violence."

"I don't think you'll talk them into returning your cattle."

"I'm going," Daniel said.

"Suit yourself." Noble clucked at the stallion and set him into motion.

They did not follow the canyons, instead cutting a direct route across the Rafter. They came up out of the broken west range onto the expanse of open plains.

Noble couldn't remember the last time he and Daniel had covered this country. There was a time they'd been inseparable. They'd ridden all over the ranch, the surrounding mountains, the broad plains. Nowhere had been barred from them.

For Daniel, the Rafter and the valley had been enough. For Noble, it had only been a start.

They drew close to the amphitheater. Noble dismounted, drew his rifle, and approached the rim. Daniel walked alongside him.

"You aren't just going to shoot down at them, are you?" Daniel said. "You'll give them warning."

Noble had no intention of giving them anything of the kind. When the first man took a round to the gut, it would be warning enough for the others.

The brothers eased up to the edge and looked down on the empty basin below.

"Empty," Daniel said. "Are we ahead of them or behind?"

Ahead or behind . . . Noble stopped to consider. He and Daniel had a choice to make if they wanted to find the Rafter cattle. Were the rustlers already south at the Webster place? Or north, still coming up through the canyons?

"What do you think, Daniel? North or south?"

"Why should I decide?"

"You're the cattleman," Noble shrugged. "Could they have driven them so far so quickly?"

Daniel looked in either direction. "Webster's."

Without answering, Noble took to his horse, and they were off for the Circle Bar.

They rode slowly now, keeping the horses fresh. The plains were broken by a series of creeks and draws, laying like a rumpled blanket draped across the floor.

"Whatever happened to Old Eli, anyway?" Noble said.

Daniel cleared his throat. "His boys died. Most

of them anyway. J.R. had a horse roll over on him. Brett got into it with a gambler in Riggins. They said it was a fair fight, but he lost. Someone shot Samuel in the back, riding home from Bigsby one night."

"They never found out who?"

"No."

"And Josiah?"

"No one knows." Daniel shrugged. "He rode to Denver last fall. Never came back. Eli believed he had been killed."

They rode another mile before Noble spoke again.

"You and Father got a lot done on the Rafter."

Daniel glanced over at him.

"I've seen a lot of ranches," Noble went on. "Traveled all over. You've done well."

Daniel straightened in the saddle. "We've worked hard for it. Everyone has. Grace and Mother too."

"Something to be proud of," Noble conceded.

"In two years, we'll make our first big cattle sale. We've done a few already, small stuff, needing enough cash to see us through." Daniel shifted in his saddle. "You could have stayed. Owned a part of it."

"I had to leave." Noble scowled. "And you know why."

"You could have come back. After enough time passed and people forgot."

"It wasn't only that. I needed to see new country. To drink from wild streams and ride over high trails."

"Always the dreamer," Daniel said. A hint of scorn hung in his voice.

"And my brother, ever the dutiful son, afraid to step out of father's shadow." Noble's tone carried his own feelings on the matter.

Noble heeled the stallion faster. The cause of his leaving, the true cause, was well known to them both. Nothing could be gained by going over plowed ground.

They came to Webster's place from the north, Noble leading the way, snaking through the scattered hills and staying low off the skyline. Finally, he brought them where they could look down onto the home place and nearby pens.

The house was quiet, no light showed, and only a faint trace of smoke trailed from the chimney. The pens were empty.

Where are the Rafter cattle and what did they do with the cattle they'd already stolen?

"Not here," Noble said. "Place looks deserted."

"Back to the amphitheater, then?" Daniel asked.

"Yes, but we'll ride back along the canyon. They won't slip by us then."

They set out west, toward the rustler trail Noble had discovered. They saw no one. Noble led the way down from the prairie into the canyon. His scalp and shoulders itched. He couldn't help but think about the hidden marksman and how close he'd come to catching a bullet. Was someone watching them even now?

He can't be everywhere at once.

In the bottom of the main canyon, beside the crude fence, they stopped. Noble struck upon an idea.

"Watch for them," he said, and dismounted.

He took his belt knife and sawed through the ropes that bound the posts and rails together. He let the rails fall where they may.

"Let's ride up into those trees." Noble pointed to a grove of mixed aspen and pine that clung to a wide shelf on the canyon wall. The shelf had easy lines of escape, all hidden from view below, and offered plenty of cover to fight from.

Noble tied his horse deep in the trees where it couldn't be found. Daniel followed his lead, even going so far as to draw his rifle from its scabbard. Noble then stretched out behind a fallen pine to wait.

"What do we do?" Daniel asked.

"We wait for them. When they realize the fence is gone and they can't get the cattle turned up into that branch canyon, we'll make our move," Noble said.

Noble draped his hat over his face. The sun shone down, warm and bright. A fly buzzed around his hat, but he soon dropped off into sleep.

He didn't sleep long. All too soon he woke to the crack and rattle of cattle coming down the canyon. He lay still for a moment, listening, thinking about what would soon come.

"They're here," Daniel whispered.

Noble could hear the tension in his brother's voice. Had Daniel ever fired a shot in anger or in defense of the Rafter?

"Just back me up," Noble said, and rose. He cracked the breech on his rifle. A brass cartridge shone ready in the chamber. "Move off a ways, not too far, behind that tree trunk there."

Daniel slipped off moments before the first cow came into view. Her woolly red hair stood out in stark contrast against the brown creek bottom. More cattle followed.

That first cow came to a post and sniffed at the fallen railing. Then she passed on by, a dozen more following, and shouts came up somewhere behind the herd. A rider stood in his stirrups, trying to see what had gone wrong.

Noble sighted in on him. He touched the trigger, aiming for the rider's right shirt pocket. Before he could fire, a shot sounded from his left, a miss that scored the canyon wall well above the rustlers.

Daniel.

What is he thinking?

"Stop," Daniel boomed.

More of the rustlers came into view. One started for his rifle.

"Hold it," Daniel shouted. "Reach for that gun and we'll put you down."

"What do you want?" a man riding a palomino horse said. He wore a tanned cowhide vest that Noble recognized from watching the Circle Bar.

"These aren't your cattle," Daniel said.

"You sure about that? Come on out and let's look them over."

"No need for that. Those are Rafter cattle," Daniel said.

The man in the cowhide gestured to a pair of his men, and they tried to break away to get behind Daniel.

Noble snapped off two quick shots; a bullet striking each. Neither shot looked fatal; one held his shoulder, and the other took the bullet in his arm.

"Ride back down," Daniel ordered. Noble heard the anger in his voice. "Ride back down with the others or we'll open up."

The man who seemed in charge nodded, and the two wounded rustlers rejoined the others. "Now what?" he said.

"Ride off," Daniel said.

"That it. You'll just let us ride off?"

"Ride off and never return," Daniel said.

"How do we know you won't shoot us when we turn around?"

"We haven't shot you yet. We could have. We could have cut most of you down."

The rustlers seemed to consider for a moment. "You win, friend. We'll ride."

They turned then and rode up the branch canyon toward the Webster place. Noble waited a good ten minutes before speaking.

"You should have killed them," he told his brother.

Daniel looked at him in disgust. "We got the cattle back, and no one was killed. You didn't have to shoot those two though. You could have given them a warning shot."

"And then they would have thought we couldn't shoot. They would have swarmed us." Noble hadn't wounded them on purpose. He'd planned on killing them. He didn't tell his brother he had meant to kill the pair, and he'd stopped only because they did. Otherwise he'd have gunned down as many rustlers as he could.

"They're gone now," Daniel said.

Noble eyed his naïve brother. "You're sure?"

Daniel ignored him and went off toward the horses.

Noble watched after his brother. Today accomplished nothing. They'd just given up their best chance to cut down a handful of the Rafter's enemies. He doubted they would have gotten them all. Several could have escaped up the canyon, but the survivors might have scattered if he and Daniel had killed the rest. Failure today would only make things worse in the long run.

The rustlers were intact. Worse, they knew they were hunted.

With a sigh, Noble followed his brother. The violence Daniel and their father preached against would only be worse now. Rather than a quick bloody end, this would go on for much longer now.

Noble watched his brother reload his rifle and place it back in the scabbard.

He thinks he did what's best for the ranch. How could anyone be such a fool?

Chapter 12

Gage Banier looked around the dingy room of the only hotel in Riggins and winced. The place was a dump. Why his boss chose to meet here when they could have used their usual place in Bigsby he did not know, but he was sure he'd learn the reason tonight.

He stood and paced to the window, dusting himself off as he'd done five minutes ago. The window's glass was stained the same brown as the mirror, the curtains, the sheets, and even the once-white porcelain of the washbowl. Everything in this town bore a permanent stain from the dusty mines. Never mind that, despite the new ore findings, most of them hadn't operated in years. Even the people, especially the people, seemed to have that brown-stained look about them.

One of the locals joked that they didn't bother burying the dead here, just laid the body in a hole and let it fill up overnight with heavy dust.

Gage could well believe it. His companion, a man known simply as Pelton, didn't seem to mind or even notice any of this. Gage supposed that to a man who spent most every night sleeping outside, Riggins was an improvement.

Pelton was a lean man—average in height—though his lankiness made him look taller. His face was dark from the sun, except for a few white whiskers on his chin and cheeks.

Pelton sat on a chair watching the street outside, waiting with the patience of a lion stalking a deer. His rifle lay across his lap, one hand wrapped around the action. The other fumbled at a matchstick, turning it over and over between long, calloused fingers.

The hunter was a thin man with straw-colored hair and a complexion like tanned leather. He sat with his head resting back on the wall, eyes half-closed, and looking completely like a man on the verge of sleep to anyone with a casual glance.

Not for a moment did that fool Gage. Pelton was a hunter and, just like that waiting lion, while he seemed idle, he was actually fully alert to every sight and sound.

Boards creaked under Gage's boots as he crossed the room again. He looked at himself in the dingy mirror, ran a hand through his hair, and replaced his hat.

Gage sighed. There was no point trying to brush it clean until the boss arrived and their business was done. He took out his pocket watch to check the time. A quarter to seven. A half hour late and no sign of him.

Where is he?

Gage took a seat on the bed and a cloud of fine dust lifted from it and then settled on his fine black coat. He looked down at the coat in disgust, considered batting the dust away, then decided against it.

Just like the hat, it's better to knock it all off outside. Until then, I'll just keep collecting it. Might as well have rolled in the stuff.

When Gage looked up, Pelton was staring at him. His face held no real expression—no anger, no fear, no joy, just a flat nothingness. The kind of look Gage might give a steak dinner. The hunter was an odd fellow. No man breathing could make Gage Banier feel fear with a pistol, but there was something about the marksman. Something unnatural.

"What?" Gage asked.

"He's out front," Pelton replied.

Gage didn't argue. There was no point; the marksman had a sixth sense about him that had proved right too many times.

The floor beyond the closed door creaked. The handle rattled, and the door opened.

"Gentlemen," the boss said. "My apologies for keeping you waiting."

"Your money either way," Gage said.

Pelton didn't bother responding at all. He usually didn't. On their end, Gage would do all the talking.

"Yes, I suppose it is." The boss frowned at the room's remaining chair. He ran a hand over the seat and wiped the gathered dust on the nearest curtain. Not that it did any good. The curtain was far worse than the chair. With a sigh at his dirty hand, he finally sat down. "We have a problem. There's a new player out at the Rafter, a man called Gabriel Bartlett."

"So?" Gage said, and shrugged. The name meant nothing to him.

"Gabriel Bartlett is brother to the owner of the Rafter N, and he's come back to help them with their rustler trouble."

Gage still wasn't sure what the problem was. The Rafter had only three men. One more wouldn't make a difference. Not when they had ten, plus Pelton and himself.

"Gabriel Bartlett left the Rafter seven years ago and when he did, he changed his name. I believe he's something of a gunfighter."

Gage snorted. A likely story. Everybody who strapped on a belt thought they were a gunfighter. How many of them have actually faced a man down and killed him though?

Gage knew the answer.

Few. Very few.

The boss waited, a half smile on his lips. "Gabriel Bartlett calls himself Noble now."

"Noble," Gage said. He sat up straight. Unable to stop himself, he reached down to make sure his gun hung loose and ready.

Both the boss and Pelton were studying him.

"I take it from your reaction," the boss said, "that you've heard of him."

"I have," Gage admitted. "He's a tough man. Fast. Dangerous."

"That's what I gathered. Will he be a problem?"

"No. When the time comes, I'll take care of it," Gage said, and meant it. Noble had been in Riggins some time back. How long had that been? Two days? Three?

That's why he's here. Not for the mining or to find a job. He already has one: Protecting the family ranch.

He and Noble should have met years ago in Texas. The range war in the San Antonio country had been shaping up that way. But then Noble's boss got to talking high and mighty, and Gage had killed him for it. Gage's own employer then put a man up for county sheriff, and after he won, he declared Noble and his friends outlaws. With no one to pay them and then law hunting them, they'd drifted out of the country.

Noble was supposed to be good, but Gage knew he was better.

He'd faced good men before and always come out on top. He'd been better than Bill Thurston and Tennessee Smith. Both of them were accounted fast, dangerous men, and he'd killed them. Noble would be no different.

"It may not come to a showdown," the boss said. "There are other ways to deal with men like him."

Pelton cleared his throat. "This Noble fellow—

big guy, broad shoulders, riding a black stallion?"

"Big yes, and with broad shoulders. I saw him in Bigsby, but not what horse he was riding," the boss said.

"I seen a fellow like that a while back, creeping around that big bowl where the boys were rebranding some of the cows. They weren't there though, so he followed down the canyon until he found the fence."

The boss chuckled. "Noble knows this country well. I should have expected him to find where we've been moving the cattle. Anything else?"

"I didn't much like the way he looked. Thought he was a marshal or something. I took a shot at him. Missed."

"Missed?" Gage said. Pelton did not miss. Not so far, anyway.

"He leaned over to check his horse. Bullet couldn't have missed him by more than a couple inches. Lucky."

"Lucky," the boss said.

"I tried again, but he got out of the canyon at a run and on the trail to the Circle Bar."

"You missed that time, too?"

"Moving too fast and too far. It was worth a chance, but not much more than that," Pelton said. The hunter didn't seem particularly upset by his failures, nor did their employer.

"Very lucky indeed," the boss said with a strange grin. "He always has been."

"You want me to take a crack at him?" Gage said.

"Not yet, though it may come to that. For now, keep him at a distance. Pelton, if you see a shot, you take it, but we'll move forward as planned. How are Tom and Lonnie coming along?"

"They sent word back from Cheyenne. Your cattle are headed east as instructed," Gage said.

"Good. Go ahead and hire a couple more men, locals. I want to speed things up."

"There's not too many in this town worth hiring," Gage said. "Should I do some recruiting in Bigsby?"

Riggins was a dump, and he would take every excuse to go to Bigsby he could get.

"No, strictly off limits. There's too much talk in Bigsby as is. Here in Riggins all they care about is their damned mines. There's no one to talk to and no risk."

Gage licked his lips. He had news to share with the boss, news that wouldn't please him. "Some of the boys hit the Rafter a few days back. They were bringing fifty head up through the canyon when a couple men stopped them."

"A couple?"

"They said four, but I think it was more like two."

"You think it was two?"

Gage nodded toward Pelton. "He saw the tracks afterward. Said it was just two."

"Did they have any idea who it was?"

"Saw one of them. Big man, shaggy hair. He gave them a warning shot. Two of our boys tried to circle them, and the other one opened up. Long shots, but he wounded both. That shaggy man, he seemed upset by it."

"That'd be Daniel Bartlett. And I'd bet the other one was Noble."

Pelton gave a nod. "Tracks were from the same horse as I seen in the canyon after I took a shot at him."

"Our men?"

"They let them go." Gage shrugged.

The boss smiled then. "Daniel for sure. I doubt Noble cared much for that. I wouldn't think he'd follow Daniel's lead though."

The boss rose then and moved to the door. He eyed the long sleeves of his coat, now coated in dust, and frowned.

"Gentlemen, I'll let you know if anything changes," he said. "Otherwise, continue cleaning out the Rafter once the rest of your boys are back from Cheyenne. Pelton will keep watch for Noble. I'll throw in a thousand-dollar bonus for each of you once he's dead."

"For that kind of money, I'll ride out to the Rafter tonight and call him out," Gage said.

"No need for that," the boss said. "I've no doubt you'll both get your chance once we start hitting the Rafter proper. I want that place cleaned out. I want the Bartletts gone."

A thousand dollars to kill one man.

No matter how good he was, Gage would kill anyone for a thousand dollars. He might even kill Noble for free. Noble was a known man. Whoever killed him would be right up there with Hickok, Bonney, or Clay Allison.

"We'll take care of it," Gage said, smiling.

Four weeks passed, and they saw no further sign of the rustlers. Noble spent his days riding and checking the cattle, usually on the west range, pushing them ever away from the canyons where they could be easily stolen.

If the rustlers wanted them, they would have to work hard for them.

The rains were plentiful, and the range improved dramatically. The cattle fattened on the rich summer grass. They grew quickly, putting on pounds and growing in number, with most dropping calves.

Clarissa too, seemed to come into her own. She put on more weight and filled out into full womanhood. Noble marveled at the change. How had he ever thought her to be childlike?

For the most part, they avoided Daniel and everyone on the Rafter. Noble saw them at times, riding the home range, keeping an eye on the more numerous cattle there.

They did not go to another of the famous Bartlett family dinners.

Emilia came to visit often. Like Noble, she too knew the relief from the rustlers was, at best, temporary. Grace brought Little Jack and Ester by to see them. Jack liked to ask about places Noble had gone or people he might have seen. Noble tried to keep clear of any stories about gun battles or hangings, but he slipped once or twice. Ester spent her time with Clarissa and Grace, usually cooking or sewing.

Clarissa seemed to enjoy the company, and Noble was grateful for it.

When the women got going, Jack usually went out riding with Noble.

"I've never seen this part of the ranch," Jack said on one of their rides.

"Your father hasn't shown it all to you?" Noble said.

"No, he doesn't spend much time on the west range."

"The home place is rich in grazing. Here you see how the soil is. All rough and rocky. The grass is weaker and less nourishing. The cattle do fine on it, but there isn't nearly so much."

They were on a ridge overlooking a wide swath of range down below. Noble brought them to a stop. From here they could see the wild, broken country all the way to the base of the Bitterroots.

"I know you said the grass isn't so good, but there are still a lot of acres though," Jack said.

"Are there?" Noble asked. "To the west

the foothills along the mountains are jagged and rough, thick woods to the north—so dark little will grow—and arroyos and dry washes splitting the rest all apart into small pastures and meadows. Not much good range left after all that. Not much left for cattle, anyway."

"I guess not."

"This was the country your great-grandfather preferred."

"Big Jack?"

"He settled the home place to keep his cattle on, but this was what he really loved. A man can do well enough raising cattle here. But it's not so much for them. The elk, the deer, and the bear though—they all prefer the rough country."

"I haven't seen a bear."

"Best not to. They're dangerous at the best of times, though if you go on your way they'll generally go theirs. Cactus hasn't taught you any of this?"

Jack hesitated, then said, "He's too busy."

Noble heard the hesitation for what it really was. A lie, or at least a stretching of the truth. Cactus was kept away, likely by Daniel.

He wouldn't want his son hearing wild talk about the Rafter's history. Especially not Jack Noble.

"Cactus knows a lot. He's lived here a long time, and he's wise in the ways of this place. That old man taught me most of what I know, him and Big Jack."

The kid studied his pommel for a moment. "Uncle Gabriel, why did you go away?"

Noble thought for a long time before answering. "See those mountains?" Noble nodded to the snow-capped Bitterroots. "When I was your age, I'd stare at them and think about what might be on the other side. 'More of the same,' everyone would say. More mountains, more deserts, more forests, more grasslands. I vowed to climb them one day and look to see for myself. One day I did."

"What was on the other side?"

Noble smiled. "More mountains, deserts, forests, grasslands—an ocean, even."

The boy grinned at him.

"But they were all worth seeing." Noble sighed. He looked at those foreboding peaks.

"You didn't miss it? The Rafter, I mean."

"I did," Noble said. "But there was always another mountain to climb. Another river to swim. Another desert to cross."

"Why does Clarissa call you Noble? Mother calls you Gabriel. So does Father and everyone else."

"My name is Gabriel, but when I left, I called myself Noble."

"Why?"

"I'm not really sure." Noble shrugged. "To honor the old man, I guess. It seemed like a good idea at the time."

Noble swung around toward the cabin and the home place beyond.

"What's that?" Jack said. The boy pointed to a long finger of smoke rising south and east of them.

The fire was miles distant, but still close enough to be either on the ranch or at the very edge.

"Let's go see," Noble said.

They dropped into a wide valley, following the trail down until the ground grew flat and even. Much as it may have looked open, the prairie held a number of draws and dry creeks. Noble knew them well. He'd hunted or played Injun with his brother and Grace in them often enough.

It took him several hours to work his way around to a wide draw, where they could safely leave the horses.

"Stay here and be silent at all times," Noble said. "We're just here to look and see what this is."

"What if it's the rustlers?" Jack said.

"Doesn't matter. Stay silent and listen only. Do not leave this very spot." Noble pointed to the ground to make his point. "If anything happens to me, if you hear any shots, you ride down that draw. Two miles along, there's a creek, lined with willows and cottonwoods that joins into this one. Turn and follow it east. Stay out of sight and walk your horse through the water. It tapers out at a spring, maybe five miles from the turn. From there, your home is just a mile north. You'll see it."

Jack nodded and said, "I know the spring."

Noble slid his rifle out. He took the riding strap off each pistol and stalked forward. If it were the rustlers, even if he got close and had a good shot, he wouldn't take it. He couldn't risk Grace's son like that.

The boy had to be kept safe.

In hindsight, it had been a mistake to bring him even this close. He could have—should have—taken the boy to the cabin and then come back to trail the rustlers. In his mind, there was no doubt that these were rustlers. No one else should be on this part of the range, and it was the wrong time of year for Daniel to be doing any branding. The Rafter always did that in the fall, just before the snow flew.

Why would they send up such an obvious signal though? And why strike in the daytime where they could be easily seen?

The smoke was just ahead. There was a narrow rise between it and Noble. He got down and crawled on hands and knees between clumps of sage and high grass until he could see.

There were three of them down in the clearing. He recognized the man whose shoulder he'd clipped and one other in a buckskin shirt. He had never seen the third man before. The man with the wounded shoulder retrieved a branding iron from the fire and brought it to where the other two held down a young calf. The calf bucked and bellowed when the iron singed its hide. The air stank of burned hair and charred flesh.

Noble snaked his rifle forward.

He desperately wanted to fire. He might not have another opportunity like this, but he could not risk the boy.

The wounded man stepped from the calf and the other two eased their ropes and turned him loose. A fourth man appeared then, mounted, driving another calf and twirling a rope overhead. The rope sailed out and dropped around the calf's neck. He reined up and snapped the rope taut, jerking the calf around to face him. The two men afoot pounced, wrestling the calf to the ground and securing his feet with piggin string.

Frustration ate at Noble. These men were here, on the home range, stealing Rafter cattle again. Daniel should have never let them go.

The four men below looked up then, all staring toward the north. A dust cloud rose in the distance. Too much for a single man.

The rustlers ran and drew their rifles. One of them came straight toward Noble. He picked out a spot to Noble's left and leaned down on his haunches, hidden from the riders' approach by a thick clump of brush.

The other three remained in the open.

At the base of the rising dust, riders appeared, three of them, coming up fast. Noble recognized them by the size of the lead rider. Only Daniel could be so large. Cactus and Vern Ollie trailed him.

The men of the Rafter slowed when they saw the three rustlers.

"You seem to be confused," Daniel said. "These are my cattle."

"No, these are Double Eight critters," the wounded man said. "This is double-eight range. We've taken over from old man Eli."

While Daniel spoke, Cactus studied the surrounding hills. Then he drew his rifle; Vern Ollie took his lead and did the same.

The young cowboy might be smarter than Noble first assumed.

"Regardless, these are my cattle. That one there," Daniel nodded to the calf they held down, "his mother wears my brand. Rafter N."

"I don't think so, friend." The wounded man smiled. "Rudy," he called.

The man near Noble raised up and cycled the action on his rifle. "Right here, Tom."

"Rudy, if any of these men start toward that calf, you cut them down," Tom said. He grinned up at Daniel. "Now, you were sayin'?"

Between the three in the open and the rifleman on the flanking hill, they had the Rafter men boxed and everyone knew it. More mobile as they were, at that range men on horseback were disadvantaged against an armed man on steady ground. Firing from a horse was tricky business. A gunfight now would see the Rafter wiped out entirely. Several rustlers would die, of course, but the Rafter would be finished.

The lead rustler was about to push the issue further when Noble cycled his own rifle and raised up enough to be seen. He had the gun aimed dead-center of Rudy's back.

At the unexpected move, everyone froze.

"I think he was saying that those are Rafter cattle and you boys are just a bunch of damned rustlers. We like to hang rustlers in this country," Noble said.

Tom's smile slipped. From the corner of his eye, Noble could see him weighing his chances.

"Rudy, you'd better convince him to lay down his guns unless you want a bullet in the spine," Noble said.

Sweat rose on Rudy's forehead as he turned his head just enough to see Noble behind him. "Tom. He'll do it, Tom. I recognize him. That's Noble there in the brush. I saw him kill Spade Carter down in Tucson. He'll kill us all."

The fight seemed to go out of Tom then.

"If we give ourselves up, you'll take us to the sheriff?" he said. "Won't be no hangin'?"

"I give you my word," Daniel said.

"Lay 'em down, boys," Tom said. All four tossed down their rifles.

"Pistols too, and slow," Noble said.

They drew out their pistols slowly—all but the fourth man, the one Noble hadn't seen before.

"I don't think so," he said. "I heard about you, Noble. I heard you were fast. Give me an even break, and let's see just how fast."

"Gabriel," Daniel warned.

"Stay out of it, Daniel," Noble growled. "This is my affair. You heard him. He asked for an even break. I'll give him one."

Noble set his rifle down. His hand hovered near the pistol on his hip. The fourth man licked his lips. His friends edge away clear. They did not try to talk him out of it. Evidently they too wanted to see if the stories were true.

"Gabriel, this isn't the way," Daniel said. "Gabriel, I forbid it."

The man went for his gun. He didn't have a chance. Noble's first bullet took him in the chest before he cleared leather. The second sent him to the dust.

"Gabriel!" Daniel said. "I gave these men my word."

"They gave you their word last time," Noble said. "They said they'd leave, but here they are, stealing more cattle. There's a big cottonwood down on Mason Creek. Take them there and hang them as a warning to the rest."

"No. They gave themselves up freely. I'm taking them to Bigsby and the sheriff."

Cactus and Vern looked uncomfortable. Cactus pointed his rifle at the surviving rustlers. "You three come out here and get on your horses. Vern hogtie them to the pommels. I'll cover you."

The three rustlers did as the old cowboy ordered.

Noble and Daniel stared at each other. Noble flipped open his pistol and replaced the spent cartridges. Behind him, something rustled in the brush. He snapped the loading gate closed and spun to face it.

Little Jack walked through the brush, leading their horses.

"You should be halfway home by now," Noble said. He wasn't much surprised though. He wouldn't have run either at that age.

"I couldn't leave you." The boy had enough sense to look chagrined, but he kept his chin up.

"Jack?" Daniel said. He turned to Noble, face a fiery red. "You put my son in harm's way. You've no right."

"He was never in danger."

Daniel charged his horse up the hill. "Of course he was. He should be miles from here—"

"Grace brought he and Ester by to visit Clarissa. I've been taking the boy riding over the wild country," Noble interrupted.

"It's too dangerous. I forbid it."

"You seem to forbid a lot of things. You can't keep him locked away forever. He's got to—"

"You will not tell me how to raise my own son. You're a tramp gunfighter. You don't have that right." Daniel's fists clenched. He looked mad enough to take a swing.

"Careful, little brother. Best not let that temper get the best of you," Noble said. "What would Father think? You fighting on the range and all?"

"Jack, come over here," Daniel ordered.

The boy did as he was told.

"You know you aren't allowed to ride the west range."

"Uncle Noble was just showing me around. He told me stories about when he was my age."

"Stories," Daniel said.

Little Jack had grown distracted by something behind them then. The boy was staring at it. Noble followed his gaze toward the dead rustler.

"Is that a rustler?" Jack said.

Daniel turned toward the body. "Don't look at that," he said, but the boy couldn't seem to tear his eyes away. Daniel moved between Jack and the dead man. "I said don't look at it. Now get up on your horse. We've got to go to town to take these men to the sheriff."

Noble studied the boy. He seemed to be neither upset nor excited by the dead outlaw. Just curious.

"You want me to take the boy home?" Noble offered.

"You've done enough," Daniel snarled. "Vern, take Jack home to my father, and him alone. Cactus, you and I will take these men in to town."

Vern rode over while Cactus held a rifle on the prisoners. "You sure just you and the old man can handle it?"

"We will," Daniel said. He was angry, and evidently Vern knew enough of his boss not to push it.

"C'mon kid. Let's get you home," Vern said. He gave Noble a look and then started with the boy toward the home place.

"Cactus, let's get these men moving," Daniel said.

Noble didn't ask to accompany them but did so anyway. He rode a few steps behind the group, whistling. He wasn't proud that he'd killed a man, but he felt like he'd finally accomplished something there. Daniel ignored his presence while Cactus glanced over his shoulder occasionally; neither spoke—not to him and not to each other.

Noble sighed. It was going to be a long ride to town.

Chapter 13

Noble led Clarissa up around the back of the home place, much as they had when the pair had first snuck into the valley to meet with Grace and Emilia.

There was something he very much needed to do, something he'd put off so far. All day Clarissa had begged him for a chance to go riding—she'd been cooped up at the cabin for weeks now—and so he'd brought her along. Like the girl, the little buckskin horse had done well in the early Montana summer, gaining weight, and even looking a little taller to Noble's eye.

They followed the creek up into the hills that lay behind the house. Twilight was but a few hours off yet, and the sun gave off a reddish-gold light.

He'd come the long way around on purpose. He didn't want to see anyone. Escorting their prisoners into Bigsby, Noble spoke to Cactus about the local law.

The sheriff hadn't impressed Noble. When he was a kid, Tom McCandles wore the badge, and he'd done a good job. He wasn't a gunfighter by any means; he carried a shortened shotgun though, and few troublemakers wanted any part of those hard barrels. Unlike his successor, Tom had often intervened in country business. He'd known that trouble on the big ranches would always lead to trouble in town. He'd even cleared out some of the worst riffraff in Riggins. Tom had been promoted to deputy US marshal and moved to Bozeman.

Cactus said McCandles still came up occasionally, but mostly he kept to the territory's bigger settlements.

The new sheriff, Kyle George, was an older man, almost the same age as Noble's father. Cactus said he usually held down a chair in front of the jail, making sure it wouldn't run off or blow away. He never went out into the country. Cactus doubted he could find the Rafter with a map.

They'd explained the situation with the stolen cattle, handed over the prisoners, and told the sheriff about the dead man. Daniel did most of the talking, and that suited Noble. Daniel had been sore the whole way to town and, once the outlaws were deposited in Bigsby's jail, Noble had quickly gone his own way home.

Two days had passed since the shootout, and Noble had seen no one.

Clarissa and Noble came to the foot of a small mesa. Without a word, Noble dismounted. They were above the ranch house now; the mesa lay between it and them. The stream was just a few feet wide here, bubbling up from where the ground birthed it before circling around the rising slope to flow by the ranch buildings.

They left their horses and climbed atop the little mesa. There wasn't much of a trail here—not on this side anyway—but the slope wasn't too great. Noble offered a steadying hand to Clarissa and helped her along.

The mesa's top was not bare. Scattered fir, pine, and aspens all grew in places.

"Where are we?" Clarissa said.

"You'll see." Noble kept moving. They went south toward the mesa's edge. Through the trees they could see the Rafter's headquarters below. Daniel's house was there, the newest building, less than a hundred yards from their parents'. Noble wondered how much Grace liked having Emilia and Sam so close.

Just fine, knowing her. She always got along well with Ma.

At last they came to a cleared space. Tall trees crowded in all around, but the south side, overlooking the ranch, was kept clear.

Grandfather wanted a good view, though he might have enjoyed an overlook on the west range more.

There were stone markers in the clearing, seven of them now. When Noble left, there had been only five. Grady and Yancy had both been alive back then. Alive and tough as old leather. It seemed impossible that only Cactus remained of the rough bunch. The markers were all of equal size, all made of the same gray granite. A handful of dried wildflowers lay at the base of each. His mother's doing, no doubt.

Noble came to a stop in front of one. He pulled his hat off and held it over his chest. "This is where my Grandfather is buried."

"Big Jack?" Clarissa said.

"Jack Noble." Noble nodded.

Clarissa knelt down in front of the stone. She ran a hand over it. There were carvings there. "Jack Noble. Born: Texas. Died '73 Montana Territory."

"That's him," Noble said. "And a harder man never lived."

Noise to their right drew his attention. There was a good walking trail up the mesa from the buildings below, and something or someone was coming up it.

Noble moved in front of Clarissa. He drew his left-hand pistol, keeping it out of sight, tucked in tight behind his leg. He saw a flash of tan buckskin and the black of a coat.

After a few moments, his mother walked out into the clearing. His father was with her. Sam's face was red; he looked out of breath. Emilia jumped at the sight of Noble and Clarissa, but quickly recovered. When had Noble ever seen anyone catch her unawares?

Never. Nothing ever fazed Ma.

"Excuse us," Emilia said.

Sam gave Noble a sharp glare and tried to catch his breath. "Come up here to see him then?" he finally wheezed. "Your brother told me he watched you kill a man who'd surrendered. Said it was murder."

Emilia went white and rigid with the accusation.

"Daniel told you wrong then. That man never surrendered. He had his chance, and he took it," Noble said. "I never murdered anyone."

"Is that so?"

"If you're meaning the night I left, ask Daniel about it," Noble said. "Ask him what really happened. Maybe your church boy isn't so clean as you think."

Sam's face reddened. "You . . . don't you talk to me about—"

"Sam, not here. Enough, please," Emilia interrupted. She had a hand on her husband's arm.

Sam looked at her for a moment. He patted her hand finally and nodded.

"The flowers are nice," Clarissa offered.

"Thank you," Emilia said. "Ester and Grace and I picked them in the meadow below the house. I'm afraid there'll be no more this late in the year though."

"Noble was just telling me who all is buried here."

"The men from Texas," Emilia said. "The men

who built the Rafter. They came from all over. Rusty there . . ." Emilia nodded toward a stone. ". . . he was from Nacogdoches. Bull was born in San Antonio. His real name was Francis. He hated it when you called him that. Chase, yonder, was the only one who could get away with it."

One by one Emilia went through the list of them. James Henry and Chase. Yancy, the cook, had died three years ago. Noble remembered his homemade rolls and biscuits. Grady, who could fix almost anything and knew every card trick ever invented, had been the last of them. Fever got him a year back.

"Each came to Montana with the old man, each had their own stories, each fought Indians, blizzards, drought, and floods to make the Rafter. It belonged to them as much as it did the Noble, and now Bartlett, family. This was their home," Emilia concluded.

"So many," Clarissa said.

"And I'm sure you've met my father." Emilia nodded. "The man with the dream."

Sam coughed, and Noble ignored him. His father and the old man had rarely seen eye to eye on anything. Especially the raising of Big Jack's grandsons.

"Someday Sam and I will be up here with them. We two and Cactus are the last. The last of the pioneers anyways."

Sam coughed again, and this time it took him some time to stop.

"We need to be going. The night air isn't good for your father," Emilia said. "You're always welcome down at the house."

"I won't—" Sam said between coughs "I won't have them in my home. A murderer and his—"

"Shush," Emilia said to her husband. "I said not here."

"His what?" Noble said. He felt his anger boil up like a thunderhead. "A murderer and his what?"

Sam's coughing fit finally subsided. He glared at Noble but said nothing.

"Let's go," Noble said.

Clarissa took a step forward. She stood proud and tall.

"Mr. Bartlett, I can promise you, your son has been nothing but a perfect gentleman to me. He saved me from a horrible situation and for that I am grateful. In no way has he brought shame to you or yours. He is a man of the highest character."

Sam looked down his nose at her. "Young lady, I can promise you, my son hasn't got a shred of character. He is the vilest of men. A murderer without conscience."

"A murderer who's going to save your ranch while you and Daniel hide behind your morality, Father. A murderer who has the courage to do what these men did. A murderer willing to fight to protect what's his."

"The Lord will—" Sam started, and then the coughing resumed.

Noble turned and left, Clarissa following.

He didn't need this. He didn't need contempt from his own father. He came to do a job. He'd do it, get his reward, and move on where he could be left alone. He didn't need family. He didn't need anyone.

Gage Banier sat in a private dining room at The Benton hotel, shuffling a deck of playing cards and scowling. They knew him here, knew his tastes and needs, and they went out of their way to make him comfortable—or as comfortable as he could be in Bigsby.

He didn't care for Montana.

Too cold, too much snow, and too few women. But he did like being paid, and his boss paid him very well. Even better, the work was easy. Recruit a few men, rustle a few cows, kill anyone who asked too many questions.

Easy. Simple.

Only now it wasn't proving so simple. His best man, Tom Shannassey, was sitting in Bigsby's jail, along with Rudy Hannon and Pete Stinson.

Gage had other men, of course, but those three were his best. Worse, Pete had a talkative streak, and if he started flapping his mouth, Gage might have to deal with the law.

Not that local law would pose a problem.

He'd met and measured Sheriff Kyle George his first day in town. There was nothing to fear there. Kyle was perfectly content to put in his time and draw his pay. More than once, he'd turned a blind eye to things. But if Kyle or the citizens sent for the marshal, there would be trouble. A marshal might know about Gage Banier. A marshal might know about what happened back in Kansas or Nebraska.

Gage flipped over the top card. An ace. What was the best way to keep poor Pete from talking?

It was Noble's fault, of course. That damned Noble. He should ride out to the Rafter and have it out with the man just to get it over with. Sooner or later, it would come to that.

Noble had avoided their fight in Texas, but here, defending his home, he wouldn't run. Even after Gage's men cleared the last cow out of the Rafter, he'd fight.

Gage dealt cards to four imaginary players, then picked up the nearest. Two queens. He could work with that. He discarded the rest and drew three cards. Another queen.

He started to turn over the other hands when Lonnie Willis and three more of his men entered.

"Lonnie, turn over that hand will you?" Gage said.

Lonnie did as he was told. A pair of deuces.

"And the next."

Two pair. Eights and jacks.

The last hand had four clubs and the five of diamonds.

Gage smiled. His luck was in. He gathered the cards and began shuffling. "You know why I sent for you?"

"Tom got hisself caught," Lonnie said with a smile. Sometime back he'd lost his left front tooth. "Told you he was reckless."

"Yes you did," Gage said. Before riding into Montana, Lonnie and Tom were the only two men Gage knew. The three of them had held up a few stages down in Colorado the year before, the rest had all been locals they'd recruited out of Riggins.

"But Tom isn't the problem. Tom knows not to talk. Pete Stinson though . . ." Gage dealt the cards again, this time with five hands, one for every man in the room.

"Pete's got a wagging tongue," one of the other men said.

Gage picked up his hand and gestured for the others to do likewise. He discarded and replaced two. The others each played their own hands.

"So are we going to bust them out?" Lonnie said.

"Something like that, but we've got to get the town looking the other way first," Gage said, and laid down his cards. "Straight."

"Four kings," one of the other men said, and the others groaned. "What do I win?"

"You get to bust your friends out of jail while the rest of us rob a bank." Gage frowned.

"Rob a bank, huh?" Lonnie grinned. "Beats rustling cows."

"Tomorrow morning," Gage said. "Be in town before sunrise behind the old church."

The four went out and several minutes passed before a fifth man entered. As usual, Pelton was dressed in buckskins, head-to-toe, and carried his Henry in his right hand. Other than the rifle, he seemed to be unarmed, but Gage suspected he had a pistol stowed beneath his jacket. He'd seen it once when Pelton leaned over to pick up a pot of coffee.

"Robbing a bank wasn't part of the deal," Pelton said.

"I won't need you for it," Gage said. "Not in town, anyway. It would help if you laid in the hills east of here. In case some upstart citizen decides to ride out after us."

Pelton didn't speak. The lean marksman didn't actually work for Gage; the boss had hired him too, and as such, he was able to choose which orders he did or did not follow. So far it hadn't been a problem, but now?

"Half mile out of town, there's a flat-topped hill. If your men skirt behind that, there's an old streambed. Way the rains have been, the water's running about a foot deep. Good place to lose anyone following you," Pelton finally said.

"And you?" Gage said. It irritated him that he had to ask, but Pelton was an odd man and he'd proven his worth with that rifle more than once. He'd almost single-handedly delivered the Webster ranch into their hands.

"I'll cover your boys until they get there," Pelton said. "You did clear all of this with the boss?"

"His idea," Gage said.

Pelton lifted a brow.

"Surprised?" Gage gave him a light smile. "So was I. I suspect we won't get much out of the bank. Once we finish with the bank, the boss has a task for you. Something on the Rafter."

"Something about the other fellow? The one he warned us about? Noble?"

"Have you seen him?"

Pelton scowled. "Not lately. He's careful, and he keeps to that rough country near the mountains. Tough to get a shot up there. If I'd known about Tom and his crew, I could have been ready for him."

There was a tone in his voice Gage didn't care for. It hadn't been his fault Tom got caught, or that Pelton had been out on a hunting trip instead of covering his men.

"Tom was rash. I didn't know he was going out there," Gage said. "Shame you missed Noble in the canyon."

That one had scored the hunter's pride. Pelton's face went slack and cold; he didn't bother with a response.

Serves him right for thinking it was my fault.

"I don't think you'll get an easy shot from any kind of distance. Have to get in close with his kind," Gage said.

"That's your game," Pelton said.

"Yes, it is," Gage admitted. "And when the time's right, I'll get it done. I'm looking forward to it."

Chapter 14

"Cactus, will you saddle a pair of horses for us?" Grace said.

"Yes, ma'am," the old cowboy answered with a tip of his hat.

The day was clear and bright, with all the makings of a hot one. Daniel, breaking from his usual routine, had stayed near the house this morning. She saw him riding across the pasture below.

Last night he'd spent an hour on the front porch talking with Sam. Grace didn't know the whole of it, but she'd interrupted them once to ask if they wanted coffee. Both had gone silent at her approach, and neither took her offer.

Retreating to the kitchen, she'd only gleaned bits and pieces of their talk, an unusual thing in itself. Both were notoriously loud when roused, and to be sure, they were angry now.

Angry over Gabriel, it seemed. Angry that he was back and that he'd killed one of the rustlers. Angry that she and Emilia were the cause of his return.

She'd braced herself when Daniel came inside to bed. He hadn't said a word, though his face betrayed his mood. He'd never been able to mask his emotions. None of the Bartlett men ever had.

In the morning, she'd risen and set about their meal. Jack and Ester, sensing trouble in that instinctual way of children, kept silent and hurried through breakfast. Daniel had stopped long enough to stuff down a bite or two, then hurried out without so much as a word.

"The horses are ready," Cactus said when he returned. "I'll hold them while you get situated."

"Thank you," Grace said.

Little Jack needed no help to climb into the saddle, but Ester still had to have a hand up. Once Grace was in the saddle, Cactus passed her the reins and swung Ester up behind her. The girl wrapped her thin, warm arms around Grace's middle.

"Ride safe, little one," Cactus said, and gave Ester a slow wink.

"Thanks, Uncle Cactus," she answered.

Cactus turned to Grace then. "Want I should ride over with you?"

The old cowboy knew where she was going, of course: to the old cabin. He would have seen the tracks. Cactus could follow sign better than anyone on the ranch, excepting Emilia.

"Not today," Grace said. Then she and the children left the ranch at a trot.

She shouldn't be doing this. She shouldn't be riding to the old cabin, not after what happened, but she'd promised Clarissa a visit today. Tough as she may have been on the outside, Clarissa was sensitive, and Grace had gotten used to their talks.

It was nice having another woman to talk to. Back when the neighbors had still come by for Sunday dinner, she'd had lots of friends. Now, even with a few acquaintances in town, she rarely spoke to anyone outside the ranch. With the downfall of the Circle Bar and now rustlers preying on the ranches, the whole valley seemed to have grown hard and callous.

Clarissa, too, seemed to need these talks. She'd come into her own these last weeks, blossoming like a wildflower after a spring rain.

Her relationship with Gabriel was an odd one. The girl was completely infatuated with him, and he seemed totally oblivious to it. Grace had seen the way Gabriel looked at her though. He was starting to see her less as some girl he rescued and more like the young woman she was quickly becoming.

Their ages weren't that far apart. Clarissa was a few years older than she looked; Gabriel would be five years older. She and Daniel were a little closer, but Sam was seven years older than Emilia.

Lost in her thoughts, Grace didn't hear the rider coming up behind until he was right on top of them. She turned and her breath caught.

Daniel.

There was a line of angry furrows across his brow. "Where are you going?"

"To see my friends," Grace answered.

"Not today you won't," he said.

"I will. I told Clarissa I'd be by this morning."

"You don't care about her. You only want to see him," Daniel snarled.

Grace felt Ester's grip tighten. She was trembling.

"This has nothing to do with him," Grace said.

"You regret your choice, don't you?" Daniel said. "You wish you'd chosen to go off with him instead of staying here with me."

Grace felt her anger rise. *How could he be so stupid?*

"Daniel, I have never once regretted being your wife."

"Then why do you not obey me?" he said. "Take the children home. I don't want them near that filthy killer."

"Gabriel is their uncle. He's here because we needed his help. You can't use his help and then try to keep everyone away from him."

"I didn't ask for his help—not now, not ever." Daniel leaned down to grab her horse's reins.

Grace turned the horse, and it danced quickly away.

"You don't think I can save us? You don't think I can protect us?" Daniel said.

"Not this time, Daniel. This isn't like before. This isn't a blizzard or a drought or bears killing calves," Grace said. "Men are taking what you and your father have built. Men who have to be stopped before they ruin the Rafter completely."

Daniel's face reddened. His mouth pressed into a hard line.

It had been a mistake to say it. She'd known that, but she'd been angry. Though she loved him, Daniel could be a pigheaded fool. He thought he could defend the Rafter from everything. She knew otherwise, but now that she'd voiced that belief, her anger melted like snow before summer. He'd hurt her, and now she'd hurt him back.

What had she done?

"I see," Daniel said. His voice was lower now. She'd cut him to the core. "Come with me, Jack. You too, Ester. If your mother wants to go, she can."

He started for Jack, and the boy spurred his horse behind Grace's. Daniel frowned. Then he rode closer and reached for Ester.

Grace felt Ester's arms cling tighter. Daniel took her around the shoulders and started to lift. The girl let out a piercing scream. Daniel jerked his hands back as if he'd been burned.

"Ester, darling, I—"

"You're frightening her, Daniel," Grace said.

Without another word, he spun his horse and spurred him into a run.

Grace watched him go. What was she to do now?

Part of her wanted nothing more than to return home. That was what he wanted. That would mend things. But she didn't regret the things she'd said. They weren't lies. She wasn't wrong. Daniel was a good man, too good for the times. Dutiful, faithful, loving—the best kind of man and husband. But right now the ranch, her children's future, needed more.

If she went home now, she would never ride this way again. Every time she did, Daniel would be waiting for her, armed with angry words and hurt feelings.

She would do as she planned. She would visit Clarissa and Gabriel. She would return to the Rafter afterward. Then she would talk with her husband.

A shot in the distance changed her mind.

It echoed through the hills and lodged in her heart. It had come from behind. Daniel. Had her Daniel been shot?

The children. I have to get them to safety. I have to get them to someone who can keep them safe.

Noble was out on the ridge when he saw them, two horses, three riders. Two of them young and small. Grace. It could only be her and the children.

They were traveling fast, almost recklessly, through rocks and ridges and thickets. It was a good way to maim a horse.

Grace knows that. If she's running hard, there must be a reason for it.

Noble moved the stallion to cut her off. He dropped down behind several boulders, crossing a trickle of a stream, then passed through an expanse of stately white aspen. At the lower edge of the aspen, he met Grace.

"What's wrong?" he said. He watched her back trail, rifle drawn. Trouble would come from that direction. He saw nothing.

"It's Daniel," Grace said. "Take the children to the cabin, Gabriel. I have to go back to him."

"I'll go. If there's trouble, it should be me."

"No!" Grace answered. "Please, Gabriel, I beg you. Take Jack and Ester. Keep them safe."

"I will," Noble said. There was genuine fear there. Instead of arguing with her though, he would do as she asked. He could drop the children off with Clarissa, then track her back to Daniel. They would be safe at the cabin.

"Swear to me you won't come to the ranch, Gabriel. Not until I come to you," Grace said.

Noble swore inwardly. She'd always been able to see what he was thinking.

"Swear to me, Gabriel."

Noble ground his teeth. If he swore he would not break his word to her. And she knew it.

"Swear it," Grace said.

"I swear," Noble growled.

"Jack, you and Ester go with Uncle Gabriel.

He'll keep you safe. I've got to see about your father," Grace said. She kissed Ester on the head and passed her over to her brother. Then she patted Jack on the head. "Don't worry. I'll make things right again."

The boy nodded. His eyes were damp, on the verge of crying, but he held himself together.

"Thank you," Grace said with a last look at Noble. Then she was off, riding hard, back the way she'd come.

Noble watched her go. She went up a long rise and passed over and out of sight. Then he looked at the two frightened children.

"Let's get you two to Clarissa," he said.

"Are you going after her?" Jack said. "You should."

"I said I wouldn't."

"You swore," he said.

"I did," Noble said. He sighed. "Your mother has always been able to keep me in line. She and your grandmother might be the only ones to do it." Grace would not be pleased if he broke his word and left her children unprotected.

The cabin wasn't far.

Noble set a quick pace, and they reached it quickly. When they arrived, Noble hurriedly explained the situation to Clarissa.

"I should go see about her," he said. He paced the short porch end to end.

"You should stay here," Clarissa said. "Grace

asked you to take care of those two. She won't be pleased if you abandon them." She tilted her head at the children.

Jack had Ester on the back of his horse and was leading it around inside the corral. Ester had both hands on the pommel and was smiling. Jack smiled up at her, but when he turned from his sister to look toward the cabin, he didn't look nearly so happy.

"Grace might be hurt. So might Daniel. The boy said they heard a shot after Daniel rode off. They could need me." Noble didn't like not knowing what was happening.

"So might these two," Clarissa said. "It might have been someone out hunting."

She wasn't wrong. A single shot could have been anything: a hunter out taking a deer or elk, a cowboy killing a rattlesnake, or just someone out sighting in a new rifle. But it could also be the silent marksman.

"You've been promising to teach me to shoot," Clarissa said. "If you want me to protect myself and them, I need to know how."

He had promised her. She needed to be able to defend herself. She'd done a fair job with Papa Clemsen, but not everyone would stop after you shot them in the hand.

"Get your pistol," he relented.

Clarissa smiled and went inside. She came out with the pistol and a box of shells. Noble drew the rifle from its scabbard and set out behind the cabin, toward the woods. Jack saw what he was doing and helped his sister down. Then they both followed.

"You want to learn?" Noble asked the boy.

He answered with a solemn nod.

"I do too," Ester said.

"All right," Noble said. There were a few discarded cans behind the house, and he tossed them out a ways. "Clarissa, go ahead. You two cover your ears."

She lifted the heavy pistol with both hands. The barrel wobbled, and she squinted and squeezed off a shot. The bullet fountained dirt almost a foot to the left of the can.

"Did you close your eyes?" Noble said.

"No," Clarissa answered.

She wasn't telling him the truth, but he let it go.

"Here, let me show you." Noble lifted his pistol with one hand, fired, and the can sailed farther out.

"Easy for you," she said. Her gun came up again. She fired. Another miss.

Noble moved up behind her. He wrapped his arms around her and helped her hold the pistol up. He leaned down where his mouth was near her ear. That close he could smell the warmth of her, the soap and sweat of her.

"Line up the sights and squeeze the trigger firmly," he said.

She nodded. The gun steadied for just a moment. This time, she scored the can along its rusty edge.

"Jack, your turn," Noble said. He handed the boy one of his own pistols. They were lighter and easier to aim than Clarissa's old gun. He did not tell her that.

Jack lifted the gun carefully. His first shot was an inch high.

The boy looked at Noble for advice, but Noble said nothing. Jack licked his lips and aimed down the sights again. The can went sailing this time. The boy grinned at his success.

"Nice one," Noble said. "You may be a natural."

The boy's chest swelled with pride at that. He looked down at the gun, examining it closely.

Ester took her turn next. Noble held the gun for her and let her line up the sights and squeeze the trigger. The pistol bucked. She missed completely but seemed pleased with the results nonetheless.

They spent another hour practicing. Noble let Clarissa take a turn with the rifle, a more practical weapon for defending the cabin. Jack took a turn with the rifle as well, but it was far too heavy for Ester.

Jack proved himself quite the shot. Clarissa improved enough to be decent. She quickly came to prefer the rifle, and near the end, Noble let her take a turn with his own pistol. She did well with it, striking the can on four out of six shots.

Noble reloaded his pistols and the rifle, then they all went back toward the front of the cabin.

Emilia met him there. She did not look pleased.

"I don't know what's happened between your brother and Grace," she said. "But I'm to fetch the children home."

"Daniel's all right?" Noble said. "Little Jack said they heard a shot."

"He isn't hurt. I heard the shot, but I don't know where it was."

"And Grace?"

"She isn't hurt either, but . . ." Emilia looked at Little Jack and Ester coming up around to the front of the cabin. "Your mother wants you home."

A dark cloud passed over Jack's face. Whatever was wrong with his parents, the boy knew about it.

"Uncle Noble and Aunt Clarissa were showing us how to shoot. I hit a can," Ester announced.

"That's very good," Emilia said. She held out her arms, and the girl giggled and ran over. Emilia lifted her up to where she could swing into the saddle behind her.

Jack kicked the toe of his boot into the dirt. "Can't we just stay here? I don't want to see Pa yelling anymore."

"What?" Noble said.

"Jack, whatever your father said, he didn't

mean it. He and your mother are fine. They argued a bit, but now they're fine. They both want you and your sister home now."

"What do you mean? What happened?" Noble said.

"Not now, Gabriel. I can't explain."

"Then I'm going with you," Noble said.

"No, you aren't," his mother answered. "You will only make things worse, son. Grace is your brother's wife. Let them sort this out together."

Noble started for the barn. He'd have the stallion saddled in a minute. Clarissa caught his hand, and he stopped.

"Not this time," she said. "Please, just stay here with me."

Noble looked from her to his mother and then back again. His mother's glare was hard as ice, but it was the tears building up in Clarissa's eyes that swayed him. He'd never seen her so upset. It bothered him in some deep way he hadn't expected. He never wanted her to cry again.

"I'll stay if you want me to," he relented.

Clarissa nodded and gave him a little smile in return. She began dabbing at her eyes.

"Let's go, Jack," Emilia said.

"I don't want to. I want to stay here with Noble and Clarissa. I don't want to see Pa. Not ever again." His hands were balled into fists.

Emilia looked pleadingly at Noble.

"Jack, you need to go home now," Noble said.

"Your mother and father miss you. Besides, someone has to look out for your grandmother. You wouldn't want her riding off alone and defenseless, would you?"

"I want to stay with you though."

"I want you to stay as well, but the point of me teaching you how to shoot was so you could protect yourself and the people you love. Now you need to go with your grandmother to protect her."

"I guess so." The boy dropped his head and went to his horse.

Soon all three were gone.

In the deepening evening, Noble and Clarissa stood alone on the porch.

"Are you all right?" he asked.

"I'm fine." Clarissa kept dabbing at the tears.

"You're sure?"

"I'm happy is all." She moved close to him and wrapped him in her arms. "Just hold me."

Noble did as she asked. She sobbed against his chest, and he gently stroked her hair. He didn't understand what had just happened. He felt like he'd made some sort of choice, one he didn't even realize.

How could that be? How can I make a choice I don't even know I'm making?

Chapter 15

Grace fell rather than sat in her chair.

It was late and she was exhausted. She and Daniel had spent hours talking—arguing—and neither had budged. Grace believed they needed Gabriel to help them drive off the rustlers. Daniel believed the sheriff would sort matters out eventually and peacefully. Barring that, he didn't know how they'd hold on to the Rafter.

"Violence is not the answer," he kept repeating. He had few ideas beyond that. None practical. He wanted to move the cattle into the far pastures, to hide them. That or send them all to market. "Sell them, and there'll be nothing to steal. Nothing to fight for. The rustlers will move on," he argued.

"What about next year? How will we hold the Rafter without cattle?" Grace had asked.

Daniel did not know.

Neither knew who fired the shot; Daniel hadn't even heard it. She'd found him walking home, unharmed, leading his horse, head down and bare. His hat was nowhere to be found.

He told her he'd tossed it into a ravine.

She'd convinced him to ride along with her toward home. Once there, though, the argument had reignited. They'd kept it civil and polite. Grace had gone out of her way to keep her voice down, and to his credit, Daniel had followed her lead.

Grace sighed. She was done now. That didn't mean she'd admitted being wrong or that he was right, but she couldn't talk about it anymore. Arguing with Daniel was like wrestling with a bear. A very big bear. There hadn't been many arguments in their marriage. Content to let him have his way, Grace knew when to give ground and when to hold fast.

If he was a bear, though, then she wasn't some boulder to be crushed. She was the stream flowing around bear and boulder both. Rage as he might, the bear could do nothing to harm the stream.

If only it were that simple. Streams didn't have feelings; they didn't love the bear, even as he tried to harm them. They didn't share children with him.

Grace did.

In frustration, Daniel had finally retreated outside. Grace hoped Cactus and Vern knew enough to keep clear of him.

Hoofbeats outside caused her to raise her head. Daniel had asked his mother to bring the children back from Gabriel and Clarissa's.

Ester burst through the door as Grace stood. She hugged Grace tight around the waist.

"Mama," she said.

Jack entered then. His head hung down, eyes to

the floor, and he walked slowly toward his room. Grace moved to intercept him and gave him a hug as well.

He did not respond and continued on into his room.

"I'm getting too old for all this riding," Emilia said as she entered. She threw her gloves on the table and plopped down.

"Get dressed for bed," Grace said. She looked at her mother-in-law. She couldn't remember a time Emilia had ever complained about riding. The woman always seemed made of iron and rawhide.

Rawhide breaks if it's pulled hard enough, and even iron slowly wears away.

"Take a rest," Grace said. "I've got coffee."

"Coffee," Emilia said. "Yes, I suppose I'll have a cup."

"Daniel is out in the barn," Grace offered.

"We saw him. He looked like he'd wrestled a bear all afternoon."

"Just me." Grace gave a sad smile at how close Emilia's choice of words matched her own thoughts.

Emilia grinned at her then. "Good for you, dear. If he were still a boy, I'd give him a good switchin'. But he's too big for that. He's a good boy, but too pigheaded and stubborn."

"That's one thing your boys have in common, Daniel and Gabriel."

"Sam too," Emilia said with a laugh. "He and Big Jack used to go rounds. Bellowin' at each other like two bulls."

"And you two?"

Emilia took her hands and squeezed them. "Sam and I too. We had our problems, rare though they were. You and Daniel will come out of this just fine. You two are good together, and you've got Jack and Ester. When this is over and the rustlers are gone, things will settle down."

"And when will that be?" Grace asked. The end seemed very far away.

"Tomorrow," Daniel answered from the door. "It will be over tomorrow. I'll ride in for the sheriff. I'm going to insist he call in the marshal. Then it will all be over. Gabriel can go about his murderous business elsewhere."

"Don't speak of your brother that way," Emilia said.

Jack and Ester reappeared from their rooms then. Daniel bent down to scoop up Ester and plant a kiss on her forehead.

"I missed you," he said.

"I missed you too," Ester replied with a giggle. "But we had a good time at Uncle Gabriel's."

"You did?" Daniel's face darkened at that.

Ester nodded.

"What did you do?"

It was Jack that answered. "Uncle Noble showed us how to shoot."

"He what?" Daniel's eyes widened then narrowed down into black points.

Grace felt her chest tighten. She'd left her children with Noble to keep them safe. Not so he would teach them to shoot.

"He let me shoot his pistol," Jack said. "He said I was a good shot."

"A good shot?" Daniel's voice shook the walls.

"You're squeezing me too tight, Pa," Ester cried.

Daniel's face reddened as he set her on the ground.

Jack went on. "I hit the can, and he said I was a good shot. When I'm bigger, I'm going with him to see the mountains." There was defiance in his little voice. He took a last look at his father, grabbed his sister's hand, and took her into his bedroom. The door slammed behind him.

Daniel turned to Grace.

Emilia darted between them. "Now Daniel. Son."

"You did this." He pointed at Grace. "You brought him here. You begged him to come and save the ranch. We didn't need him. We never needed him and now he's . . . he's . . ."

"He's what?" Emilia said. "He's started teaching your boy how to protect himself. Seems like that's what he needs."

"You would think that." Daniel looked down at his mother. "You always loved him most. But I'm the one who stayed. I'm the one who took care of you and Father. He abandoned us."

Emilia reached back to slap him, but he caught her hand. "Not this time," he said. "This time he has gone too far. He's a murderer. He killed that man on the home range. I watched him kill him in cold blood. And now he's corrupting Jack. My son!"

Emilia tore her hand loose and moved back. She rubbed at her wrist where he'd held her.

"Enough," Grace said. She stood and faced her husband. She took two steps forward and stared up right at him. Less than a foot separated them. "This is my home. You will not raise your voice in my home. You will not speak to your mother in this way."

"Yours? You would have nothing if it weren't for me. You had nothing when you came here," Daniel said. "THIS HOME IS MINE."

Grace slapped him with all her might. His head flew to the side. Grace's hand stung like it was on fire. She ignored it. "I'm glad he did it. I'm glad Gabriel shot that man. I'm glad he showed Jack how to use a gun. You should have done it. Jack should have learned about guns years ago. When did your grandfather teach you? Seven? Eight? Jack is old enough to learn. He needs to know how to protect himself, and if you won't teach him, then I'm glad Gabriel did."

"How dare you," Daniel said. His hand started back.

Grace's eyes never left his. "Go ahead. You won't fight to protect the ranch, but you're willing to hit me, your wife."

Daniel's hand dropped. He spun on his heel and stormed out. The door slammed behind him, so hard the shelves rattled.

Grace's knees weakened. She started to fall, and Emilia caught her from behind.

"Here now, I can't carry you. I'm too old for that. Let's get you to a chair," the older woman said.

"I've done it now." Grace began to sob. She took a handkerchief from a pocket on her dress. "Everything is falling apart. My husband hates me."

"Oh dear." Emilia patted her on the head and smoothed her hair. "Daniel does not hate you. Never think it. He'll come around."

The door opened, and Sam entered. He raised a hand, finger extended, toward Emilia. He started to speak, looked at Grace, and thought better of it.

"You have something to say to me?" Emilia stood up straight.

His mouth opened again, the hand and extended finger came up, but he paused. His eyes went from Emilia to Grace and back again. They softened.

"No," he finally said.

"Nothing at all?" Emilia asked.

Sam shook his head. "Nothing at all. There has been enough trouble already."

"Yes, there has. Now go talk sense into Daniel. He needs you." Emilia tilted her head toward the outside.

"I think I'll do that," Sam said. He retreated like a scolded cat, closing the door gently behind him.

Grace looked up at Emilia then. She'd never seen anyone make her father-in-law back down. Emilia usually seemed content to let Sam have his way, and no one else ever stood up to him.

"What was that?" Grace said between sobs.

"Took me thirty years of practice to do that," Emilia said with the trace of a smile. "Now let's get you cleaned up."

Daniel did not come to breakfast. He'd spent the night sleeping in the barn. Though the last few days were warm, even in the peak summer, Montana nights were bitter cold and often damp.

Grace thought about taking a blanket to him but decided against it. Tired as she was of arguing, her position still hadn't changed. If Daniel wanted to sleep with the horses, he was welcome to it.

She was up and preparing her usual breakfast when she saw him through the window. Still wearing yesterday's dirty clothes, he had his favorite horse saddled and led it out into the open. Then he swung up, took a long look at the house, and rode south toward the open pastures below.

Neither Cactus nor Vern were up yet. At this hour, she and Daniel were the only ones awake. He had to have seen her through the window. Grace had only narrowly resisted the urge to wave at him.

If he doesn't have the sense to come in and eat or wash up, then why bother.

Cactus stuck his head out of the bunkhouse and looked down after Daniel. He disappeared for a moment, returning only when he had his hat in place, and then drifted over to the main house.

"Ma'am," he called after a knock.

Grace went to the door and opened it. Cactus never knocked; he certainly didn't need to. He was family.

"Cactus, you've known me since I was Jack's age. There's no need to call me ma'am," she said.

"How are you this morning?" Cactus said. He entered and took his hat off, turning it over and over in his leathery brown hands. "Do I need to ride out and look after him?"

"He's big enough to take care of himself," Grace said.

Cactus studied the floor for a moment. He cleared his throat and rubbed the toe of his boot on the hardwood.

"Seems to me I've never seen a man grown up enough to take care of himself. Most flail around like newborn calves without a woman's help."

"Have a seat, Cactus," Grace said. "Breakfast is almost ready."

She poured him a cup of hot coffee.

"Thank you." Cactus set the coffee on the table and held it between his hands. For a long minute he studied the contents. "I never been married you know."

"I know." Grace flipped the bacon and went back to the eggs. The biscuits were almost ready.

"Had me a girl down in Texas. I wrote to her a time or two—sent letters from Bigsby—but by the time I got around to that she was married with a baby on the way. She didn't want no part of Montana. All the snow and wind and cold. She wanted a lot more than I could give her," Cactus said.

"Her loss," Grace said. "I'm sure you would have made a good husband."

"I don't know about that." Cactus cleared it throat. He shuffled in his chair. "Point is that you and Daniel are lucky to have each other is all."

He looked up then, and Grace met his eye.

"And it would be a shame for two people like that to stay mad at each other. My ma was always mad at Pa. He wasn't much hand on the farm. Pa liked to gamble and visit the saloons. That's when he wasn't runnin' around with—well, never you mind that. Daniel isn't that sort."

"No, he is not," Grace agreed.

"Though here lately he has been a fool," Cactus added.

"A fool?"

"This business with rustlers and all. He needs to cut Gabriel loose and let him have at it. Be the best thing for this to just have done with it. Then it'll blow over. Gabriel's been holding back. He's tried to honor Daniel's wishes, and Sam's of course, and then, well . . ." Cactus's voice trailed off as he looked at her. "In the old days Jack would—"

"The old days are gone and so is Jack," Grace interrupted. "That's the problem."

"Yes, they are and no, they aren't." Cactus's eyes hardened. "Daniel is a civilized man. So is Sam. Those rustlers and whoever is behind them isn't. Someone has to go down there and clean them out."

Grace looked out the window after her husband. "Someday this will all be settled, and we'll have peace in the valley." She sighed.

Cactus's eyes narrowed. "You believe that?"

"Of course. The law will come. More people will come."

"Yes, they will. And they'll bring more problems with them. They'll fight and argue about who got here first or who gets the water or who owns what. Those eastern towns aren't civilized. They just fight with different weapons is all. They use the law like a cudgel."

"It won't be so bad as this though. Men being shot in the pasture."

"Men been fighting and dying over land for a long time. I was young when they fought the War Between the States. When it was done, they said we'd have peace. We didn't though. They came from the North to take the land and punish anyone who'd fought against them."

Cactus hesitated then said, "There will always be a need for men who can take action. Men who will rise up and do what needs doing."

"You don't think Daniel can?"

"He can in some ways," Cactus said. "In other ways a fellow like Gabriel is what's needed. It don't make either one better than the other. Fact is the Rafter will need both, and they'll need each other too."

"I'm not sure they see it that way," Grace said. "Either one."

"Guess it's our job to show them then." Cactus gave her a smile. He stood and moved to the door. "I'll go wake Vern up. That boy can sleep through a tornado. Me though? A man like me can hardly sleep when a body tears off through the morning like the Comanches was after him."

"I'll tell Daniel not to make so much noise when I see him," Grace said.

"I hope you see him soon," Cactus said, and stepped out.

After breakfast was done, Grace left the children with Emilia and rode out after Daniel. She'd thought a lot about Cactus's words. She wouldn't back down from Daniel, not when he was wrong, but she could try and make peace with him.

She found her husband sitting his horse atop a ridge overlooking the very edge of the Rafter. Cattle—Rafter cattle—milled on the plains below, grazing and growing fat.

"You missed breakfast," she said.

"Wasn't hungry," he mumbled.

Grace patted a basket tied behind her saddle. "I brought you a few things for lunch then. Will you eat with me?"

Without answering, Daniel climbed down. He helped her out of the saddle then untied the basket. She'd packed an old blanket, and they stretched it on the ground. There were several strips of leftover bacon, biscuits, butter, and cheese.

"I remember when we used to do this all the time," Grace said.

"So do I," Daniel said.

"When did we stop?"

"After Ester was born. She was sick all the time, and we kept her inside."

"I remember," Grace said. They'd both been worried about her. She was so thin, so frail. "She came through fine though."

"She did," Daniel said. "Do you remember the first time we came down here?"

"I do. It was all of us. You, me, Gabriel, your parents . . . even Big Jack came."

"He did," Daniel said. "He used to come all the time."

They were both silent for a long time until Daniel cleared his throat.

"I knew. Even as a boy I knew I'd never measure up to Big Jack. Gabriel, wild Gabriel, that was Big Jack's grandson. I was too . . ."

Grace reached over and clasped his hands.

"Too soft," he said. "Gabriel was a fighter, and I was soft, like my father. I wanted so badly to prove him wrong, but then I realized he was right. So I became my father. I worked hard. I built this place up best I could. Father did as well. Gabriel couldn't have done better."

"You've done well, Daniel." Grace gave his hands a squeeze. "I'm sure if your grandfather could see you now he'd be proud of all you've accomplished."

"It isn't enough though. I can build and build and build, but I can't keep them from taking it all from me." He was on the verge of tears now. Grace had only seen him cry twice, the day each of his children were born.

"Let your brother help," Grace pleaded. "He wants to help you."

"I don't know if I can. I don't even know if

there's time," Daniel looked out over the cattle below. "We lost another fifty head last night. Taken from the home range. The home range! We can't stand to lose more."

"We will make it through this." Grace gave his hands another squeeze. "Together."

The crack of a large rifle echoed in the distance. It came from the north, the direction of the house.

"Was that a—" Grace said.

"Yes," Daniel answered. "We've got to get home."

Chapter 16

Noble rose to a gray, rainy morning. By the time he made it outside, the rain had withered down into a drizzle, and clouds pressed down low against the land, thick and the color of cold iron. They rolled east, dipping their long, misty fingers over the hills and ridgelines.

The cool morning air carried the heavy smells of moisture and damp grass.

Clarissa followed him outside.

"Sure you want to ride today?" Noble said. "Looks like a wet one."

"I'll be fine," Clarissa said. "You promised to show me more of the ranch."

"Up to you." Noble shrugged. Then he fetched the horses while Clarissa waited beneath the dry porch.

They started out north. This was some of the best cattle country on the west range. There were large flats of prairie with only a few creeks and streams separating them. Pine, spruce, and fir grew along the waterways, with the ever-present cottonwoods alongside. Their wax leaves clapped in the faint breeze. All but a few head of the cattle were here. Noble's efforts to push them out away from the big canyon had accomplished that much, at least.

Noble led the way over it all, crossing shallow streams, flatlands, low hills, and rocky crests. Finally he topped a low hill and pointed farther north.

"The Rafter ends at that tree line," he said.

"Why there?" Clarissa said. "Does someone else own that?"

"No, there's almost no grass beyond what you see. Lots of trees and woods. Technically, I guess the ranch boundary goes farther up, but there's nothing but trees and more trees. Good timber country. Nothing for cattle to eat though."

"Could you cut the trees down?"

Noble laughed. "I guess so, but it would take an awful long time. They're thick as weeds up there."

They stood and watched the clouds for a moment, then turned south and east before setting off again.

"There's a lake up ahead. It's on the dividing line between the home place and the west range. The ranch houses aren't too far beyond," Noble said. "We might catch a fish if we're lucky."

"Fish?" Clarissa crinkled her nose.

"You've never had a mountain trout before?"

"No. Why would I eat a slimy fish?"

"They're not so bad. Butter, onions, salt. Good change of pace from all the beef."

Clarissa frowned. "I've never had a fish."

Noble picked up the pace into a quick trot.

Morning had given way to noon when they reached the lake. The sun was a faint ball of white through the churning clouds.

The lake was full with spring runoff, and Noble rode down to the sandy shore. The still water reflected the trees and mountains beyond the far bank and even the clouds above.

"It's pretty," Clarissa said.

"It's nicer when it isn't so cloudy. Almost like a mirror," Noble said.

"It's not bad now. I like how the trees shine off the surface."

"On the other side, you can see the Bitterroots in the reflection. I learned to swim here."

"I don't know how to swim," Clarissa said.

"Really?"

"Never had much need for it. After Ma and Pa died and then Chet, I never learned to swim. Never learned much at all, actually." She patted Bailey's neck. "Just how to ride a bit and how to cook."

"You got a knack for that," Noble admitted. He'd have to watch how much he ate of her cooking.

"Thanks," Clarissa said, and smiled. She turned a little red around the cheeks. "Emilia and Grace have been teaching me a few things."

"Oh?"

"Sure. A little writing and reading. I'm not so good at numbers though."

"That's good."

"You can read and write?"

"I can. Though I haven't done much of either. Not in a very long time."

"Could you teach me, then?" Clarissa said. She was looking down at the sand when she said it, but Noble thought her cheeks had grown a shade brighter.

"Don't know how much of a teacher I am. Grace and Ma would be better."

"Well, maybe you could teach me to swim?"

This time she looked right at Noble, and he felt his breath catch. He licked his lips and took his time before answering.

"That is, if you want to?" she said and lowered her eyes.

"Clarissa, I—"

A gunshot interrupted them.

"That came from the home place," Noble said. He held his breath, listening for another shot.

"Maybe they shot a deer?" Clarissa asked.

"We'll go ride and see," Noble said. It could have been a deer or elk, but he was thinking of the mystery sharpshooter. There were a lot of places around the home place where a man with a rifle might hide.

They came in from the north, circling around the mesa and the cemetery. Noble paused in a grove of spruce trees and studied the hills around the cluster of buildings.

A rifleman might be laying atop any of them. *If we charge out in the open, he'll take a shot at either of us.*

Clarissa didn't ask why they'd stopped. The girl continually surprised him with how practical she was. She might not have a proper education, but she had a great deal of good sense.

"The rustlers have a rifleman. He took a couple shots at me. I haven't seen any sign of him in weeks, but he might be here."

Clarissa nodded. "What do we do, then?"

"It's been a long time since we heard the shot. He's likely gone, but we'll circle that boulder there and keep low and fast when we ride in," Noble said. "When we ride in, be sure to keep some room between us. I don't want you getting shot on accident."

"All right," she said. "I can help though."

"I know you can," Noble said. "But keep clear of me all the same."

Another woman, or most men for that matter, might have argued, but the girl just took it in stride. She'd argued with him occasionally—never over anything important though. He liked that about her. He liked too that she was willing and able to help. After their practice, she could shoot well enough, and she had the judgment to know what to shoot at.

Noble set out at a fast pace. The stallion was quick, and it ate up the distance, first to the boulder, then they raced down the draw toward the house, and finally into the cluster of ranch buildings.

He swung down behind his parents' house and snatched the rifle from its scabbard. Clarissa hopped off her horse but kept a healthy distance between them.

Noble crept alongside the house until he could peer out into the front yard.

He saw his mother first. She was on her knees over a body, crying and screaming.

Noble didn't hesitate; he ran out to his mother's side.

It was his father. Sam was alive, but the bullet had caught him in one lung. His face was gray. He seemed to be conscious and breathing with difficulty.

"Emilia," he panted. "Emilia."

"Let's get him inside," Noble said. He passed his rifle to Clarissa and knelt over his father. His mother looked around at him then. She didn't seem to recognize him at all. Her eyes were red, and blood covered her hands. She looked at them and wiped them on the front of her buckskins.

Noble tilted his father up; Sam let out a pained groan. Then Noble wrapped his arms around his father, picked him up, and dragged him to the house. He was a heavy man and tall.

Emilia seemed to steel herself. She scrambled around them to open the door.

"Put him in here," she said, and led the way to their bedroom.

Noble half-dragged, half-carried his father inside and lowered him onto the bed.

"Sorry," he said. It had to hurt like hell being carried like that.

Sam was breathing hard, trying and failing to catch his breath. Pink froth bubbled on his lips. Noble had seen the signs before.

His lungs are filling up with blood.

The sound of more horses came from outside.

"Cactus and Vern went to town for supplies. I don't know where Daniel and Grace are," Emilia said. She was at Sam's bedside now. Jack and Ester were with her. Noble didn't know where they'd come from.

"Stay here," Noble said, and drew a pistol. "Clarissa, watch over them."

Clarissa nodded. She laid his rifle on a table and checked the breech to make sure her own was loaded and ready.

Good girl. She'll keep them safe.

Daniel and Grace rode up as he reached the front.

"Gabriel, who's hurt?" Daniel said.

"Pa," Noble answered. "He's been shot."

"Where are Jack and Ester?" Grace shouted.

"Inside, with everyone else," Noble said.

Daniel jumped down and bolted inside. Noble

waited a moment to help Grace down, then followed her in.

"How bad is he?" Grace said.

"Bad."

When he reached his parents' bedroom, his brother was kneeling at their father's side. His mother hovered near. She had placed a damp rag on Sam's forehead. Sam's breath came in hard, labored gasps. There was more of the pink froth on his lips; Emilia wiped it clean.

Sam's eyes met Noble's in that moment. He beckoned Noble to come closer.

Noble shuffled his way over and took Daniel's place. He reached for his father's hands and clasped them tight. His father's lips moved and there was a mumbling of sound. What was he saying? Noble took off his hat and leaned over his father with an ear close to Sam's lips.

"I . . . did not approve . . . of your life, son, but I want you to know . . . I want you to know . . ." Sam said. "I wish . . . I wish . . . we had a little more time. I wish you had never left."

Noble's eyes began to sting.

"I . . . I know why you left. I know the real reason was . . . for your brother . . . for what he did in anger. I am . . . grateful to you for that . . . I never told you . . . should have . . . I am sorry. I know it never seemed that way. I forgive you everything."

Noble shook his head. He couldn't believe it.

No one but he and Daniel knew the reason for his leaving. For seven years, he'd never told anyone, and he was certain Daniel hadn't.

How long had Father known?

"A little more time . . ." Sam's voice fell. His breathing slowed, and he was gone.

Noble straightened. He went outside without speaking.

I know the real reason was . . . for your brother . . . for what he did in anger. I am grateful to you for that. I forgive you everything.

Those few precious words, how they changed everything.

Daniel and Emilia were crying. Grace too. The children were too frightened to cry. Did they understand that their grandfather was gone now? Jack might have, but young Ester could not.

Noble remembered the day Big Jack died. There were no goodbyes, no final words. He'd simply gone to sleep and never woke. A man who did whatever was required of him, violent or not, died peacefully, while a man of pure faith who lived in peace died from a gunshot.

This world is not a just one. They both would have agreed on that.

Noble waited patiently for the others. He moved away from his father's side. He'd had his moment, let them have theirs.

Daniel was the first to recover himself. He looked at Noble and said, "I'm taking this to the sheriff, and I'll have no argument from you."

"You won't," Noble agreed. Father would have wanted it that way. Kyle George wasn't much of a sheriff, but they would take it to him, and Noble would give him a chance to see the killer hunted down and brought to justice.

And if I'm not satisfied with the results, I can always do it myself.

Daniel was looking at him, expecting a fight, apparently.

"It's what Father would have wanted," Noble said. "When do we leave?"

The ride to Bigsby was the longest of Noble's life.

Noble wasn't in the mood for talk, and it didn't seem like Daniel was either. He'd loaned Noble a fresh horse—the stallion was tired from the morning ride—and they'd come in to Bigsby after assigning Cactus and Vern to watch over the womenfolk.

Little Jack had asked to ride along, but Daniel and Grace forbade it.

Daniel led the way through town. Nightfall wasn't too far off—an hour maybe two—and the streets were abnormally silent. Even the saloons seemed less rowdy than usual.

Noble sensed the town's mood. He wasn't sure what caused it, but it felt like Bigsby was holding its breath, waiting for an oncoming storm. He'd seen this before. You couldn't live by the gun as long as he did and not see it. On a night much like this one he'd left New Mexico, and two days later John Tunstall had been killed in the opening shots of the Lincoln County War. That time, he'd missed the storm. Other times, he hadn't. Texas was like this right before the final showdown at the end.

Whatever storm came this time, he would be at the center of it. Whoever killed his father would pay.

Light came from inside the sheriff's office.

Daniel and Noble hitched their horses out front. Before they could go in, Noble caught his brother's eye.

"Tread careful. Something about the town tonight. I don't like it," Noble said. He checked both pistols.

Daniel nodded. "I feel it too." He stopped and took in Bigsby with a long gaze. "The air feels like before one of those big lightning storms out on the plains."

He led the way inside.

Kyle George was sound asleep when they entered. His feet were propped up on his desk, chair leaned back against one wall with his hat down low, covering his face. The light gleamed off the badge pinned to his chest, and a sawing snore came from beneath the hat.

"Sheriff," Daniel's voice boomed. In the small of the jail, it echoed like cannon fire.

The sheriff's feet jerked back, and his chair slammed to all fours. He dropped instantly behind the big oak desk.

"What? What?" Kyle said. Hatless, he peered over his desk at them.

"It's Daniel Bartlett. I want to report a murder."

"Oh . . . Oh," the sheriff said. He rose slowly from behind the desk, picking his hat up from the floor. "I see. Well, why not come back tomorrow and we'll file a proper report."

"We aren't staying in town," Daniel said. "I've got no time for reports. My father was just killed, and I want the killer found."

"Mr. Bartlett, I am very busy, much too busy to investigate anything out in the *county*." He said county like a dirty word.

Noble shifted on his feet. They didn't have time for this.

"I'm aware of just how . . ." Daniel paused to look around the empty jail ". . . just how busy you are. But my father's murderer must be brought to justice."

"Look, Mr. Bartlett I'm—"

By then, Noble decided he'd had enough. "What you are . . . is a sorry excuse for a sheriff or any other kind of lawman," he said. "A lazy, shiftless, incompetent bum is all you are, unfit to wear Tom McCandles's badge. But he's not here, and you're what Bigsby has. So you'll take Daniel's report now, tonight, before we leave."

Kyle's mouth fell open in shock. He closed it, and his face flushed red. "Now see here, I'm the sheriff here. I'm in charge."

Before Noble could act, Daniel grabbed the sheriff by the shirtfront and shook him until a bone button popped free and spun on the floor. "Kyle, I don't care if you're in charge. My father was murdered today on his ranch in front of his grandchildren. You will take my statement now, before I lose my temper." Daniel finished by throwing the sheriff back. The Sheriff bounced off the back wall and caught himself on his desk.

Noble hadn't seen his brother that upset in a long time—not since they'd both been a lot younger. The simple truth was, for all Daniel's preaching against violence, he could break an awful lot of stuff when he was properly riled. He was a big man, after all. Rough, too. Noble wondered if Daniel had ever really lost his temper since that day seven years ago.

"I'll take your statement then," the sheriff agreed. His hands shook as he took out pen and paper. He tried to write the date. His hands shook so badly, though, it came out as an illegible blob.

"Here, I'll write it down for you," Noble said, and took over. They'd be there all night otherwise.

Noble wrote out a quick statement for himself, signed it, then did another for Daniel. He explained about the shot the day before—the sharpshooter taking a practice shot to gauge his aim, Noble was now sure—and then how they found Sam. He examined his penmanship for mistakes and was satisfied there were none. Ma always said he had a gift for writing. In his line of work, he didn't get much chance to use it. He folded the two statements neatly and set them on the sheriff's desk.

"Now," he said, "when does the marshal arrive?"

"The marshal?" Kyle repeated.

"When does he next arrive? And where are those rustlers we left with you?" Noble asked. The two cells were empty, each of their doors hung open.

"Escaped."

"Escaped," Noble said. "How?"

Kyle licked his lips. "Outlaws hit the bank. They made off with three thousand dollars. I went after them and when I got back, the rustlers were gone."

"Gone," Daniel said. His big, hammer fists clenched tight.

The sheriff nodded. "Truth is, boys, I'm on the verge of quitting. I'm not leaving town until the marshal comes. I sent word for him day after you brought those rustlers in. I've had enough. Three of the other outfits have all complained about the rustlers. There's only so much one man can do."

"One man?" Noble said.

"What can I do by myself? I've got the town to

watch over. The county will have to take care of itself."

"That's just how range wars start," Noble said.

"I don't care. I hired on for town sheriff. No more than that." Kyle was adamant. He'd recovered a sliver of pride from what Daniel had shaken out of him.

"Which outfits complained?" Daniel said.

"Double V, Lazy Six, Four Diamonds."

Noble wasn't familiar with the Four Diamonds, but he knew the others. Each had arrived in the years following the Rafter's founding. They were east of Bigsby.

"Between those three, us, and Webster's that's everyone," Daniel said.

Kyle nodded. "It's too big for one man, you see?"

"All I see is a waste of a badge," Noble said.

"You think you can do better? You wear it then," Kyle said.

Noble laughed. "You'll never catch me wearing one of those damned things."

"When's the marshal due?" Daniel said.

"Two, three days. No more than that."

"We'll be back then," Daniel said. "Give him our statements."

Kyle didn't answer, only scowled at them as they left.

Noble followed his brother outside and to the waiting horses.

"For a man who doesn't like violence, you sure can put a man into a wall," Noble said beside the hitching rail.

"I lost my temper," Daniel said. "Won't happen again."

"Before this is all over, you might have to lose it again," Noble said. He'd been glad to see some fight in his younger brother.

"I'm not like you," Daniel said with a glare. "I don't go around killing people."

"Not even the man who killed our father? Seems to me he might deserve it."

"No, I won't be a party to killing. That wasn't Father's way. I won't betray his memory that way. He wouldn't want it."

"Good for you, brother. You do that. When the time comes, I'll be the one to take care of it."

Daniel grabbed Noble's shirtfront, same as he'd done the sheriff. "No, you won't. I won't let you."

Noble looked down at the hand holding him. "Big as you are, Brother, you never saw the day you could whip me," he said. "Best remember that."

"I will stop you," Daniel said. He let go of the shirt though. "I'll have him brought to justice, not murdered in vengeance."

"We've got to find him first," Noble said. "I don't think the sheriff will be much help."

Noble got into the saddle and headed toward

home. Daniel came along behind him. Noble hoped when he caught up to their father's killer, his brother wouldn't be there.
And if he is, I'll just have to fight him, too.

Chapter 17

Grant Hickman showed up on the Rafter the following day driving a new wagon.

Noble and Daniel came out to greet him.

"Boys," Grant said. He wrapped the reins around the wagon's seat back and set the brake but did not climb down. "Never imagined I'd see the day when the two of you were back here together. Feels like old times."

"It does," Noble said.

"What brings you all the way out here, Grant?" Daniel said.

"Heard about your father. I'm awful sorry," Grant said. He took off his hat and fanned his face with it. "I also came out to tell you Kyle George left town last night. Sold everything he had and pulled up stakes. He owed a good bit on his house, but I took over the remainder of the loan and paid him the difference for traveling money."

Noble exchanged a look with his brother and said, "I'm not surprised."

"No. Kyle wasn't much of a sheriff, and with these cattle rustlers rampaging through the country and all, he just wasn't up to it," Grant said. "He did write to the marshal though. Tom McCandles should be here any day now. After I heard from Kyle, I sent Tom a telegraph as well. I asked him to appoint a replacement sheriff for us. Someone salty enough to clean this country up. Rigsby is big enough to support a marshal full time, and we've got crime enough to keep even a top man busy."

"Seems like it," Daniel said.

It struck Noble that Daniel didn't have much to say to Grant. They'd never really been friends; Noble couldn't remember why. Grant had spent a fair share of his time prowling over the country with them. He and the Webster boys, too.

Grant shook his head. "I just can't believe it. Sam Bartlett gone. A good man murdered on his own place. It can happen to anyone."

"How's your bank?" Noble said.

"What?" Grant's head tilted to one side.

"The bank. I heard you got robbed. We brought in a group of rustlers and their friends busted them out. Sounded like they hit the bank at the same time," Noble said.

"Oh," Grant dabbed sweat from his forehead. "I didn't make out too bad. Lucky for me the vault was closed, and I was out seeing about a loan at the time."

"Very lucky," Daniel agreed.

"Don't know as I'd say that. They made off with three thousand dollars. Would have been worse if the vault had been open though. Listen, boys, I just came to tell you how sorry I was to hear about Sam and to let you know about the sheriff. I'd also like to offer my services if you need them."

"Services?" Daniel said.

"Well, I can't do much, of course. Not against the rustlers, but I can promise to send you word when the marshal arrives."

"We'd appreciate that," Noble said.

"Good, good. I'll send a rider out this way soon as he arrives. You'll both be here then?" Grant asked.

"Someone will," Noble said. "I've half a mind to ride into Circle Bar, guns blazing, and clear the whole bunch out."

"Really?" Grant said. "Why, I thought you'd already chased them off the Circle Bar." From inside his coat, he drew out a bag of coins and tossed them to Noble. They fell short and landed with a jangle. "I sent a man over there yesterday and he said the place was empty. No signs of rustlers at all."

Noble stooped and picked up the bag. He hefted it. A tidy sum. He tossed it back to Grant.

"No?" Grant said.

"Didn't earn it yet," Noble said. "I'll come by to see you when the work is done."

Daniel turned and went back into the house.

"Something wrong?" Grant said, looking after Daniel.

"No," Noble answered. "Family matter is all."

"Ahh, understandable. Well, I won't keep you all day," Grant said. He untied the reins and started to go. "One thing though. It might not be a good idea to go looking for trouble just yet."

"Oh?" Noble said. He did not like anyone, not even a friend, telling him what or what not to do. Generally it made him more inclined to do a thing.

"The marshal will be out soon enough. Let him earn his pay," Grant said. Then he leaned down and lowered his voice. "Besides, how sure are you that it was Sam the sharpshooter was after?"

"What do you mean?"

"It doesn't make much sense to kill Sam. Everyone . . . well everyone knows how he was. Peaceful and all. Why would the rustlers murder him, of all people?"

Noble had been asking himself the same question. His father wasn't one to put up a fight. But what if they weren't after Sam? He and Daniel and Sam were all of similar size. From a distance, a sharpshooter could mistake any one of them for the other. More questions came to mind. If Sam wasn't the target though, were they after Daniel or himself?

Grant straightened. "I see by the look on your face that you've had the same idea. Might be if they got the wrong man, they'll be back to try again. Makes a fella want to hole up until help arrives."

"Yeah," Noble nodded.

"Well, I've got to get back to town. Let me know if you need anything, Gabriel."

"I appreciate that."

Noble watched Grant's wagon roll back toward town.

Everyone in the valley knew Sam did not own the Rafter. It was Emilia's ranch, one of the first in Montana to be owned by a woman. Jack Noble had wanted his daughter and then grandchildren to own the Rafter, and Sam had always been content with the arrangement.

Sam could not have been the target unless it was done to get Daniel and me riled up and careless.

Noble snorted. Careless men got killed. He'd long ago lost any careless urges. Daniel though . . . If Daniel were lured to town or into a trap somewhere and killed, who would own the Rafter then? Grace. Emilia. Capable as both were, they could not defend the Rafter. In truth, his brother couldn't either.

Could not or would not?

Cactus knew how to fight. Vern Ollie seemed to have some sand to him; he hadn't blanched when Noble killed that rustler. They were good, loyal men. They'd fight, but there were only two of them. Two against what?

Nine more. At least that many.

Noble walked to the corral and leaned

against the railing. His stallion came over, restless.

"Yeah, I'm restless, too. We've been here too long, boy. Need to wrap a few things up and be back out on the trail where we belong," Noble said.

Tomorrow they would bury his father. Then he would take Grant's advice. He'd keep close to the ranch house and make sure no one else got bushwhacked. When the marshal arrived, he'd see about hunting after his father's killer.

And I'm going to start in Riggins. Someone there knows what this is all about, and if Gage Banier gets in my way, I'll erase that mark too.

Fifty-seven.

Noble counted each step between the barn, the corral, and his grandfather's old cabin. The grass was beaten down along his path, bare ground showing through in patches.

He paused long enough to call into the cabin. "Are you ready?"

"Almost," Clarissa answered for the third time.

Noble returned to pacing. Twenty-nine steps between the house and barn.

Two days he'd been waiting. He hadn't exactly been idle, but he'd spent most of his time prowling around the tree-covered hillsides that overlooked the home place or doing the same here. He found the sharpshooter's resting place the first day, found where he'd laid down and smoked a cigarette, then where he'd hidden his horse for the long wait. There was a bullet hole in the corral's top rail, just feet from where his father had been shot. A practice round, Noble was sure.

But he didn't stop there—not until he'd learned all the likely spots for the sharpshooter to hide, knew all the routes of escape, knew where a man in a hurry might hide a horse. He knew them all and had checked them often over the last couple days.

Today, though, they had family business to attend to. Today, he and Daniel would bury their father.

When he was midway between the corral and house, the door creaked open, and Clarissa stepped out. She didn't own anything properly black and had made do with a dark-gray dress and a deep-blue shawl. She drew the shawl up over her head and wrapped it tight against the morning chill.

"Ready," she finally announced.

Noble turned on his heel and retrieved their horses.

Both animals had been feeling the same idleness. They nickered in excitement at the prospect of a ride.

Noble helped Clarissa up on Bailey, then mounted the black before they finally set off.

Noble held a fast trot that matched the beating of his heart.

"They won't start without us," Clarissa said.

"I know," Noble answered. Without meaning to, his trot had grown into a gallop, and he slowed the black. "I'm just too keyed up, is all. Not used to sittin' around waiting."

"What would you do if you weren't so worried about the rest of us?"

"I'd ride out and hunt after them."

"Where would you start?"

"Riggins," Noble said. "I should have just done that from the start. Anytime there's trouble in the valley, it starts from Riggins."

"No one in Bigsby can start trouble?" Clarissa asked.

"Oh, they can all right." Noble took her meaning. "But someone from Riggins is generally involved and knows about it."

"And you'd ride into Riggins and demand answers?"

"Pretty much."

"Sounds like a good way to get shot." Clarissa frowned.

"Sometimes it turns out that way, but at least it's something. I'm not meant for sittin' around watching for trouble. I'd rather seek it out."

"And what about Gage Banier?"

Noble cursed inwardly. He never should have told her about Banier.

"If he's involved, I'll deal with him."

"You said he was fast. Is he as fast as you?"

"It's pretty close between us." Noble shrugged. "Won't know until we shoot it out."

Clarissa frowned. "So you won't know which of you is better until you meet and one of you is dead?"

"Or both of us. Sometimes that happens too," Noble said. He'd seen more than one gun battle end in both men dying. "But that's the way it has to be."

"So you'd just ride in and shoot the town up until you found your man?"

"You make it sound worse than it is. I'd ask a few questions first. It wouldn't take many. There's always folks eager to tell what they know."

"And then what?"

"Then I'd start settling scores. First for my father, and then for the Rafter."

"It still sounds dangerous to me."

Noble let it drop. She wasn't wrong. Finding the enemy and then just wading in, fists flying, guns flashing, was dangerous, and it was stupid, but sometimes it was the only way forward. Find the obstacle, smash through it, find the next one.

He'd often played the smart way. It was by far the safer route, and it worked often enough, but sometimes a man just hit a wall. Then he had to either find a way around or bull his way through to make progress. Noble had considered alternatives. But his father was killed, the Rafter's enemies had all gone underground like moles. He had to flush them out somehow. That or wait for them to come out again. And waiting galled.

I've waited enough. Waiting got Father killed. I should have ignored Daniel and shot it out with those thieving rustlers long ago.

They tied their horses to the hitching rail outside the Rafter bunkhouse. Noble helped Clarissa down, and she quickly went to the house. Noble found Cactus and Vern Ollie waiting on the porch.

"Rain today," Noble said, and swept his hat toward the gray sky.

"Cloudy enough for it," Cactus agreed. "He was a good man, a man a little ahead of his time."

"I think so," Noble agreed.

"He and Jack went rounds—they didn't see eye to eye on much—but in the end they both respected each other. The Rafter was all the better for it."

"I remember a few of those," Noble said.

"I didn't know him as well as I would have liked," Vern Ollie said. "He kept his distance."

"Yes, he did," Noble agreed, and Cactus nodded.

Daniel came out. "Ready?"

"We are," Noble said for them all.

They went inside.

The casket left the house first, carried by the men, all but little Jack, who walked at his grandmother's side. Emilia patted the boy on the head. Dressed in her finest Sunday dress, she came after the casket, followed by Grace, Ester, and then Clarissa.

They carried the casket up the little hill, which was not steep on that side. There were others gathered at the top, families from nearby ranches and a few of the old congregation from town. Noble didn't know the pastor. The man had a good voice though, strong and clear, and he did a fine job. Sam would have approved. When the sermon was done and the casket lowered with ropes into the prepared plot in the warm earth, overlooking the ranch below, the family stepped back. All but Daniel, who stood alone beside the headstone to say a few words.

"Thank you for your words, Pastor Hardin. Pa was the preacher," Daniel said. "If he were here, he'd offer up pretty words about life and love of the Lord and his mercy. I lived Pa's ways best I could, but I never could deliver much of a sermon."

He took his hat in both hands, rolled the brim tight, and wiped a thumb at each eye. "Pa liked plain things. Useful things. So all I will say is this: He was a man of conviction who did what he thought was right and just. We will all miss him."

Then Daniel stepped down. Jack walked Emilia up beside the plot. She patted Daniel on the arm as they passed and tossed in a handful of wildflowers. Grace, Ester, and Clarissa all did the same. A handful of the mourners followed their lead.

Some spoke to Daniel and Grace, words of encouragement.

Noble and Clarissa hung back a bit, content to be alone. Clarissa wrapped one arm around him. Noble put his own arm around her shoulder. He hadn't agreed with most of Sam's convictions, but he respected that his father had stood by them, steadfast and unyielding as a stone.

The crowd slowly drifted apart, making their way down the trail to their waiting wagons or horses until only the Rafter family remained.

"Good words," Noble said. "I think he would have liked them."

Daniel's eyes narrowed.

"Yes dear, you did very well," Grace said, and squeezed Daniel's arm.

"I should have said more," Daniel said. "But I was never much good at the words."

"You did a fine job," Emilia said. "He would have been proud."

Noble thought about his father's confession at the end. Sam had known all along the truth about his sons. The truth about why Noble left all those years ago. If knowing had stained his opinion of Daniel, there hadn't been any sign of it. Moreover, Daniel seemed to have no idea Sam knew the truth.

The family moved back down off the mesa toward their homes.

Daniel and his family followed Emilia into her house. Cactus, Vern, and Clarissa stood outside the bunkhouse with Noble.

"What are you plannin' now?" Cactus said.

"Not sure yet," Noble said. "How many head on the place?"

"Should be five hundred on the west place, another fifteen hundred on the home place."

"How many has the Rafter lost?"

"Three hundred total. Young stuff. They took another fifty off the home range last week."

"Young stuff," Noble said. "Not the kind you'd take to market, but younger animals like a man might build a herd with."

"Right," Cactus said.

"What's that mean?" Clarissa said.

"Means the rustlers aren't going after cattle ready for the beef market. They're avoiding those and choosing animals for breeding. Rustlers wouldn't do that. Not unless someone was directing them to," Noble said.

"And paying them for," Cactus said. "They won't be doing it for free."

"Someone in charge of the rustlers? Someone paying them?" Vern Ollie said. "I never heard of such."

"I have," Noble said. "Down in Texas. Man from Illinois, name of Tarpley, came to town with money but no cattle. He hired a gang, and in a few months he had cattle but no ranch. So then he ran out one of the local ranches, same one he'd stolen most of the cattle from. All of the sudden he has money, cattle, land, and friends who would protect him."

"Good setup," Cactus said.

"I think that's what's happening here. The rustlers aren't the real threat. The man or men behind them are."

"Who is it though?" Clarissa said.

"I don't know," Noble said. "I think Daniel plans on laying up and waiting for the marshal, but I'm going to ride the ranch and wait for the rustlers again. I'll try to take one alive and find out what he knows. That or trail them back and see where they're keeping the cattle. That should lead us to who's behind all of it."

"I'll go with you," Cactus said.

"I want to ride along," Vern said.

"Vern, you keep an eye on the boss and the home place," Cactus said. "You see anything, you let us know. That bushwhacker might be back any day."

Noble briefly outlined where all the best spots were for a marksman, how to approach them, and where he might leave his horse, with Cactus adding a couple more to the list. "I'd appreciate it if you'd ride out and check on those now and then. Even if you don't see him, a set of fresh tracks might make him decide against laying for us again."

Vern nodded. He didn't seem to like staying at the house, but Cactus trusted him to stay behind and guard the ranch proper.

"When this all goes down, you'll get your chance, Vern. Everyone will. I've a feeling it's going to get bloody before the end," Noble said.

Chapter 18

Two days after his father's burial, Noble found the tracks. He was riding the home place, four miles south of the ranch houses, when he spotted them. They were fresh. The previous day a hard rain had come, and the mud from the animal's hooves was fresh and black against the green grass.

Noble rode around the tracks, pausing often, weaving his way from one side to the other. The story they told was plain as day.

Sometime after the rain, four men had come into the home pasture, culled out thirty head of young heifers and a pair of bulls, and pushed them south and west toward Riggins. Noble followed the tracks along to a high vantage point where he could see for miles. No sign of them on the trail ahead. By that time the rustlers were well on their way south. They couldn't be too far, though, and they were traveling slowly. Otherwise the rain would have washed out all sign of their passing.

Smelling a trap, he turned and rode for the Rafter home place. If he had Cactus along for backup, they might turn the trap on their enemies.

Then at last we'll have some answers.

Noble rode into the Rafter and tied up at the hitching rail. With a fresh horse, he could catch them quickly.

"Cactus!" he said.

The old cowhand, rifle in hand, appeared from the corral.

"Saddle up a pair of horses. They've got thirty head off the home place headed toward Riggins. Tracks can't be more than half a day old," Noble said.

Cactus nodded and went for the horses.

Daniel came out into the yard then. "Where are you going?" he said.

Noble took his saddle off the stallion and set it on the railing. He led the horse to the corral. "Rustlers took thirty head off the home place. Last night or early this morning by the sign. Cactus and I are riding after them."

Noble patted the stallion's head and pulled the bridle off him, then turned him loose in the corral. "With fresh horses, we'll catch them before nightfall."

"No," Daniel said.

"What?" Noble turned to his brother.

"I said no."

"No what?"

Daniel took a step forward until only a few feet separated them. "No, I won't have you riding out after them."

Grace, Emilia, and the children came out from

the house and onto the porch then. Grace held Jack around the shoulders.

"What would you have me do, then?" Noble asked.

"Wait for the marshal. Let him sort this all out."

"Wait for the marshal," Noble repeated. "By the time he gets here, there'll be no Rafter left to save. You'll be cleaned out. Ruined."

"We'll start over if we have to," Daniel said. "But this isn't the way. This isn't how father wanted it."

Noble cocked his head to the side. "Father is dead."

The fist came from nowhere and clocked Noble like a mallet. Noble fell to his side and lay there for a moment, looking up at his little brother.

"We wait for the marshal," Daniel repeated.

Noble looked at Daniel, then at Grace and Emilia and the children up on the porch. "I'm sorry to disappoint you, Daniel, but I'm riding out."

"Not on Rafter horses, you won't," Daniel said. "Cactus, turn those two back into the corral."

Cactus shifted his feet, evidently unsure of what to do.

"Cactus, don't bother. We'll be needing them in a minute," Noble said, and climbed to his feet.

"You didn't hear me?" Daniel said. "I said you aren't taking those horses, and you aren't following those men."

"I heard you just fine," Noble said. He threw a wicked punch that rocked Daniel back on his heels. "And that's for the sucker punch."

Daniel dabbed his mouth with the back of his hand, and it came away with a spot of blood. Then he stepped in, fists flying.

Noble clinched up and withstood the onslaught. He caught glancing blows to his shoulders, head, and midsection. Then he short-stepped back and threw a hook to Daniel's huge jaw that sent his head twisting around.

Daniel roared and came in, great arms reaching, trying to wrap Noble up.

Noble popped him with two more quick shots to the head, then another to the body. It was like hitting a slab of beef. Solid and thick with muscle.

A wild fist caught Noble in the side, and he twisted away. Parted for a moment, each took time to catch their breath. Daniel knew little of fighting. His skills were limited, but Noble had learned much in his travels. He'd sparred with a few boxers over the years. He knew how to throw a punch and how to take one.

Noble eyed his brother and wiped the edge of his fist over the split in one cheek. It came away bloody.

Whatever Daniel lacked in skill he made up for in power.

"Not going," Daniel slurred.

Suddenly, both were punching away toe to toe. Daniel scored again on Noble's eye. Noble caught Daniel coming in and smashed his nose flat. Both slugged away. They fought that way for what seemed like minutes, then fell apart.

Blood trickled down from a cut above Daniel's eye. Noble had one eye swelling shut. His side ached like he'd cracked a rib.

Daniel moved in and threw a wide haymaker intended to end the fight. Noble ducked it and slugged away at his younger brother's midsection. Daniel let out a grunt and threw Noble off with both hands. He was hurt now, favoring one side, when he stepped back in. There was a determined look in his eye.

Noble let his brother walk into an uppercut that sent him to the ground. Noble stood and spit a wad of blood and gunk to one side. He turned and started for the horses when Daniel caught him around the knees and threw him down.

Daniel slugged him twice, but then Noble rolled free and climbed to his feet. His fist met Daniel's jaw as he tried to rise. Daniel rolled back, wavered, started to fall. Noble grabbed his brother's shirtfront with one hand and caught him up. Twice more he punched Daniel in the head, then let his brother fall on his back.

Grace screamed and ran for her husband.

Picking up his hat, Noble walked to the waiting horse. He set the saddle blanket in place, then slung the saddle up and tightened the cinch. When he turned back, Grace and her children were gathered over Daniel. Jack and Ester's eyes were red from tears.

"He shouldn't have sucker punched me," Noble said.

Grace leapt to her feet and stomped over to him then. She reached back and slapped him full across the face. Noble felt the bite on his cheek from her wedding ring. He reached up and wiped away the blood from where it sliced his cheek.

"How dare you," Grace said. "He was right. We never should have brought an animal like you back here. Better if you'd never come."

"You sent for me," Noble countered.

Grace's arm shot back again, but Noble caught it this time.

"You're a dirty murderer, and I hate you," she said.

Noble let go of her arm and climbed into the saddle. "When your husband wakes up, ask him what he did to your father. See if you believe him."

"What?" Grace said. "Don't speak about my father."

"You ask Daniel what really happened the night I left. Ask him what right he has to call me murderer. His hands aren't so clean. I took the blame for him all those years ago."

"You . . . you lie," she said. "You're lying. Daniel would never . . ."

"You ask him and see if he tells you the truth. You tell him our father knew," Noble said. "All along, he knew."

Noble looked from Grace to his mother. Emilia still stood on the porch. No tears from her, of course. She was too hard for that. But there was something else in that one look; he knew then that his mother too had always known the truth. That was to be expected. Different as his parents might be, they didn't keep things from each other.

I'd lay money it was her that figured the whole thing out. How did she convince Father though? It would take a lot to convince him that his favorite son was a killer.

Noble spurred his horse, and Cactus followed. Whatever his brother might think, he had to save the Rafter, to keep it safe, and catching the rustlers would be the next step.

With Vern Ollie's help, Grace got her husband into bed. His forehead was hot, so she laid a damp cloth over him.

"Grace," he suddenly cried out.

"I am here, Daniel," she said, and brushed the hair back from his battered face.

"Grace . . . I . . ." He slipped back into unconsciousness.

He'd been beaten badly, his face was cut and swollen and covered in terrible bruises. Daniel was a strong man, powerful, but he hadn't the experience fighting that Noble did.

Noble fought like a savage.

The floor creaked behind her, and Emilia walked in, carrying a washbasin and a stack of clean linen. Without a word, she set them on the dresser. Then she pulled a chair over and set about washing the rest of Daniel's wounds. The room's only sound was drops falling back into the basin.

"My poor boy," she said, and dabbed the wet linen around his eyes. The cloth came away bloodstained. She squeezed it out and streams of red tinted the water.

Grace only watched her. Emilia had caused this. All of it. Daniel's beating was her fault. She'd been the one who wanted Noble here, and she'd forced Grace to help her. If not for his return, none of this would have happened. Sam would be alive. Her husband wouldn't be lying in bed with broken bones. Her children wouldn't be in their rooms crying and sick with worry for their father.

Emilia caused it all and now she was in here worrying over her "poor boy."

Grace fought down the urge to scream at her, to force her out of the room and out of her home. Doing so would only disturb Daniel. He needed rest. He needed care.

When Emilia finished, the basin's contents

were dyed a sickening red. She took up the basin and linens and left. Grace followed her.

"You weren't worried about him while your son beat him," Grace said when they were clear.

Emilia looked at her with tired eyes and did not speak.

"You let Noble break him."

"Daniel isn't broken," Emilia answered. "Far from it. He will recover, and Gabriel will do what needs to be done to save the Rafter."

"Do you hear that? Your grandchildren are in their rooms. Crying. They think their father is dying. All because you brought him back here."

"Their father isn't dying though. I brought Gabriel back for them."

"For them?"

"What does it matter to me if the ranch is lost? I'm an old woman now. I have no need for cattle or land. I did it all for them."

"And I suppose you'd do it again, wouldn't you?" Grace said. She couldn't believe what she was hearing. How could Emilia be so careless after what she'd done?

"I would," Emilia said quietly. "What would you do to save your children?"

"I wouldn't let one of them beat the other to death."

"Daniel isn't dying. Far from it." Emilia sighed. "He took a beating, is all."

Anger filled Grace to the bursting. This stubborn old woman.

"And what was all that talk about my father?" Grace said.

Emilia only stared at her.

"My father? Noble said to ask Daniel about him."

Emilia sat down at the kitchen table. She let out a long, tired breath. "I had hoped this secret would stay buried."

"What secret?"

"You remember coming to us from Riggins? Your father couldn't feed you. The man was a shiftless drunkard, and so he threw you out into the cold. It was wintertime. A storm passed through, and snow lay piled up high around the eaves of the house. Sam and I were out riding. It was the first clear day in a week, with more snow moving in. You were huddled beneath an old pine tree, soaked to the skin and shivering. You'd gotten a fire started somehow, but not much would burn. It was all too wet."

"I know all that," Grace said. "I remember how you found me. I remember how cold it was. I thought I'd lose my toes with frostbite."

"Sam and I raised you as our own. I always wanted a little girl. We thought we were done having children. The boys both loved you from the moment they saw you. . . ." Emilia's voice dropped off.

"What does that have to do with my father?" Grace said.

"Nine years you were with us," Emilia said. "You were with him for seven years in Riggins. You were more ours than his, but he came for you one night. Drunk as usual, he came out here and wanted to take you away."

Grace felt her breath catch. She'd never seen her father after he'd thrown her out in the cold. She thought he'd died soon after. To learn only now that he had been alive and that he'd come for her . . . Was he alive still?

"I wanted to fight him," Emilia went on. "I told him I'd shoot him if I ever saw him again. Sam though—Sam was a man of peace. He said you belonged to him, and we should give you up. Your father changed his mind by then though. He came by a day later and said we could keep you if we paid him. Said for twenty dollars he'd leave and never return."

Emilia scowled. "Twenty dollars. That's all you were worth to him, Grace. Sam paid though, I begged him not to, and your father left. We didn't see him for another year. I told Sam he would come back, that he'd want more money, and I was right. Three more times he came, and three more times Sam paid him."

Twenty dollars. My father gave me up for twenty dollars.

A tear rolled down Grace's cheek. It was

worse than thinking she'd been abandoned. She couldn't imagine selling Ester or Little Jack for twenty dollars. Not for any amount.

"The last time he came, we weren't home. We were in Helena buying more cattle for the ranch. You'd come with us, but the boys stayed here with Cactus and the others. When your father arrived, he ran into Daniel first. Your father asked where you were. Said he wanted pay for use of his little girl. He was an ugly drunk. He implied . . . he implied some awful things about you."

Emilia paused and cleared her throat.

"Daniel lost his temper. He was bigger than your father, even at seventeen. He beat your father, and he kept beating him. When Gabriel found them, your father was dead, and Daniel was soaked to his elbows in blood. Together Gabriel and Daniel buried your father in one of the ravines in the west range. I don't know where. Gabriel cleaned Daniel up and then took him to the house. When we got back from Helena, he was gone."

"Gabriel took the blame for it." Grace was clearly upset. "That's why he left. That's why he went away without a word."

"Gabriel always wanted to see the world. Daniel never wanted anything more than the Rafter. Gabriel loved his brother so much he took the blame for your father's disappearance. So Daniel could stay."

"But they could have both stayed. They could have kept the secret."

Emilia shook her head. "Your father told too many people where he was going and why. Said he was off to collect money from the Bartletts. There would have been questions. Everyone knew Gabriel had a temper. Everyone knew how dangerous he was. He left, and they assumed he'd killed your father. Sheriff McCandles came out and asked a few questions, but with Gabriel gone and your father missing, everyone was content to let the matter drop."

"How did you know? If Daniel didn't tell you, how do you know all of this?"

"Cactus figured it out. He'd been out with some of the other hands, away from the house when your father arrived. When Gabriel and Daniel didn't come in for supper, he went out and tracked them. He found your father. He saw your father's wounds. Daniel's swollen hands."

"Everything I know is built on lies," Grace said.

"No, dear." Emilia rose and helped Grace into a chair. She held Grace close and stroked her hair. "You have a home. You have a husband and two children that adore you. You are loved here. None of this changes that."

Grace buried her face in Emilia's shirt.

"My father sold me for twenty dollars," she said. Tears welled up in her eyes and spilled over.

Chapter 19

Noble set a blistering pace after the rustlers.

The fight with Daniel had delayed him, but that would not stop him. He and Cactus rode hard for several hours, crossing off Rafter range, swinging east around Riggins, and continuing south toward the Wyoming border.

At last the rustlers had turned again, this time along a dry wash. Noble reined in and studied their tracks.

"They've gone east now," he said.

"Looks like it," Cactus grunted in agreement.

"Do you know where this wash goes?" Noble asked. Cactus had ranged over this country for years; he knew every swell and draw for forty miles.

"East another mile, then south. Ends at the very southern edge of the Webster place."

"Doesn't make sense," Noble said. "When he was out at the ranch, Grant said the rustlers were off the Circle Bar."

Cactus shrugged. "Must have been mistaken."

Noble considered the problem. Grant wasn't one to make mistakes. The rustlers might only be passing through this time, or they could be using it only when no one was around. Grant had business in town. He might not know the place well enough or be out often enough to catch them.

"How far behind them are we, you figure?" Noble said. He picked up a clump of mud the stolen cattle's hooves had disturbed and squeezed it between his fingers. Still damp.

Cactus studied the sun, then the tracks. The day had grown hot, and the mud from the rain was starting to bake. "Couple hours, no more'n that," he said.

That matched Noble's own thoughts.

"Can we save time going overland? Maybe get out ahead of them?"

"Sure," Cactus nodded. "There's an old trail the Sioux used up over those hills there. Should shave some time off."

"Lead the way," Noble said, and then they set off again.

The afternoon was edging in toward night by the time they saw the end of the wash. They were coming down out of the hills two miles south of the Circle Bar corrals, where Noble had seen the rustlers working over stock earlier. The stolen Rafter cattle were just coming out of the wash. Four rustlers were driving them, all well within rifle range.

Noble drew his rifle. Firing from the saddle was tricky, but he'd done it before. To have much chance of hitting anything, you had to either stop completely or time your shots with the horse's strides. Being close helped.

He took aim at the lead man, held a breath, and squeezed. His first bullet took that lead rustler in the shirt pocket. Cactus's shot wounded a man on a short black-and-white pinto mare. Noble cycled the action and swung to his next target. He recognized this one, the one who hid in the brush when they'd tried to ambush his brother; the one they'd called Rudy. Noble's first and second shots missed. Smoke rose from Rudy's own rifle. Noble heard an angry buzz pass overhead.

Noble adjusted his aim and squeezed the trigger a third time. Rudy took the bullet in the side and spilled from the saddle.

Smoke rose from the last man's rifle, but Cactus's aim proved true. His bullet took him in the throat, and that left only the one wounded man on the pinto mare. He was riding hard, heading back up through the wash. Cactus lined up for a shot when Noble called out.

"Let him go."

Cactus eyed him and said, "Thought you was all for wiping them out."

"I am. But he'll leave a nice trail to wherever the rest are hiding."

"Good thinking," Cactus said. "What about this other one?"

In his tumble, Rudy had lost his rifle. He lay on the ground, one hand on his wounded side, the other palm open in surrender. Noble sat his horse, looking down at Rudy. He held his rifle in one hand, barrel pointed at Rudy's midsection.

"No prisoners this time, Rudy. Nobody is here to save you," Noble said.

"I can help you," Rudy said. "I can tell you where he's going."

"I can track where he's going," Noble said. "Cactus, where's the nearest tree tall enough for a hangin'?"

"Back up those hills. Take some time to get there though."

"Bad news, Rudy, we don't have much time. We need to be along after your friend."

"Wait . . . Wait . . . Wait. Please," Rudy said. "He's going to Riggins. We're meeting the boss there."

"That don't tell me nothin'," Noble said. "Tell me something useful or I'll tie a rope around your neck and let your horse drag you to death."

"Gage. Gage Banier. That's who Tom's going to meet. He's who we work for, but he's not the man in charge."

"Who is?"

"I don't know. I don't know. Please!" Rudy said. There was blood on his lips now. Noble's shot had gone deep. Rudy wouldn't need hanging. He'd be gone soon enough.

"Cactus, get me that horse. We'll tie him by the neck like the Sioux used to."

"Please. Please, no," Rudy said with a cough. "I don't want to be dragged."

"Then tell me something useful," Noble said. "Who's in charge? Where are they keeping the stolen cattle? Who killed Sam Bartlett? Who killed my father?"

"Bartlett," Rudy said. His breath became ragged now, chest heaving. "Pelton killed . . ." He started to say more, but the words were lost as his head dropped slack.

"Pelton," Noble repeated. He knew the name. He knew the man as well—a remorseless killer out of Arkansas. No good with a pistol, but deadly with any kind of rifle. He'd been a marksman during the war, and a good one. They sent him after the Union officers. Legend said he'd killed five colonels and even a general at Bull Run.

After the war, he'd gone hunting buffalo and when they were gone, he'd discovered hunting men paid better.

Pelton was not a good man to have on your trail.

Gage Banier was one of the rustlers' leaders. That wasn't much of a surprise. Gage had fought in the cattle war in Texas. He'd been on the opposite side from Noble. The two had not met during that particular mess. Gage had killed Noble's boss though. That killing had brought about the end and resulted in Noble being wanted for murder.

Since then, Gage had built up a fearsome reputation. He'd fought all manner of gunfighters, east and west. He always sold his gun to the highest bidder. Gage wasn't the type to do this on his own though. He didn't care for cattle, and if he was working for someone they had deep pockets.

That narrowed the list down. There were few men in Bigsby with any kind of money. But did they have to be from Bigsby? What if it was someone from the outside looking to get their start in ranching?

Gage had done it before. That had been just the way it began down in Texas.

Someone like the cattle buyer Grant had introduced me to? Or the new man in town? The one with money but no one knew how he'd come by it?

There could be others, of course. The country had changed since Noble left, and so had the people.

"You can follow the trail?" Noble asked Cactus.

"Easy enough. I winged him pretty good. He's bleeding a lot. I don't think he'll stop to patch himself up. Not the way he was running."

"Let's go then," Noble said. "I want to know who's behind all this. Gage Banier will know, and if not, we'll have to find Pelton."

"I heard about both of them. Bad ones. Real killers."

"You heard the right of it," Noble said. "Guess we'll just have to get them first."

• • •

Noble and Cactus followed the trail up the dry wash and out onto the plains and then to the mountains.

Once he left the dry wash, the wounded rustler took a hard left and rode straight for Riggins. He'd ridden hard; hard enough that Noble was surprised he'd managed to stay in the saddle. Noble and Cactus followed at their own much slower pace until they lost the trail at the edge of town.

"Too many people coming and going," Cactus said. The rustler's tracks blended in with a dozen others. "But he won't go much farther."

"Is there a doctor in town?" Noble said.

"Man named Fleck calls himself a doctor, but he's not much more than an old sawbones. Think he served in the Reb army hacking off limbs and such," Cactus said. "If I was sick, he wouldn't be my first choice, but he's all Riggins has."

"Any idea where we'll find him?"

"Office in the middle of town. Rundown, like everything else."

"Seems to be more people here than I remembered." Noble had noticed that on his earlier visit, and it was even more pronounced on this night. The streets ran full of miners and freighters. A line of men waited outside the Aces High saloon. The place was packed too full to admit them.

"Must be payday for the mines. They hit a vein of silver two years ago. It ain't much, but it's been slowly drawing people in. Got the old mines headin' down deeper. Everybody dreamin' of being rich again. Even the Three Timbers is operatin'."

Three Timbers, the biggest, deepest mine from the old days, sat halfway up the mountain. In the growing dark, Noble could see lanterns at the shaft entrance.

"They still think it's haunted?"

"Some do. Locals refuse to go in, but there's a lot of new, desperate men in town willing to take the risk," Cactus said.

Riggins's slow death had begun with the accident in Three Timbers. It was a gold mine, the only successful one to operate in the valley. Men who'd been inside said the vein was two inches wide for the first three hundred feet, high-grade ore, and after that they were seeing signs of the mine growing richer yet. Four more smaller veins intersected it, though each of them had played out after another hundred feet. Three Timbers's end had been quick.

Noble had been five at the time.

Two days before Christmas, on the verge of what they claimed was a huge discovery, thirty-seven men died when the main shaft collapsed. It had been a wet year. Some said the ground soaked up so much moisture the rock grew unstable. Others claimed a charge went off while they were hauling explosives down.

Whatever the cause, when the smoke and dust finally cleared, thousands of tons of loose rock blocked the main tunnel for at least two hundred feet. They tried sinking a second entrance. It collapsed after a hundred feet and showed no signs of ore.

Ownership changed hands several times that Noble knew of. Each group promised to reopen the mine. One managed to drop a shaft and intersect one of the branch tunnels. Miners tried getting back into the main tunnel where the vein had been, but it remained blocked. Search as they might, they never found any gold, and that finally killed the Three Timbers and the mines in Riggins.

Or it did until now.

"Are they pulling much out?" Noble said. He'd been to gold camps before—the signs of a boom were here—but most booms played out within a few months.

"Just enough to tease them," Cactus said. "Or so I hear. I'm no miner. No gold, but some silver. I wouldn't know the stuff if I saw it. Heard it was a gray-purple color."

They tied their horses at a hitching rail beneath a sign that said simply Doc Fleck's.

"I don't know if he can rightly spell doctor." Cactus laughed.

The town was lit up from all the saloon-hall lamps. Noble swept the toe of his boot along the dusty walk in front of the doc's office.

"No sign of blood," Noble said. He knocked on the door, and no one answered.

"Maybe he found his friends, and they fetched the doc to him."

"Maybe," Noble grunted. "Let's check the saloons first. I'm guessing we'll come across someone I recognize."

"Your party," Cactus shrugged. "You know what Banier looks like?"

"I do. Him and Pelton both. You'll know them when you see them." Aside from those two, there was also the chance that they'd find more rustlers from the Circle Bar. Noble remembered several from his time studying the place.

"Where do we start?" Cactus asked.

There were at least five saloons, another three hotels where they could hide a wounded man, not to mention the numerous shacks and shanties on the back streets.

"Up one side and then the other," Noble said. "I'll look inside each. You keep an eye on the street. If I'm not out in five minutes, follow me in. What's this Doc Fleck look like?"

"Short, wiry, glasses, like most every other doc I've ever seen. Carries a black bag loaded down with tools and bottles," Cactus answered. "Not sure he knows how to use most of them."

The bag at least would stand out in the crowd.

The first two saloons were full up to the rafters. Noble pressed between poker tables, saloon girls, and outright drunks, but he saw no one he recognized.

The third saloon, Miner's Hole, was the fullest yet. They had an old upright piano against the wall and a greasy man in a vest banged away at it. The notes were well out of tune, but the crowd didn't seem to notice as they raised their glasses and sang away. Noble stepped to the side and looked out over the crowd. A man at the bar tickled his memory. It could have been one of the rustlers he and Daniel had run off back in the canyon. Then he saw it. A black bag lay half open on an empty poker table in the back. The only empty poker table he'd seen so far that night. He shouldered his way through the crowd, jostling miners aside until he reached it.

He opened the bag. He recognized several tools and number of bottles, some filled with powders, others with dark liquids.

"I'll thank you not to touch that," a man said behind him.

The man was on the short side, maybe five-four, lean and spare, with spectacles and some sort of medical instrument hanging around his neck.

"You're Fleck then?"

"I am Doctor Fleck. And those are mine."

"I'm looking for a friend of mine. He rode in here wounded about an hour ago. Had some trouble out on the plains and caught a bad one."

Fleck adjusted his spectacles higher on his nose; his eyes fell on Noble's guns.

"I see," he said. He licked his lips and went on, "I removed the bullet and left him in the care of his other friends. I'm not sure where they took him."

"You're certain of that?" Noble squared up to face him, and Fleck seemed to shrink in on himself. "You don't have any idea where they might be?"

"I know right where they are," a new voice said.

Noble turned to face the newcomer and knew him at once.

Gage Banier. The gunman laid a hand on Fleck's shoulder. "No need to bother the good doctor here, Noble. I'll be happy to answer your questions."

Noble shifted slightly, enough to square himself up against Banier. There were four other men in Banier's wake, each looking right at Noble. Five against one, and one of those was Gage. Poor odds.

Noble eased his hands closer to his pistol grips.

"No need for that now," Banier said. "Doc, why don't you collect your bag and be on your way. Your services won't be needed here."

Fleck hesitated, clearly frightened of Banier, then snatched up the bag and disappeared into the crowd.

"Now then, Noble. Where were we?"

"Last time I was here, you bought me a drink. Seems like a good time to return the favor. Will your friends be joining us?"

Banier grinned. "They're not the thirsty types. They'll just keep an eye on things. Johnny, go get us a bottle and two glasses. I've been thinking about Laredo lately. I think about it a lot."

"I don't," Noble said.

"Oh? But you and I, we never got to finish our game."

Johnny returned. Staying clear of his boss, he set the bottle and glasses on the table and moved back out of the way.

"Was it a game? Some good men died there— one at least—and others got the law set after them," Noble said.

"Casualties of war," Banier said. With his left hand, he pulled the cork from the bottle and then filled both glasses. He hoisted one in salute.

Noble took the other with his right hand. One of the men in the back twitched.

"Not now!" Banier stopped them.

But the man behind him was slow to listen. His hand fell on his holstered gun. Noble didn't slow. He threw the whiskey in Banier's face and drew his left gun. He shot the man who'd moved first, and then kicked the table into the rest of them. He snapped off a hasty shot at a falling Banier but knew instantly it had missed.

"DOWN," Cactus said.

Noble dropped to the floor a split second before a scattergun erupted into the group of rustlers. Noble sprung to his feet. By now miners and dancing girls were fleeing the bar, and he joined them. Cactus came out just behind him.

"Get to the horses," Noble said.

They ran for the doctor's office then. Behind them, one of the rustlers reached the street and fired. The shots were wild, striking the ground, the buildings ahead, or nothing at all.

Noble snapped off two quick shots, and the rustler screamed before vanishing back inside. Noble jerked his horse's reins loose, and then he and Cactus were off and running out of town. As they passed the last house, Noble saw a lean man in buckskins walking down the street, carrying a long rifle over his shoulder.

Pelton.

Noble drew and fired three times. The range was far and the chances of scoring a hit low, but the manhunter dove behind a water trough.

"That was Pelton," Noble said. "We've got to get out of the open."

Though it was dark, the moon shone bright and clear, and they could see for a long way. Long enough for Pelton to get a shot off.

A rifle boomed behind them, and Noble heard the bullet buzz by.

Cactus turned a little to the left, and they dropped down into a sandy arroyo. Noble followed. They kept the horses to a run for several minutes, then eased up. Running in the deep sand would tire them quickly. Cactus led the way up an old cow trail onto the hard plains.

"They'll be after us," Noble said, and swore.

The tables had been turned. What started out as a hunt after a wounded man had turned into a desperate escape. They needed to lose their pursuit and get back to the ranch, where they at least had more help.

"Tough to figure out where we climbed out of that arroyo given all that sand. It'll take them some time," Cactus said. "I got an idea though on where we might lose them."

They rode north and west until they dropped into the big canyon at the base of the Bitterroots. They kept their horses in the stream for a good half mile, then turned onto a flat span of hard gravel. The gravel pack stretched out east into a side canyon. This branch of the canyon wasn't long; it ended in a slope of hard talus. The horses scrambled up the talus and out onto the plains again.

"By the time they find where we came out, we'll be back on the Rafter," Cactus said.

Noble wasn't sure how much good that would

do. He couldn't face down all of them at once, not with Pelton and Banier involved. It was too much for him. He needed help, and game as Cactus was, he was long in the tooth. The Rafter needed more fighters.

Or I need to put Pelton and Banier out of it.

He'd have to get them alone; together or with their men they were too dangerous. Pelton wasn't a gunfighter, but out on the plains or in the woods, he was by far the worst of the two. Banier would at least come straight at you. He'd always put himself into the most favorable position, sure, to have the sun in your eyes, make sure he had backup handy, but when he thought he had enough of an advantage, you would see him coming.

With Pelton, you would never know. Still, they had accomplished much this day. Four of the enemy were out of it: Three dead and one severely wounded.

He and Cactus would be needed to protect the ranch. In a fight, Vern Ollie was an unknown quantity. Cactus said the kid had sand, and Cactus had always been a good judge of character. But he couldn't expect an unproven kid to guard the Rafter alone.

We'll have to wait until they make their move.

Action would be better. Force them into making a mistake. But in this case, outgunned and outmanned as they were, he couldn't see any other way but to wait.

Maybe the marshal would arrive and be of some help. Grant had said the town had sent for him. He should be due to arrive any day now. Even as he thought it, Noble knew it wouldn't be enough. The Rafter wouldn't be safe until the rustlers were gone and the man behind it all dispatched along with them.

McCandles won't be enough for Banier. He might thin out the rest, but Gage is beyond him.

What was it Banier said? "We never got to finish our game."

We didn't finish in Texas, but it ends here, in Montana.

Chapter 20

His grandfather's cabin was quiet when Noble arrived home. It was late, well after midnight. Clarissa would be asleep.

Noble crept inside, taking care not to make enough noise to wake her. The fire was low. Clarissa had forgotten to bank it against the chilly night. Usually she wasn't so forgetful; no doubt she had a lot on her mind.

He started for the fireplace, pausing when he noticed a shadowy figure sitting in his grandfather's chair.

"Who?" Noble asked. It wasn't Clarissa; the figure was too short and too spare. Clarissa had filled out the last few weeks.

"I wish you would have spared Grace that," Emilia said.

"Seven years I spared her. I was tired of living a lie while he . . ."

"While he what?" His mother's voice was smooth, but he heard the anger she held back. "Married Grace and lived the life you wanted?"

Noble didn't speak. He didn't trust himself to say anything.

"Would you have done what your brother has?"

"No. Not that. I never would have stayed."

"And Grace could not live a life on the trail."

"I shouldn't have said anything. I was just tired. Tired of him always looking down on me like I'm worthless. Tired of the judgment and lies." Noble took his hat off and set it brim up on the table.

"You never cared what anyone thought. Not even when you were a boy. Are you more upset with Daniel or Grace?"

"I couldn't take the way she looked at me. Like I was nothing but a killer."

"And now she knows her husband killed her father. What you really wanted was to hurt your brother, and you wanted to hurt her."

Again. Noble said nothing.

Emilia leaned back and sighed. "Grace knows the truth now. The whole of it."

"I wanted not to be the bad brother," Noble said. "Just once, I wanted her to look at him the way she looked at me. Father knew the whole time. All that preaching about violence and truth and how I was the evil son, and he knew. He knew what Daniel did."

"Your father never thought you were evil, Gabriel. He didn't understand you. He couldn't understand how one of his sons could do the things you did."

Noble's pistol appeared in his hand. "That I could use this? That I could fight? That I could kill? I didn't want to. Never really did. But I didn't have a choice."

"All of that, yes," Emilia said. "But also that

you could leave. That you could go out and start over on your own. Your brother and father aren't like that. The Bartletts are builders, not explorers. Your father understood violence well enough. He didn't agree with it, but he understood."

"I've wasted my life. Roaming town to town and fight to fight, barely scraping by. I haven't explored anything. I haven't started over."

Noble slammed the pistol back into the holster.

"That's why I need to save the Rafter. I need the money. So I can start over. I know places. Places where a gunfighter named Noble can disappear, and I can leave him far behind."

"And her?" Emilia nodded to the closed door. "What about Clarissa?"

"What about her?"

"That girl loves you."

"She thinks she does. She doesn't know me. I'm no good. The best thing I can do is leave her with some money and get her started on her own. Then I'll vanish, and she'll be better off."

"She wouldn't say that."

"She doesn't know. I do. I've done bad things, terrible things. The truth is, everything Father said about me is true. I've fought. I've sold my gun. I've killed for money. I'm no kind of man fit for her." Noble straightened. "And I'm willing to admit it. I won't saddle her or anyone else up with a man like me. At least I can spare her that."

"Is that it?" Emilia said. "Because your

Grandfather Jack was all those things. He changed. He found love. He found a life and started something grand."

"He got out. I'm not sure I even want to. I'm not sure once I have the money that I won't try and fail utterly to break free from this. Or maybe I'll just blow it all in a poker game. I should just give it to her and go on my own way. Might be for the best."

Emilia rose. "One thing is clear: Neither of my sons understands women. That is my fault, I suppose. I wasn't much of an example. I was so concerned with both of you learning what the ranch needed that I didn't spend enough time teaching what each of you needed."

"You did fine," Noble said, and kissed his mother on the forehead. "You were everything we needed."

Emilia smiled. "We both know that isn't true. But it's nice of you to say." She moved toward the door.

"Tomorrow we need to group up. Cactus and I followed the rustlers. We stopped them. Three of them won't trouble us again, but the cattle they stole need to be recovered."

"I'll tell them," Emilia said. "Anything else?"

"Tell Daniel . . ." Noble hesitated. "Tell him I made a mistake. I shouldn't have told Grace. I am sorry."

"It shouldn't have been a secret for so long.

Grace should have been told years ago. But it was easier this way." Emilia smiled. "The right way is rarely easy."

"Tell him I'm sorry all the same."

Emilia nodded and then closed the door.

"How many are there?" Emilia asked.

She and the rest of the Rafter family—Grace, Daniel, their two children, Vern Ollie, and Clarissa—all listened while Noble and Cactus had outlined the danger they were in. They'd told it all, the catching of the rustlers, the shootout, following them into Riggins, Gage Banier, and then their desperate escape.

"Around eight. Six rustlers plus Banier and Pelton," Noble said. Numbers alone didn't represent the true danger. The rustlers would be hard, tough men. Worse yet, Gage Banier and Pelton were each worth five of the others. "Banier and Pelton are by far the most dangerous."

"You think this Pelton fellow killed Father?" Daniel said. His face was bruised and puffy, but his eyes shone clear and bright. He sat in a big, padded chair with Grace holding his hand.

"I can't say for sure," Noble said. "But it fits."

"Was he after Father or one of us?" Daniel said.

Noble swallowed. They wouldn't like the answer, but the truth would keep them alert and possibly alive. "Best guess is he mistook Father for you."

"That can't be," Grace said. "These men have no reason to come after us."

"No, they absolutely do," Noble said. "The Rafter has cattle and land, and men want both. Men like Pelton and Banier won't fight fair. They'll kill and murder to get the Rafter. They wanted to get Daniel. They missed and got Father instead. At a distance, it would be easy to mistake them."

"I don't believe—" Grace started.

"He's right," Cactus said. "This isn't a Sunday social we're talking about. These men aim to kill all of us and take what's ours."

"What do we do, then?" Grace said.

They all looked at Noble. He in turn looked at his battered brother.

"These days I work for the ranch," Noble said. "Daniel is in charge of the Rafter. What do you plan on doing?"

Daniel's broken lips curled. "Ready to listen to me now? Why?"

"It's your family on the line. Seems like it should be your decision. I've only got to worry about me. I can ride away tomorrow, and it won't make a bit of difference. You have a family to care for," Noble said. Clarissa shifted in her chair at that. A frown crossed her face.

Noble didn't like this, not a bit. He and his mother had discussed it though. Responsibility for the ranch fell to Daniel. They couldn't afford to fight among themselves anymore, and it fell to Noble to compromise. Daniel never would.

Daniel started to speak, then stopped. "The marshal should be here any day now. He's a good man. He can sort all this out. We can hole up here until then and stay safe."

Grace let out a long, relieved breath.

Noble shifted his weight from one foot to the other.

"You don't agree?" Daniel said.

"I do," Noble said. "Much as I might like to, we can't defend the Rafter properly if I go out after them. We don't have enough men for it. So we wait for the marshal and hope he can bring us some help. Even one more gun would make a difference."

For a long time, no one spoke. The children shuffled their feet, resting weight on one foot and then the other. Grace wrung her hands. Emilia's rocking chair creaked.

"We should ride to town tomorrow," Daniel finally said.

Noble didn't think he'd heard his brother correctly. First Daniel wanted to do the right thing, to hole up and wait, and now he talked about riding into town, where trouble would be waiting. The idea was a sound one.

He wasn't the only one taken by surprise.

"You aren't well enough to ride Daniel," Grace said. "We've got to wait here."

"I'm fit enough, or I will be tomorrow," Daniel said.

"Daniel Bartlett, this is foolishness. You can barely stand, much less ride to town."

"Cactus will hitch up the team. By now the marshal should be here. We need the law's help. To get it, I need to meet with McCandles."

"But Daniel, dear, I—"

"I won't stand for being coddled." Daniel's voice rose. "Especially while everyone else is out working. Tomorrow I am riding in, one way or the other."

"Emilia, speak sense to him. He doesn't know what he's saying," Grace pleaded.

"I think it's a fine idea," Emilia said.

Grace looked around for support. Vern Ollie and most of the others just stared at the floor. "Cactus, surely you don't."

"He's the boss," Cactus said, and shrugged.

She skipped over Clarissa entirely, and her eyes fell on Noble. "You did this. You convinced him to go to town with your talk of fighting."

"He did not," Daniel said. "We need supplies if we're to stay near the ranch. We need to speak to the marshal too. He needs to be told what's been going on out here."

"Grant can do that," she said. "He'll take care of it."

"Grant is Gabriel's friend, not mine. I never cared much for him, and I don't trust him,"

Daniel said. "Besides, the responsibility is mine and mine alone."

"I'll ride with you," Noble said. "Everyone else can fort up in the houses. They can't clean the Rafter out in a single day."

"All right," Daniel said. "It's settled then."

Chapter 21

The wagon rattled and rolled over the grassy plains, bouncing over the occasional rock or rut. The trail from the Rafter to Bigsby wasn't a smooth one. Other than the monthly supply run, no one ever used the wagon much.

Daniel sat stiffly in the seat. He coaxed the two horses on at a steady pace. Less speed didn't seem to make any difference in the jarring ride, but more would at least end it quicker.

Grace came along. She'd demanded it. Daniel tried to talk her out of it, but she rode on the wagon seat beside her husband, fussing over him like a hen with her first newborn chick.

Daniel looked like he'd rather be anywhere else. He groaned and complained at first, but between subtle scoldings, smothering affection, and alternating hurt or stern looks, Grace wore him down.

Noble rode alongside the wagon—far enough away so that he didn't catch every word, close enough to chuckle at his brother's misery. That brought a scowl from Grace. Noble wondered if Clarissa might behave the same way to her husband.

I very much doubt it. More likely she'd hold

him at gunpoint or tie him up and sit on him if he went against her wishes.

He'd asked Clarissa to stay behind with his mother and the others. The girl could fight in a pinch, and staying on the Rafter would be safer than in town. He hadn't told her that, of course. Instead he'd asked her to protect his mother and the children. If she thought he was keeping her away from harm, she would've insisted on going.

They passed through the hills north of Bigsby, crossing scattered streams and winding around thick stands of aspen, cedar, and ponderosa pine. They'd started early and arrived on the outskirts of town just before noon.

Daniel reined up before they went on in.

"Gabriel, will you ride ahead and make sure it's clear?"

Noble answered with a nod and spurred his horse. His eyes swept the streets as he rode through town, scanning for danger—an open window where a rifleman might fire, a stranger who seemed to be paying too much attention to them.

He saw nothing. He tied his horse at the hitching rail in front of the sheriff's office, then took off his hat and gave an overhead wave to his brother.

While Daniel and Grace came in, Noble kept a sharp eye on either side of the street. Daniel brought the team in quickly, set the brake, and secured the horses. Noble helped Grace down, or rather tried to. She gave him the same deep scowl she would have given a rabid dog, and he took a step back before she jumped down from the wagon.

She landed badly—though she tried to hide it—and winced when her ankle rolled. Noble gave her a little smile.

Serves her right for refusing my help.

Noble turned to keep from laughing and walked over to knock on the sheriff's office. No answer. He knocked again, louder. Still nothing. He tried the door, and it swung open easily. Everything inside was covered in a layer of dust; no one had been in here for at least a week. On the desk lay the shining tin star he'd last seen pinned to Kyle George's chest.

Noble picked it up and rubbed the dust from it.

He heard Daniel's heavy steps and turned. "Seems like Bigsby needs a new sheriff," he said, and handed Daniel the badge.

Daniel scowled at the tin star, then set it back on the desk and followed Noble out.

"What now?" Daniel said.

"Ask around for the marshal, see if he's here," Noble said.

"Grace and I will go to the general store. We'll buy a few things for the ranch and see what they know."

"I'll go and see Grant. He'll have heard something. See you at the store afterwards."

Noble crossed the street, then walked down until reaching the First National. Grant was waiting on a customer when he entered, the cattle buyer from Colorado. They were deep in conversation, and after catching Grant's eye, Noble took a seat in a chair near the back wall.

When Grant finished up, he escorted the cattle buyer out the front and parted with a handshake. Then he came over to see Noble.

"It's good you came in, Gabriel," Grant said. "It's been a busy few days."

"How so?"

Grant dragged a chair over and leaned in conspiratorially. "The sheriff's gone."

"You thought he was gone earlier," Noble said. That wasn't exactly news.

"I thought he was. Now I'm sure of it. No one's seen him for days. Worse, the marshal has been killed."

"What?"

"Someone shot Tom McCandles down in Eagle Pass. Stagecoach found him. One shot center of his back."

McCandles dead. Their hope for help was lost and gone. "They'll send someone else," Noble said.

"Yes, but when?" Grant shrugged. "Might take

a while, and their first task will be to find who shot Tom, not drive off a few rustlers."

Noble didn't like the thought but could find no fault with it. Grant was right. It might take weeks to get another marshal up this way, and then he wouldn't be interested in the Rafter's problems. Noble couldn't help but think the murder of McCandles and the rustlers were related. Especially given how he'd been murdered. Shot in the middle of the back?

That sounded like Pelton's work.

"Look Gabriel, I didn't want to speak of this before, but your father had several debts."

"Debts? My father?" Noble didn't believe it. More than once, Sam Bartlett had preached against the wickedness of banks and debt. But Daniel and Grace each talked about how bad things had been the last few years. The Rafter had cattle and land, but little in the way of cash money. Noble remembered how surprised Grace had been when Emilia offered to pay him.

"Times have been hard. The Rafter hasn't shipped beef in years. Sam came to me and signed the loan. It wasn't much, not then, but it's grown over the years."

"How much?"

"You need to ship cattle next year. If you do that, the Rafter will be fine. I know you've got a lot riding on you right now. I wish there was something I could do to help."

"Hold off on the loan," Noble said. "Let it wait for another year."

"Sam already asked me that once. More than once, in fact. If I hold off any longer, the debt will only grow larger. My hands are tied. The bank is struggling. You heard about the recent robbery?"

"Surely you can do something. You run this place."

"It isn't my money. I only manage the bank for other people, it's the town's money. I extended the loan out of respect for your father, but there are a lot of newcomers in town. People who aren't from here. People who don't know the Rafter and its history. All they see is an open note and a lot of money owed on an overdue debt."

"Dammit Grant," Noble said. He needed to move faster. He needed to break these rustlers, find where they'd taken the cattle, and return every head he could.

"There is something I could do," Grant said. "If the Rafter doesn't ship cattle next year, the bank will want to take possession. I might convince them to leave a portion of the home place alone. I need to convince them the Rafter's worth more than the loan. There isn't another ranch like it anywhere."

"How big a portion?"

"Say a thousand acres. I could hold that for your family. Keep your mother there, and then there should be enough money left over to care for her."

"A thousand acres." Noble fumbled over the words. How could his father have let the loan grow so large? What had he been thinking?

"I hate to see your family go through all this. Especially after losing your father like that," Grant said. "I swear to you though, I will hold on to something for your mother's sake."

"It'll break her heart to lose the ranch," Noble said.

Grant licked his lips and shifted uncomfortably in his chair. "There's one other thing, Gabriel. I didn't know how to bring this up, so I'll just dive in. I haven't asked you about your past, but . . ."

"Go ahead."

"Did something happen down in Texas? Something about a range war?"

Noble only looked at him.

Grant spread his open palms in a gesture of peace. "There are rumors in town that you're wanted for murder. Worse, they're saying you killed the marshal."

"Me? That's crazy. I've been too busy with Rafter business."

"They're saying Tom knew about Texas and was coming up to take you in."

"That's a lie. We called him in to help with the rustlers. You saw to it yourself."

"I've told everyone that," Grant said. "But

I don't know if they believe me. They know we're friends from the old days. Someone is out there telling them different. They're even saying you're the one behind the rustling."

Gage Banier.
All of this fits the way he operates.

He was dividing the Rafter from the rest of the valley. He'd sent Pelton to kill the marshal, then spread the lie that Noble did it. Then he'd spread those stories about what happened in Texas.

The man doesn't lack for brains.

"Look, Gabriel," Grant said. "You really did me a favor out at the Circle Bar. I sent a couple of men out that way yesterday. They said someone had cleaned out the house, but everything else was in good shape. I feel like I didn't pay you enough for the job."

"I didn't do much," Noble said.

"Regardless, I know things are bad. Nothing's gone the way you planned here. Given all that's happened, you'd probably like to just ride on to the next town."

Grant had that right. How had it all gone so badly?

"I've got an extra thousand I can give you for traveling money. That's on top of what I promised you earlier."

"Traveling money?"

"Put all this behind you. When the marshal arrives—whoever they send—I'll explain everything, and if he stops the rustlers, then great. The Rafter is saved. If not, and your brother doesn't get his cattle to market, I'll see that your mother keeps something." Grant took out a fat stack of new greenbacks. "Either way, there's not much left here for you. Might as well ride off with a little in your pockets."

No one spoke on the long ride back to the Rafter. Noble had told Grace and Daniel about the sheriff's disappearance, the marshal's death, and that he was under suspicion of killing the latter.

Once the townsfolk get to thinking about it, they'll probably decide I killed Kyle George, too.

Some distance apart, Noble followed Daniel and Grace. He let his thoughts roam like a herd of mustangs over the events of the last few weeks.

What was he still doing here?

No one wanted him here. The town thought he'd killed the local lawmen. His brother thought he was a violent gun thug; Noble wasn't sure he was wrong. Now Grace knew it, too.

Noble studied Grace's back as she sat beside his brother. She leaned against Daniel, her head riding on his shoulder, all her earlier anger melted away. The years had been kind to her. She still looked like the girl he'd grown up with.

He hadn't come back for the money. Not really. He'd come back for her. He'd come back thinking he could show her that she had chosen wrong. She would have been better off with him, that the Rafter too would have been better off with him in charge.

The notion was foolish when he thought about it.

She and Daniel had each other; they had their children. Noble had a gun, a fast horse, and no kind of life for a woman like Grace.

And Clarissa? What about her?

His mother's questions had raised the subject. Before, the plan had been simple: ride in, save the Rafter, show them they needed him, show them all that he was the better brother, and then ride off with enough money for a clean start. Clarissa he could leave with a stake and her own fresh start.

Only now he found that he didn't want to leave her in some rundown town or mining camp. He didn't want to leave her at all.

That kind of thinking gets a man killed.

They crested a little rise and saw lights from the ranch house in the far distance. Too many lights. Something was wrong. Then Noble knew what it was. Gouts of flame were rising from the barn.

"Daniel," Noble said.

"I see it," Daniel growled.

"What?" Grace said as she came awake. Then she too noticed the flames. "What's happening?"

"Someone has set fire to the barn," Daniel said.

"Jack. Ester," Grace said. "We've got to get to them."

Daniel whipped the team to speed. Noble's stallion overtook them in three strides and flew out ahead. He didn't hear any shots. Whatever had happened was over by now. The thought sickened him. Clarissa, his mother, Grace's children. They'd been under attack, and he hadn't been there.

The stallion must have sensed his need. It ate up the space in what seemed like moments.

Noble had his gun drawn when he cleared the yard. If anyone had been hurt, he'd kill every man responsible.

He saw his mother first, her face stained with black soot. He jumped down and looked her up and down.

"Ma, are you alright?"

Emilia only nodded and stared at the burning barn. "Your grandfather built it. Hauled the lumber in from the west range. Took him three years. Your father helped. Said it was the one thing they agreed on: the need to build something lasting."

"Where are the others?" Noble said.

No answer.

"Mother, where is Clarissa?"

"She took Jack and Ester to the graveyard. Took them up there to be safe."

Cactus came out from behind the bunkhouse

then, limping on his left leg and using a rifle with a busted stock for a crutch. Someone had tied a rag around the leg to staunch the bleeding, but his pants were stained a wet, black color. His face was pale as the moon.

"Hit us an hour ago," Cactus said. "Caught me out fetching water."

Noble was already back in the saddle. He spurred the stallion for the mesa behind the houses. Clouds of dust rose with every footfall. The horse was out of breath when they crested the top.

"Clarissa," Noble said. "Clarissa!"

The night was still and dark, the flames from the barn lit only the high treetops. Deep shadows stirred behind his grandfather's headstone, the largest one up there.

"We're here," Clarissa said from behind the stone. "We're safe."

Noble leaped off the horse and ran to her. He embraced her and kissed her, hard and long. Then he said, "I wasn't sure what I'd do without you."

Clarissa caught her breath and smiled up at him. "Your mother and Vern and Cactus held them off. I shot one. He won't bother women no more. But then more rode down from the east. Your mother said to take Jack and Ester and come here."

"I'm glad you did," Noble said. He looked at Ester standing beside Clarissa, and Jack a little farther behind.

"I didn't have a gun," Jack said. "I should have had a gun. I need a gun."

"You did well enough to get your sister and Clarissa away and keep them safe," Noble said. "That was the job, not to get yourself shot at."

"She kept us safe." Jack pointed to Clarissa. "I didn't do anything."

"You looked after your sister while I watched," Clarissa said. "That was important."

"No, it wasn't. I didn't do anything," Jack said. His face was wet with tears.

"Jack, Ester!" came Daniel's big voice.

He was on the mesa top then and rushing past Clarissa and Noble. He wrapped up Ester in his enormous arms. On his heels, Grace went to Jack and bent over him, kissing his head and holding him tight.

"I didn't do anything," Jack said. Despite his mother's attention, he looked only at Noble. "I need a gun."

Chapter 22

By morning nothing remained of the barn but a pile of black and gray cinders.

"It's gone," Emilia said. "All gone."

It wasn't. The ranch houses, the bunkhouse, they all still stood. Except for a section of railing, the one nearest the barn, even the corral survived.

The horses ran loose. Vern Ollie had managed to free them before the fire got too high. Some were singed by the flames. Two had to be put down.

Clarissa told them what had happened.

"They came in just before dark. No more than an hour before you returned. Five of them riding abreast up the valley," she said. "We weren't sure who they were. They didn't start firing until they were close. They shot Cactus in the leg. We fought back."

She glanced at Noble then. "Your mother killed one. I think I killed another. We were winning. They shot Vern after they set fire to the barn and he freed the horses. Then there were more of them. They came riding down from the hills. That's when your mother sent me to take the little ones away."

They found Vern Ollie a hundred yards south of the barn. He'd been shot three times, once in the front, twice in the back. Then they'd trampled his young body beneath their horse's hooves for good measure.

It was beyond cruel, and Noble knew who had done it and what message Vern's body had been intended to send. The man he'd worked for down in Texas had been murdered in exactly the same fashion.

Gage Banier had killed him, too.

Whatever his faults, Vern died for the Rafter. He'd earned his place of honor among the men from Texas. They buried him in the Rafter cemetery after a small ceremony.

At the end of the burial, Noble caught Clarissa's hand and waited for the others to leave.

"We should leave," he said. He held his hat in his hands, turning it round and round by the brim.

"Yes, the others are waiting," she agreed.

"No, I mean really leave," Noble said. "Go somewhere else, away from here."

"Where would we go?"

"Anywhere but here. We can start over fresh."

"Both of us?" Clarissa said. "You won't leave me, will you? You talked about it."

"No."

She looked at the buildings below. "What will happen here?"

"Does it matter?"

Clarissa didn't say anything. She took Noble's hand and waited for him to replace his hat before they started down.

Tomorrow. Tomorrow they would put all this—the Rafter, his brother, Grace, all of this—behind them. They could ride on. Ride on and start again. Just him and her. Grant had given his word. His mother would be taken care of. Daniel and Grace would find their own way. Daniel had skills enough to make it.

Would it be home though? Would it be the Rafter?

No, but they'll all be alive. Alive and together, and that's what matters.

"I've got two pack animals from the Rafter. Daniel won't mind us taking them. He owes me that much," Noble said. "We'll take only what we need. Food, clothes, supplies."

Clarissa moved quickly, wasting no time. She piled up what they needed on the table while Noble sacked it all up and carried it out to the waiting horses.

"Where will we go?" she asked.

"Don't know. West. Idaho or Oregon, maybe."

"I've never seen the ocean," Clarissa said. "Is it really so blue and deep, like they say?"

"Blue and deep and frothing at the edges."

"How wide is it? Like a lake?"

"Wide enough you can't see the other side. Biggest lake you ever saw."

Clarissa brought out more supplies. Between their four horses, they could carry a considerable amount. Noble listened as she moved. He stared at his grandfather's chair. Clarissa had draped a dyed wool blanket over it, a Navajo pattern of blocky red, black, and turquoise.

His own chair rested beside it. For a moment, he considered putting both chairs into the fireplace. It wasn't right that someone else should sit in his or his grandfather's chair. It wasn't right that someone else should live here, in his grandfather's home.

Clarissa interrupted his thoughts. "What about the money?"

"Money?" Noble said.

"What will we do for money?"

"I have money, enough to get us going," Noble said absently.

Noble left the chairs as they were. It wasn't in him to burn them. He needed to leave something behind, some sign of the Rafter, of his grandfather, of himself. This cabin wasn't much. Two chairs were even less, but they would have to be enough.

The horses climbed the long, winding trail up out of the little valley. Noble looked back once, at the very crest, before moving on. They crossed the Rafter quickly; Noble caught sight of the home place only once, between the trees and hills. He hadn't told Daniel about his plan. He hadn't told Grace or his mother or Cactus or anyone else. No one.

Just like all those years ago.

They dropped into the canyon, making their way through and coming up the other side. Then they climbed up onto the overlook at the edge of the Bitterroots. The same one they'd paused at on the ride there. They stopped for one last look over the edge.

"It's a pretty valley," Clarissa said. "I can see why your grandfather settled here."

"It was empty back then. A few Indians is all," Noble said. "No towns, no other people. Not even another cow."

"I bet it was beautiful."

"Yes. Wild and free," Noble said.

"You said you had money enough to get us started?"

"I do."

"I thought you were broke."

"I was."

"Where did you get money, then?" Clarissa looked at him askance.

"Grant. My friend Grant gave me some. Said I'd earned it running the rustlers off from the Circle Bar."

"Did he give you a lot?"

"Not as much as I would have earned for saving the Rafter. Enough to get us off to a good start though."

"Why would he pay you so much?"

"Does it matter?"

"I suppose not," Clarissa said. She went back to studying the valley below. "You didn't answer my question yesterday. What will happen next?"

"Does that matter?"

"It does," Clarissa said. "What will happen to your family?"

"The rustlers will win. They won't kill anyone else; Daniel won't put up a fight. They'll steal the cattle, but once they have them, they'll move on."

"And the man behind it all?"

"He'll get what he wants. The cattle, the Rafter. Then he'll leave my family alone."

"You're certain of it?"

Noble hesitated.

"Nothing is certain," he said. "But Daniel won't fight. He won't allow Cactus to either."

"What about the Rafter, your grandfather's legacy?"

"The Rafter will fall."

"And your family?" Clarissa said. "What happens to them?"

"Nothing."

"Nothing? They'll lose everything."

"Not everything," Noble said. "My father owed money on the ranch. Grant will take the land for the bank. He said he'd take care of my mother. Make sure she always has enough."

"Your family—your brother and Grace—they'll be ruined."

"They'll be alive." Noble choked the words out.

"Alive and owning nothing," Clarissa said. "I know what it is to have nothing. To have no hope. No future. You said you wanted a place of your own. Someplace you can raise your own cows and watch them grow."

"I do."

"You have all of that right here."

"Here?"

"On the Rafter. You had your own house, your own range, your own cattle. Everything you wanted is here."

"No, it isn't," Noble said. "All this belongs to Daniel. Here I have nothing."

"Unless you fight for it," Clarissa countered. "Your brother and your mother would give you the west range if you saved the Rafter."

"There's no chance. They've got no chance. They'll only get killed."

"Not if you stay and help."

Noble didn't argue with her. He couldn't.

"I'm going back," she said.

"Going back?"

"I'm going back to fight for them."

"Why? You can't save them," Noble said. "They aren't your family."

"No. They're yours." Clarissa started her little horse back down the way they'd come.

Noble couldn't believe it. He'd offered to take

her with him. He'd promised not to leave her alone. Now she'd left him.

He watched after her. There was nothing she could do. If she tried, she'd only get herself killed. Noble started the horses west over the mountains toward Idaho. Riding late, he could be down in the foothills before making camp.

Through the aspen and pine, Noble rode down the Bitterroots' western slope.

If Clarissa wanted to fight a losing battle against rustlers, she was welcome to it. He hoped, for her sake, she'd keep her head down and stay out of their way.

Chapter 23

Noble made camp off the mountain in a hollow, surrounded by a thick screen of juniper and out of the wind. It made a good camp. A cold mountain creek trickled just a few yards away, and the hollow held enough grazing to keep the horses content. Their packs were stored under an overhang of dark branches in case of rain.

Noble cooked but didn't feel much like eating. Nothing seemed to taste the way he wanted. Instead, he stared at the low flames and held out his hands to warm them. The wind whistled overhead, tussling the treetops.

"Why did she go back?" he asked the wind.

He leaned forward to pour himself another cup of coffee.

The move saved his life. From somewhere behind him, a bullet tore into the fire, sending ashes and embers flying. Noble dove over the fire and rolled into the brush. He lay on his stomach deep in shadow, pistol drawn. Only a hint of daylight remained, and he could see nothing.

Pelton. It had to be him.

Against a rifleman, the pistol made a poor weapon. He would have to get close to have any kind of chance. That would be a problem. From the direction of the bullet he knew Pelton was up on a long ridgeline of rock and scattered brush.

Noble's rifle lay in its scabbard just a few feet across the open hollow. He would be exposed if he went for it. Pelton would know that.

He's watching.

A distraction, Noble needed something to draw Pelton's eye long enough to get the rifle and get back into cover. Pelton would be watching for that too. The distraction would have to be a good one.

Noble could think of nothing that would work.

"Rifle's awful tempting ain't it," Pelton called out.

Noble didn't answer. For his voice to be so clear, the bushwhacker had to be closer than the ridge. Quite a bit closer.

"Course you might just give it up and take out, but I don't think you will. You set store by that black horse of yours. Then there's all your supplies. Wouldn't want to walk away from all that."

To Noble's left something crashed through the trees. Pelton had thrown a rock. Noble was too experienced to fall for such a trick, but it revealed something about the marksman. Even a strong man couldn't throw a rock much beyond pistol range. Pelton had to know that, and yet he'd done it anyway.

What is he up to?

Another crash sounded then, this time on Noble's right. Then he smelled the smoke.

Through the trees, he glimpsed a hint of orange and yellow flame. It wasn't a rock he'd thrown, but a lit branch. Pelton was setting the hollow on fire!

Noble licked his lips. The hollow wasn't very large, and it was packed with dry timber. The flames wouldn't take long to reach him. He'd either burn to death or, if he moved, Pelton would see him clear against the backdrop of flames.

He saw what might have been light from Pelton's own fire beyond a rock outcropping. The rock was large enough to hide a man and shelter a small fire from view. Noble cocked the pistol and waited for Pelton's next throw.

There was only one direction left open to him. He could retreat west, toward the stream. Something moved near the rock, and he fired. The bullet whined off harmlessly. A burning branch arced high overhead and disappeared. Noble fired twice more, hitting nothing but rock. From directly behind him, the branch clattered as it fell through the trees. Noble considered his next move. Pelton wouldn't give him any more opportunities.

Burn here or take a chance on running.

Noble could still make it. The fire would take time to spread and close him in completely, but the risk was high. What if Pelton anticipated the move? What if he circled back near the stream and was there waiting? Time was running out.

Noble crawled back on his hands and knees. When he was deeper in the trees, he rose to his feet and ran for the stream. As he ran, a pair of gunshots sounded from behind him.

At least Pelton wasn't somewhere ahead.

Noble crashed into the water. Most of the stream wasn't deep, but there was a pool where scattered boulders formed a dam of sorts. Lifting one pistol clear of the water's surface, Noble moved into the pool. Two of the boulders were large enough to form a shadowed overhang. Slowly, so as not to make a sound, Noble moved up against them and into the darkest shadow. Then he waited.

Everything to the east was now ablaze. Fortunately the rock blocked the light and kept the pool hidden.

Despite the heat of summer, the water was snow-fed and biting. Noble's teeth chattered, and he forced them to still.

Something moved against the backdrop of flame. A man-sized shadow creeping closer. Noble brought back the hammer on his pistol.

Pelton carried his rifle low across his body. He came to the edge of the creek, peering across. He was searching the bare ground directly across the water. Pelton put a hand on the tree Noble had passed beside. Then his eyes shifted to the pool. Too late. Noble's gun bucked. The bullet took Pelton in the side and spun him around.

Pelton vanished.

Noble swore. He knew he'd hit the man, but how had he gotten away?

A wild spray of shots sent water flying up in a geyser all around Noble. Evidently, Pelton had kept hold of his rifle.

Noble fired three times more toward the muzzle flash from Pelton's rifle. Two hit nothing. But the third, final shot connected with a metallic whine; Noble recognized the sound.

He moved to the stream's edge and crawled out onto the bank as quietly as he could.

"That sounded like a bad one," Noble said.

"Bad enough, you bastard," Pelton replied. "Busted my rifle, too. I'm unarmed."

"Forgive me if I don't take your word for it."

"Come see for yourself then," Pelton said with a laugh.

Noble thought he knew where the voice had come from. He circled wide around it, keeping away from the blazing fire so he'd be unseen. Finally, he crept in around the trunk of an old, twisted pine.

Pelton lay sprawled on the ground, face up. Noble saw where his first bullet had hit, just below the man's ribs.

The rifle lay discarded several feet away. Noble's bullet had smashed the action.

The fire blazed up for a moment, and Pelton saw him.

"I'm done," Pelton said and lay still. "Lucky shot, that last one. It hit the action and went down into my leg."

"Where'd I put the first?"

"Ribs, same side," Pelton said between clenched teeth.

Keeping his pistol on the wounded man, Noble moved closer. He'd never known Pelton to carry anything other than the rifle, but a man couldn't take any chances.

"I'm unarmed, like I said," Pelton went on. "Take me in to the law."

"I'm not the law," Noble said. "I don't think there's any law left in Bigsby."

"I'll testify. I'll testify to everything. I killed the marshal. Killed your pa too," Pelton said. "Just take me in to the sawbones, and I'll tell it all."

"I don't think so," Noble said. "Your friends will spring you before the law arrives. Just like they sprung those others. Besides, those wounds are bad. You wouldn't make it back to town anyhow."

"What? You'd leave me here?"

Noble raised his pistol. "You shouldn't have killed my father."

"I'm unarmed. I surrendered. This is murder," Pelton pleaded.

"Just like you murdered my father," Noble said, and raised his pistol.

. . .

Grace was the first to see Clarissa. She'd been in the barn talking to Daniel and helping him feed the horses, and on her way back to the house she saw the girl riding in.

"What's happened?" Grace said when Clarissa was closer. "Where is Gabriel?"

Clarissa seemed not to hear her. She rode on, staring at the pommel and crying. Her eyes were red, and the front of her dress was soaked with tears. How long had she been crying?

"Daniel. Daniel!" Grace said.

When Clarissa reached the corral, she sat her horse and shrugged off every question.

Daniel stuck his head out from the barn then ran over.

"Something is wrong with her," Grace said. "And there's no sign of Gabriel."

"Help her down Daniel," Emilia said. She'd come up from behind the house.

Daniel eased Clarissa down while Grace tied her horse to the corral railing. He tried to get her on her feet, but the girl collapsed, and he barely caught her.

"Bring her on inside," Emilia said.

Daniel scooped her up in both arms and took her into the house. He eased her down into a chair while Emilia fussed over her.

"Clarissa," Emilia said. "What's happened?"

Still the girl ignored the question. Emilia took

Clarissa's head in her hands and squatted down to look directly in her eyes. "Where is Gabriel?" she asked.

"Gone."

"Gone? Gone where?"

Clarissa licked her lips, and her eyes turned to Emilia's. "He left. Said the Rafter couldn't be saved. Said he was moving on," Clarissa said.

"He left you?" Grace said. Anger flared deep in her chest. The Rafter couldn't be saved? And he'd left Clarissa behind?

"No." Clarissa shook her head. "He offered to take me with him. I made it as far as the mountains. The overlook. But . . . but I couldn't go." She looked around at Grace and then Emilia. "You've all been so nice to me, and I couldn't stand the thought of you all losing your home."

She began sobbing again, and Emilia embraced her.

"I thought he'd change his mind. I thought he'd come back for me," Clarissa said between the tears. "He didn't though. He left me. He said he wouldn't."

Emilia stroked the girl's long hair and said. "There, there. It will be all right. It will all be all right."

Grace doubted it. Gabriel had gone again, and this time for good. She shouldn't have been surprised. Daniel had held him back from doing what he'd been hired to do, and now he was gone, and there was no one coming to save them.

"I shouldn't have been so hurtful to him," Grace said. "This is my fault."

"No," Daniel said. "The fault is mine. I didn't want more killing."

Cactus limped into the room then. "Riders coming. Looks like trouble."

"Who is it?" Grace said. In her heart, she already knew. It was them. The men who wanted to steal their cattle. Only now they weren't content to take over the cattle. They wanted the Rafter itself, and Gabriel was gone.

"I recognize two as those rustler fellows we took to jail," Cactus said. "I'll cover them from the bunkhouse."

Then he was gone, limping over to the bunkhouse on a crude crutch.

"Stay here," Daniel said, and rose. He took down the hunting rifle from over the door and checked to see that it was loaded. From the shelf beside the door, he picked up a box of shells. "I'll try to reason with them."

"And if that doesn't work?" Emilia said.

Daniel looked down at the rifle, and then back to his mother with a resigned look.

"Some men only understand violence, son," Emilia said. "If it comes to it, do not hesitate. You know what's at stake."

"I do," Daniel said, and set his jaw.

"Ester, Jack, follow me," Grace said. She

opened a locked drawer on Daniel's desk and took something out.

"Look," Ester said, and held her doll up. "She's sleeping."

"Come with me, sweetheart," Grace said, and headed for Jack's room.

Jack met them at the door. "Men are coming. I saw them on the hill," he said. "Is it the bad men again?"

"Keep your sister in here," Grace said. She closed the wooden shutters and dropped the bar in place. "Bar the door after I'm out and do not open it. No matter what you hear, do not open it unless it's one of us."

"I should be out there fighting," Jack said. He had a determined look, one of boiling anger. She'd seen that look before. Gabriel had always been like that before one of his fights.

"Stay in here and protect your sister," Grace said.

"I need a gun," Jack replied.

Grace unwrapped the bundle in her hands, rolling it out on the bed. Inside were two of Big Jack's pistols. She handed one to her son. "You know how to use it?"

He nodded. "Uncle Gabriel showed me. Is he here?"

"No. We're on our own now. Your father is out front. Six shots, and make certain of what you're shooting at."

"I will," Jack said sternly.

Grace wiped the tears from her eyes and drew the door shut. She heard Jack lower the bar in place. Her knees felt like water. She leaned against the wall to steady herself.

Did I just say my last goodbye to my children?

The first shot sounded. Grace took the other pistol and ran to the window. Emilia was already at another, sighting down the barrel of a rifle. Her shoulder jerked, and a shot echoed. Then she cycled the action and lined up again.

Grace peeked around the window's frame. There were men on horseback riding around the barn's wreckage and yelling. More rode between the main house and the bunkhouse. Grace used both thumbs to draw back the pistol's heavy hammer and took aim. When the next group of riders swept into view, she squeezed the trigger and felt the heavy gun jerk. A puff of smoke rose from the barrel. A horse screamed.

More shots came from her left. One struck the window frame, and she fell back.

"Got one," Emilia roared, and fired again. "He won't steal another cow."

Grace went back to the window. Cactus and Daniel were in the bunkhouse, firing from one window and the open door.

More riders came through, firing and shouting. Grace fired twice. She lost count of Emilia's shots. Gray powder smoke rose from the bunkhouse where Daniel and Cactus had been fighting.

Then the riders were gone, and all was quiet.

"Where's Clarissa?" Grace asked.

"Upstairs. I gave her one of the rifles and a pistol. I think she got one."

"Emilia, can you reload this?" Grace said.

Emilia scuttled over, keeping low and out of sight. She handed Grace her rifle and said, "Don't lean the barrel outside. If you do, they'll know where you are." She opened the old gun and started reloading. "I know this gun. This was my father's. Where's the other one?"

"I gave it to Jack."

"Good." Emilia nodded. "He might need it."

"It's quiet," Grace said. "What are they doing?"

"Reloading likely. Trying to figure out how many of us there are and where."

"How long will this quiet last?" Grace asked. The quiet was worse than the fighting. She wanted it to be over. She wanted to run to Jack's room to make sure her children were safe.

"Until they make up their minds," Emilia said.

"Make up their minds?"

"On how best to kill us."

"And what do we do in the meantime?"

"Wait and see," Emilia gave her a grim smile. "It's all we can do."

Chapter 24

Their respite did not last long.

A half hour after they'd gone, riders swept through the buildings again, firing their pistols, while others, on foot and armed with rifles, opened up from all sides.

"How many are there?" Grace asked. It seemed like a hundred men out there.

"Eight or nine, give or take," Emilia said between shots. "But that number's falling fast."

"Gabriel didn't think there were so many," Grace said above the gunfire.

"They must have brought friends," Emilia said. A bullet smashed the window frame above her head; she ducked down before two more struck lower down, where she'd just been. Splinters and bits of mortar fell in her gray hair.

Grace rested her pistol's heavy barrel on her own window. Shouting and shooting, a man in a flat-crowned hat raced by. She fired twice, then her gun clicked on an empty cylinder. More shots came from above and the bunkhouse, reminding her that they were not alone in the fight.

She reloaded her pistol—Emilia had shown her how—and raised up enough to glance at the bunkhouse. The rustlers had thrown torches on the roof. So far none had caught, but the walls were black and smoldering in places where torches lay piled up against them.

It won't take much longer to catch.

"They're trying to set fire to the bunkhouse," Grace said.

"I see that," Emilia said. "When it starts to go, we'll have to cover Cactus and Daniel as they cross over."

Grace saw the man in the flat-crowned hat peek around the corner of the bunkhouse. She fired and missed, but he vanished.

"One on foot behind the bunkhouse," she said.

Emilia sighted along the rifle and waited. When the man looked around a second time, she shot him in the face. "Good call," Emilia cackled.

More torches sailed for the bunkhouse. The main house was shingled with thin slate; it would take a lot for it to catch fire, but smoke started up from the bunkhouse, thick and black.

Cactus leaned out the door, fired, and then hollered, "Coming over."

Emilia went to the door and lifted the bar. Then she cracked the door open to make sure it would swing freely. "Ready," she shouted. "Grace, fire at anything and anywhere they might come from."

Both women opened up then as Cactus hobbled toward the house on his wounded leg. He hit the door with his shoulder, fell on the floor, and rolled away clear. Rifle in hand, Daniel followed him. Shots spattered the dirt all around him. When he reached the door, he slammed it shut and quickly dropped the heavy bar in place.

"Grace, see to Cactus. He's bleeding again. I'll take the window," he said.

"I'm still in it," Cactus said between gritted teeth.

"He's not," Daniel said. "One snuck in close and got him in the shoulder."

Grace went to Cactus's side. His shirt was stuck to his body, soaked with blood. The wound on his leg had torn open in the fight, but it bled only a trickle. Grace got a thick towel from the kitchen and pressed it to his shoulder.

"I'm all right. Just prop me up where I can shoot out," Cactus said.

Bullets struck the house all at once then. Daniel jumped back, but one nicked his ear enough to draw blood. The firing held for several long seconds until a torch flew in through one of the windows.

Grace grabbed it with the blood-soaked towel and tossed it into the fireplace. More shots kept coming. Grace could hear the torches clattering against the outside; she could smell their oily smoke. Another flew in. The flames died when she smothered it with the towel.

Daniel rose up and fired three shots, then he pulled back inside as more bullets struck all around.

Grace's breath came quick and hard. They couldn't keep this up. Eventually, the house would catch and burn. They all would. There was nothing they could do. The rustlers had driven them back and won.

She went to the door to Jack's room. Ester was crying on the other side. She heard Jack trying and failing to comfort her. She should be with them when the end came. She would hold them tight and tell them she loved them, and that it would all be all right.

Then the shooting lessened. Rifles kept firing, but their bullets no longer struck the house. Emilia rose up through the window and fired. Daniel did the same.

"Has help come? The marshal?" Grace said. She went to the window to look out.

A dark rider came down the hill, black horse at a flat run, pistol in one hand, reins in the other, smoke rising with every shot.

"It's Gabe," Daniel said.

A rustler stood up in the tall grass, went for his gun, and Gabriel cut him down. Another to his other side aimed a rifle. Grace held her breath. How could he fight off so many?

Gabriel's pistol came over in a smooth, unhurried motion, jerked once, twice, and the rifleman's shot went into the air as he fell.

Gabriel holstered his pistol and drew a second.

He kept firing, passing out of view behind the house. More shots rang out.

"Get them all!" Emilia said.

Grace was horrified to find her own voice shouting. Even Daniel let out a roar. He shot one of the rustlers when he came around the wreckage of the barn to avoid Gabriel's charge.

Then it was over. A group of riders bolted from behind the bunkhouse and raced their horses south. On the upper level, Clarissa's rifle roared once more, and one fell.

Gabriel came up to the house.

"Everyone all right?" he said.

Clarissa flew down the stairs and burst through the front door like a shooting star. She leaped into Gabriel's arms, holding him tight and kissing him.

"What the—" he said.

Then she stepped back free of him and slapped him across the face.

"Well, what was that for?" he rubbed his red cheek.

"Noble Bartlett, if you don't know." Clarissa reached back for another slap.

He caught her arm and spun her around so she was pinned and facing away from him. He grabbed her other hand above the wrist, and she couldn't move. She gave him a half-hearted struggle.

"Now hold still. No need to slap a man. I came back, didn't I?" he said.

"Almost too late," she said, and tore loose.

"Looks like you had it well in hand," Gabriel said.

She pouted, but only for a moment, and then went back to his side and they were kissing again.

Grace coughed, and Gabriel stopped long enough to notice the others for the first time.

"Everyone made it?" he said sheepishly.

"Cactus is wounded," Daniel said. "Mother is with him now."

"Jack and Ester?"

Grace went to their door and knocked. "Jack? Ester?"

The bar scraped, and Jack came out, gun in hand. "Is it over? Are they gone?"

"They are," Grace said, and hugged Ester.

"You gave him that?" Daniel said.

"I did."

Daniel frowned but didn't speak further. Gabriel stared at his brother with a half smile.

"Looks like you decided to fight," Gabriel finally said, and nodded to the rifle.

"I did what I had to. It's over now," Daniel said. "The Rafter is safe."

"No, it isn't. That was Gage Banier with those others. He won't give up nearly that easy. He'll keep coming until he's dead. Plus, there's the man behind all this."

"What about that other one?" Cactus said. "Pelton? The one who murdered Sam?"

"I found him earlier." Gabriel's tone was grim.

Cactus's eyes narrowed. "Good."

"Lay back, old man," Emilia said. She was bandaging his shoulder and leg.

Gabriel went out behind the bunkhouse and caught up one of the rustler's horses. The man Daniel shot lay face down between the bunkhouse and the remains of the barn. Gabriel flipped him over and unbuckled his gun belt. Then he replaced the missing cartridges in his left- and right-hand guns. Then he took the man's pistol, examined it, and tucked it into the back of his belt.

"Isn't that a bit much?" Daniel said.

"Never hurts to have an extra pistol ready," Gabriel said with grin, and mounted back up.

"And where are you going?" Daniel asked.

"Bigsby or Riggins. Whichever way Banier went."

"Alone?" Clarissa said.

"Alone."

"Gabriel, there's no need for this. They've been beat. They won't be back." Daniel said.

"They'll be back. They always come back, and with more men and more guns. Maybe dynamite to blast you out. Maybe another sharpshooter to kill one of us while we're out riding. They keep coming back until they're stopped. I aim to be the one who stops them."

"I'm going with you," Daniel said, and hefted his rifle.

"I'm not going to talk to them, Daniel. I aim to put Gage Banier and the man who hired him into the ground."

"I understand. I won't get in the way."

"Daniel, the law can handle the rest. You don't have to do this," Grace said. How could he leave her at a time like this? What was wrong with him?

"I do." Daniel gave her one of his rare smiles. "I have to see it to the end."

"Gabriel knows what he's doing. Let him finish it."

"No," Gabriel interrupted. "It's his ranch. His future. His children's future. If he wants to hold on to the Rafter, he's got to do it."

Daniel saddled one of their horses from the corral. Grace watched him and wiped the tears from her eyes. Why now, after so many years, did he decide to fight? And against a gunfighter?

He climbed into the saddle and rode up in front of her.

"Daniel, please?" she said, and reached for his hand.

"I'll be home soon," he said. "No need to worry."

Clarissa only watched Gabriel. He tipped his hat to her and said, "I'll see you when I get back."

"You will," she answered.

Gabriel turned his horse and rode south, the direction the rustlers had gone. Daniel hesitated for a moment and then followed along after his brother.

Grace wandered closer to Clarissa.

"They'll be fine," Clarissa said.

Grace didn't know how she could be so calm, so certain.

"I hope so," was all she could muster.

"Looks like Riggins," Noble said, and straightened in his saddle. The tracks were plain enough. Four men survived the attack on the Rafter. One of those was Gage Banier, a dangerous man, a killer with few equals.

Daniel grunted and looked into the distance, much as a man might look at a coming squall. Together, they rode on.

Noble would have to keep Daniel clear of Banier. Daniel was formidable when he made his mind up to it, but he wasn't a gunfighter, and he certainly wasn't in Banier's class.

"Sure you won't turn back?" Noble said.

"Not this time," Daniel answered. He gave Noble a sideways look. "Finally got me to pick up a rifle and now you want me back home and useless."

"You bring a pistol, too?"

Daniel held out one of Jack's old pistols, the one Grace had been using.

"And spare cartridges for it?" Noble asked.

"Of course," Daniel snorted. "You aren't the only one Big Jack taught to shoot."

"That might be, but I don't remember you being too keen for it."

"I'll do my part," Daniel said.

"Best to stick to the rifle, if that's what you're comfortable with."

"I plan on it."

They traveled in silence for a time.

"I can't remember the last time the two of us rode to Riggins together."

Daniel smiled. "It's been awhile."

"Remember that time we tracked that brown bear into the Bitterroots? What were you, twelve? Fourteen?"

"Thirteen. I thought I'd wounded it in the leg. I shouldn't have taken that shot," Daniel said. Then he gave Noble a sidelong glance. "If I remember rightly, someone goaded me into it."

"Must be getting old. I never goaded you into anything. That bear sure wasn't hurt when we caught up to him. How many times did we end up shooting him?" Noble asked.

"Plenty. Thought I was going to run out of shells."

Daniel shifted in the saddle. Riggins was just out of sight over the next rise.

"This won't be like hunting that bear, will it?" he said.

"Dangerous enough, but bears don't carry guns and they don't shoot back." Noble's tone turned serious. "Shoot fast, brother. Don't worry too much about honest folk. They'll scatter and hide when it starts. Likely they already have. Keep on my right and a long step behind me."

"What about this Banier?"

"If you see him, call out and get into cover. He's snake fast and mean as the devil."

"Don't know as I'd recognize him."

"You'll know him when you see him. Dresses like a dandy."

"Can you beat him?"

"It won't come to that. Most gun battles don't end in a draw in the street. This will be a running battle through town."

Daniel stopped his horse and looked at him. "Can you beat him though? Are you better than him?"

Noble paused. "Yeah, I am."

"Good." Daniel levered a round into the rifle and continued on.

They came to the edge of Riggins and dismounted. Charging a horse through town was a good way to draw every bullet in town. Not to mention kill a good horse.

Noble patted the stallion on the neck and tied him up behind an outlying shed. He drew his rifle, opened the action, then closed it again. He checked the riding thongs on both pistols, then made sure the gun he'd taken from the rustler was safely tucked in his belt.

That done, he nodded at Daniel, and they started up the street.

Noble took the lead. A pair of miners came out from one of the saloons. They took one look at Noble and then Daniel before running back inside. More men and a few women scattered up the street. A few brave souls watched the street from shop windows or behind barrels.

Riggins lay open before them, quiet as a sleeping beast.

Noble drew a deep breath, then stalked forward.

To his left, a rifle barrel eased out through an upstairs window above a saloon. Noble's rifle whipped to his shoulder. He put three rounds into the window, fast enough that the shots blurred together; the man fell forward through the window. He struck the ground with a thud.

More rifles suddenly opened up from farther up the street. Dirt fountained beside Noble and, firing as he went, he ran to the back of a wagon. He heard more fire from Daniel and hoped his brother had taken whatever cover he could find.

Noble paused his fire long enough to reload the rifle.

We have to keep advancing.

Getting pinned down would mean death. There were at least two more up on the rooftops.

Several more taking shelter in the old hotel at the very end of the street.

Gage will be in the hotel. He's waiting there to see if I make it.

The man never took chances. He didn't believe in taking chances.

One of the gunmen on the roof leaned out too far, and Daniel shot him. He slouched forward over the false front and dropped his rifle.

Two down, but by the amount of fire, there were more than the four survivors from the Rafter. There had to be at least four or five still alive in the old hotel.

"Daniel," Noble said.

Daniel's head briefly came into view from behind a store entryway. Even as he looked out, a bullet scored the wood walk.

"Come across," Noble said, just loud enough for his brother to hear. Then Noble began firing up at the hotel. He didn't hit anything, but the oncoming bullets made the rustlers duck back into cover. His rifle emptied just as Daniel reached the back of the wagon.

"We've got to take the fight to them," Noble said, and reloaded a second time. "Think you can push this thing?"

Daniel looked at the wagon. It was half loaded with barrels and sacks. He leaned on it to test the weight. "If the brake wasn't set."

Noble leaned around the edge of the wagon just

enough to see the brake. He shattered the wood with a pair of shots, and the mechanism swung free.

"There's enough downhill slope to carry it once you get it going," Noble said.

"And when it does?"

"When it does, you dive clear, between the next set of buildings. Then work your way up closer to the end of the street and around to cover the back. I'll follow the wagon in through the front. If anyone tries to escape or comes out to try and flank me, shoot them."

"I will," Daniel said. He set his rifle in the wagon's bed and pushed while Noble began methodically firing at the rustlers' position. He hit one man, sent him falling back. The wagon creaked as it started moving. Noble walked and then finally ran as the wagon began picking up speed.

Daniel snatched his rifle up and clapped Noble once on the back before running off between buildings.

One of the men in the hotel stood up to shoot at him, but Noble got him first. Another man down. How many could be left?

The wagon soon outpaced Noble, wheels spinning and buzzing over sand, rock, and packed gravel. Noble tossed his rifle in the back and ran faster to keep up. More shots struck the front of the wagon and the ground on either side, and he prayed not to catch an unlucky ricochet.

The heavy wagon struck the front of the hotel in a titanic crash. The barrels in the back burst open. Sacks exploded in a cloud of fine, white flour and grainy, yellow cornmeal.

Noble drew both pistols and slammed a shoulder into the front door. A man confronted him just inside; Noble's pistol bucked, and his attacker was dead. Another man, rifle in hand, came down from the second floor, but Noble's bullet took him in the throat.

Then Gage Banier was there, coming through a doorway in the back, white teeth shining and both guns blazing. Bullets struck all around Noble. One slugged him in the shoulder and he dropped his left-hand pistol. With his right, he fired once, twice, a third time. Two of the bullets hit.

Banier kept firing.

None of Gage's shots found their mark. Noble's bullets spoiled his aim. Noble drew the third pistol from behind his belt. He leveled it and shot Gage in the smiling mouth.

All was quiet then. Dust sifted down from the ceiling to land on the dead men. The ceiling above groaned. At least one enemy remained. The man who'd hired Gage and Pelton. The man who'd set it all in motion. The man who'd arranged the death of Noble's father. That man was still up there somewhere.

Noble went up the stairs quietly. He found the last man he needed to kill in a front room overlooking the street. He was wounded in the arm by a stray bullet and leaning on the wall.

"I'm unarmed," Grant Hickman said. "Thank God you got them."

"Got who?" Noble asked.

"Those men. They took me from Bigsby this morning. Held me hostage to get the bank's money." Grant licked his lips.

"Funny. They didn't seem like the kidnapping type," Noble said. His pistol was held low and ready.

"I heard them talking about it," Grant said. "Some of them went off to attack the Rafter, too." He kept glancing back over Noble's shoulder toward the door.

"He isn't coming."

"Who?" Grant had a confused look.

"Gage Banier. I killed him. Shot his front teeth out."

A flash of anger passed over the banker's face but was quickly gone. "I don't know who that is."

"Sure you do. You hired him to take the Circle Bar from old man Webster and then to take the Rafter from us." Noble lifted the pistol.

"I don't know what you're talking about," Grant whined.

Noble shot him in the knee.

He fell, screaming and howling. "Dammit, I don't know—"

Noble raised the pistol again, taking aim at

the other knee. "Hold still. Wouldn't want to hit something vital. Not yet, anyways."

Noble fired. Hickman flinched, and this time the bullet punched through his thigh.

"Your fault for moving," Noble said. He cocked the pistol again.

"All right, I did it," Grant said. "I did it all. I hired Banier. I hired Pelton. Only don't shoot me."

"Why? You were my friend," Noble said.

"Your friend," Grant snorted. "I wasn't your friend. I was just some town kid you spent time with. Your family was rich and mine was poor. You had cattle and land and everything. And why? Because your grandfather got here first. I had nothing because mine came to Montana and found a played-out mine. We had nothing. You had everything, and then you just left. You threw it all away. I meant nothing to you."

The floor groaned behind Noble.

"You heard all that?" Noble said.

"I did," Daniel answered.

"I'll take care of this. No need for you to get your hands any dirtier. You have to live here, after all."

"No." Daniel laid a hand on Noble's shoulder. "Leave him for the law."

"He killed our father." Noble raised the pistol.

"Yes. But it's over. You don't have to kill him."

"Are you going to fight me over this? Over

him? He deserves it." Noble went over to Grant and pressed the barrel against his head.

"Gabriel . . . Noble . . . I only ask you to do the right thing," Daniel said. He looked down at the whimpering Grant, then back to his brother. "But no, I won't stop you."

Daniel turned then and went out, leaving Grant and Noble alone in the quiet, dusty room.

Epilogue

At the tall peak of what would be the new barn, legs dangling almost thirty feet above the ground, Noble sat astride a broad pine beam.

With the hole done, he laid his hand drill aside and mopped sweat from his brow. He'd never built a barn before, or any other type of building either, and this one would have to last. He'd cut the beam four feet longer than originally planned, enough extra for a block and tackle to hang out over the barn's end. He'd seen them used before to haul hay up to the loft, and it seemed considerably easier than forking it up overhead. In his youth, he'd done plenty of that.

Overall, the replacement barn was coming along well. They might have it framed and covered by the first snow if they kept at it.

Daniel brought the team in, dragging another huge old log. That one would be sawed into crossbeams and posts for the sides.

"How many more do you think?" Noble said.

"Dozen, at least," Daniel said. "I've got two more on the ground already."

"Pity, we can't season them."

"Not much choice if we want it done this year. If we lap the joints, it should be fine."

Noble didn't argue. When it came to building

with fresh timber, or any other manner of construction, he knew absolutely nothing.

"You finished the hole?" Daniel asked.

"Just now," Noble said. "Should have done it on the ground though."

"That would have been easier."

"My first time building a barn." Noble grinned down.

Daniel backed the team and released the chain. Then he turned the tired horses loose in the corral.

Like the horses, the day was old and tired now. A fading sun cast crimson and purple over a bank of high clouds. Crowned with caps of glittering gold, the rocky Bitterroots rose up in the far west. Soon enough they'd exchange those gold crowns for pure white snow, and then the Montana winter would gradually wind its way down to lower elevations until it blanketed the plains and the Rafter.

Noble rested and took it all in.

A pair of hawks flew high overhead, wings flashing with the faint light, looking for one last meal before returning to their nests. He pulled a few swallows from the canteen he'd hung from the beam. From his perch, he could see Rafter cattle grazing in the home pasture. Rafter cattle eating Rafter grass.

He couldn't think of anything that would make the evening more perfect.

They'd lost some of course—not all had been recovered from the rustlers—but after a search of the Circle Bar, they found over half of what had been taken.

Finished feeding the team, Daniel looked up at him with a faint smile; he started to speak, then went on into the house.

Evidently, the perfect evening has an effect on him, too.

Clarissa came outside wearing a stained apron. She looked up at him.

"I think you left that hole just so you had an excuse to climb up there," she said.

"Maybe," Noble said with a grin. He moved around the beam, then wrapped his legs around the length of heavy rope he'd used to climb up. Holding the rope with both hands and legs, he quickly slid back down.

Clarissa met him at the bottom.

"That looked like entirely too much fun," she said.

"The block and tackle need to be hung next. You can climb up and do that if you think it's so fun," he said.

"Not on your life. You won't catch me any higher off the ground than Bailey's back."

Noble squeezed her shoulders and looked at the barn's skeleton.

"It'll be nice when it's finished," she said.

"I think so."

"Your grandfather would be proud. Your father, too."

"I believe they would."

They were silent for a time.

"What happens next?"

Noble sighed. "The marshals took Grant in for trial. Based on Daniel's and Mother's word they decided I was in the right and that I didn't kill McCandles."

"Will they leave us be?"

"No telling," Noble shrugged. "I've got a reputation. That won't help, but they seem to be willing to give me a chance."

"And the Rafter?"

"I'm not sure."

"And us?"

"We stay," Noble said. "We do what needs to be done to save the Rafter. There're a few lean years ahead, I'm afraid."

He hadn't taken his mother's reward, exactly. In lieu of cash, he'd taken his payment as a share of the ranch itself. The west range, including his grandfather's cabin and a few head of cattle were now his.

Mine? Ours, I think.

He squeezed Clarissa's shoulders. At this point, she certainly seemed to have distinct ideas on who owned what.

"Ready to go in?" she asked.

"You cooked tonight?"

"I did." She smiled at him.

There was nothing wrong with Grace's cooking, but everyone—Grace included—agreed that Clarissa made an excellent meal. Daniel argued that Grace's was better, but even he didn't sound convinced.

Probably for the best if he says that, anyway.

"Let's just stay here for a moment more," Noble said, and looked at the sunset again.

Carson McCloud grew up in the Texas Panhandle on his family ranch. Since then he's lived in a great deal of the West, including Wyoming, Nevada, Idaho, New Mexico, and Arizona. These days he's returned to Texas with his wife, kids, and a pair of housebroke cowdogs all keeping him busy.

Center Point Large Print
600 Brooks Road / PO Box 1
Thorndike, ME 04986-0001 USA

(207) 568-3717

US & Canada:
1 800 929-9108
www.centerpointlargeprint.com